A Controversial Cover

A CONTROVERSIAL COVER

Lorna Barrett

BERKLEY PRIME CRIME
New York

BERKLEY PRIME CRIME
Published by Berkley
An imprint of Penguin Random House LLC
penguinrandomhouse.com

Library of Congress Cataloging-in-Publication Data

Names: Barrett, Lorna, author.
Title: A controversial cover / Lorna Barrett.
Description: New York: Berkley Prime Crime, 2024. | Series: Booktown series
Identifiers: LCCN 2023058303 (print) | LCCN 2023058304 (ebook) |
ISBN 9780593549445 (hardcover) | ISBN 9780593549469 (ebook)
Subjects: LCGFT: Cozy mysteries. | Novels.
Classification: LCC PS3602.A83955 C66 2024 (print) |
LCC PS3602.A83955 (ebook) | DDC 813/.6—dc23/eng/20240105
LC record available at https://lccn.loc.gov/2023058303
LC ebook record available at https://lccn.loc.gov/2023058304

Printed in the United States of America
1st Printing

Book design by Laura K. Corless

This is a work of fiction. Names, characters, places, and incidents either are the product
of the author's imagination or are used fictitiously, and any resemblance to actual persons,
living or dead, business establishments, events, or locales is entirely coincidental.

PUBLISHER'S NOTE: The recipes contained in this book are to be followed exactly as written. The
publisher is not responsible for your specific health or allergy needs that may require medical supervision.
The publisher is not responsible for any adverse reactions to the recipes contained in this book.

For Adam Hart:
Thank you for being my friend.

ACKNOWLEDGMENTS

Many thanks to my Lorraine Train members, Amy Connolley, Linda Kuzminczuk, Debbie Lyon, and Pam Priest, whom I can count on for support. And to my agent, Jessica Faust, who is always in my corner. You ladies are the best!

You can talk to me (and make friends with some of my other readers) on my Facebook group: Lorraine's & Lorna's (Cozy) Perpetual Tea Party page. Come along for the ride!

Cast of Characters

Tricia Miles, owner of Haven't Got a Clue vintage mystery bookstore

Angelica Miles, Tricia's older sister, owner of the Cookery, the Booked for Lunch café, Booked for Beauty day spa, and half owner of the Sheer Comfort Inn. Her alter ego is Nigela Ricita, the mysterious developer who has been pumping money and jobs into the village of Stoneham.

Pixie Poe, Tricia's assistant manager at Haven't Got a Clue

Mr. Everett, Tricia's employee at Haven't Got a Clue

David Price, Stoneham's new children's librarian and Tricia's special friend

Antonio Barbero, the public face of Nigela Ricita Associates, Angelica's son

Ginny Wilson-Barbero, Tricia's former assistant, wife of Antonio Barbero

Grace Harris-Everett, Mr. Everett's wife, manages their charity, the Everett Foundation

Ian McDonald, chief of police, Stoneham Police Department

Cast of Characters

Becca Dickson-Chandler, former tennis star, ex-wife of Marshall Cambridge

Dan Reed, owner of the Bookshelf Diner

Stella Kraft, former English teacher at Stoneham High School

Betty Barnes, owner of Barney's Book Barn, children's bookstore

Amelia Doyle, Stoneham Public Library's new director

Larry Harvick, owner of the Bee's Knees specialty honey shop

Lois Kerr, former director at the Stoneham Library

Lauren Barker, author of the Cuddly Chameleon children's book series

A Controversial Cover

ONE

The metal folding chairs were arranged five across, bisected by an aisle, with another five opposite. Six rows had been set up in anticipation of sixty guests, and it was nearly a full house. The first four seats on the left had neat, computer-printed placards saying RESERVED. Tricia Miles had led her sister, Angelica; her niece-in-law, Ginny Wilson-Barbero; and Ginny's toddler daughter, Sofia, straight to the front row.

"Hey!" a male voice called out to the women and child as they took their seats. "Why do *you* get the prime location?"

Dan Reed continued to be a thorn in Tricia's proverbial side. Everything about the fifty-something man set her teeth on edge. Dan believed every conspiracy theory he saw online and held court at the front of the house at his business, the Bookshelf Diner, sharing his opinions with anyone who'd listen—and drove away those unwilling to put up with his proselytizing.

Tricia ignored the boor and studied the cover of the children's book she'd purchased before entering the Stoneham Library's community room. Betty Barnes, owner of Barney's Book Barn, Stoneham's children's bookstore, had been asked to provide the books for sale. Not only did she have piles of the current title, but others in the series for sale, as well.

"Did you hear what I said?" Dan tried again.

Tricia closed her eyes for a few seconds to draw on her reserve of patience before she half turned. "I did, and it's none of your business."

"Who says?"

"Me." Tricia turned back to face the lectern set up in front of the floor-to-ceiling saltwater fish tank.

"Isn't this exciting?" Ginny asked, passing to Sofia the copy she'd purchased of author Lauren Barker's latest offering in the children's book series, *The Cuddly Chameleon's Coat of Many Colors*.

Tricia couldn't understand why Lauren's latest addition to the series had been met with controversy. Was it because Lauren had chosen a chameleon as her protagonist—a lizard that could change colors to blend into a threatening environment—and somehow a certain segment of the population seemed to think that was somehow subversive? Tricia had read the books to Sofia several times, so she couldn't comprehend that viewpoint.

The front row where she sat had one free chair, and Tricia was pleased when Stella Kraft, a former teacher at Stoneham High School, claimed the seat. She leaned forward. "Stella, it's so nice to see you."

For a moment, the older woman studied Tricia's face in confusion.

"Tricia Miles. I own the Haven't Got a Clue bookstore on Main Street. We met a few years back and talked about one of your former students."

Stella's eyes widened. "Oh, yes. Now I remember you."

"I didn't know you were a fan of children's fiction," Tricia said.

"Only when the author is one of my most successful students," Stella said with pride.

"That's wonderful. Have you spoken to Ms. Barker recently?"

Stella's eyes practically sparkled. "Not since she was in my class. Of course, it was *I* who first encouraged her writing talent. She handed in many fine compositions and had a flair for narrative, even as a high school freshman. And now her most popular work is being adapted into a full-length movie—maybe the whole series eventually!"

"You sure keep up with her achievements," Tricia remarked.

"Oh, yes. I've taken a keen interest in her career, and I hope we'll have a merry reunion."

It was then that David Price appeared at the front of the room to check the sound system, and Tricia couldn't help but smile. He'd brought such happiness into her life during the past six weeks. David was responsible for arranging his first author appearance since he'd taken over as the children's librarian weeks before. He hadn't yet earned his master's in library science, but he was pretty close to it, which was why he'd been hired.

David had also become Tricia's much younger—by twenty years—lover. The age difference didn't bother Tricia or David, but it seemed to annoy other community members. Even Angelica seemed to disapprove. Tricia had learned not to mention her relationship with David too often to her older sister. Angelica always seemed to have some complaint concerning him—whether real or imagined. It had put a strain on the sisters' relationship. But that night, Angelica seemed to have forgiven David for the sin of youth. And she'd taken as a given that members of the extended Miles family had been given preferential treatment.

David's return smile wasn't as wide as Tricia's, and he left the podium and headed back up the aisle.

Sofia paged through her copy of *The Cuddly Chameleon's Coat of Many Colors*. "Mama—mama Cammy-le-on!"

"That's right," Ginny said, gazing at her firstborn with adoration. Baby Will was home with his father, Antonio Barbero—Angelica's son. Not many in Stoneham knew that fact. Angelica was determined to keep it that way, and Antonio didn't seem to care. At least, he'd never offered an opinion to Tricia either way. Antonio was the public face of Nigela Ricita Associates, a company Angelica owned with extensive business holdings in the village. She also owned several in her own right. Talk about a business mogul! Meanwhile, Tricia was the proprietress of a solitary enterprise, a bookstore known for selling vintage mysteries, although as each year passed, those early volumes were becoming rare. It was primarily due to the diligence of her assistant manager, Pixie Poe, scouring tag and estate sales on her days off that kept those tomes on the store's shelves.

Tricia glanced at her watch. The program should have started ten minutes ago, but there was no sign of Lauren Barker. Tricia strained her neck to look over her shoulder to see David standing at the room's entrance, anxiously looking outside the doorway, no doubt looking for his errant guest.

David had asked Tricia to step into volunteer mode. She'd advised him on what he could expect as she had scores of author signings under her belt. She'd even offered to take charge of the books Ms. Barker was to sign. As a bonus, the Friends of the Library provided refreshments of cookies and hot and cold beverages to those who attended.

David had initially expected the author to read from one of her works but was told by Lauren only minutes before her appearance that the event would be a signing only. More than a score of wee ones had been brought to the library expecting story time. David had confided to Tricia via text that he wasn't eager to pass that information to those assembled.

Tricia saw her man straighten, looking almost regal in his royal blue velvet jacket with his long, wild curls captured in a ponytail trailing down his back, looking good enough to pose for a John Singer Sargent portrait. It seemed Lauren Barker had finally arrived.

David disappeared for a minute or so before he escorted Lauren down the aisle, and the audience—at least the adults present—broke into applause, not knowing their children were about to be disappointed.

Lauren took the chair behind the table where, to one side, a beautiful gift wrapped in pink-and-burgundy floral paper sat. David took a position at the podium and looked out at the expectant crowd, his expression a mixture of apology and mortification.

"Thank you, everyone, for visiting the Stoneham Public Library tonight. It's heartwarming to see a new generation eager to read and learn and that the Cuddly Chameleon is so beloved." A smattering of applause greeted his words. And now for the bad news.

"Unfortunately, Ms. Barker has a conflict tonight. She won't be able to give a reading, but—"

"Why the hell not?" Dan Reed shouted. "Or should we be grateful? What with the subversive material that *woman* writes to poison the most vulnerable of our youth. She ought to be arrested."

The audience responded with a resounding *Boo!* And in an instant, the library's security guard, who'd been lurking on the edge of the room, charged forward. He spoke into Dan's ear and, in a moment, grasped the interloper's arms, hauling him into the aisle between the chairs and out of the community room.

The rumble of voices that accompanied the ejection was more than a little unsettling.

Once Dan was gone, David donned what Tricia knew to be a forced smile. "And now, Ms. Barker would be happy to sign your copies of *The Cuddly Chameleon's Coat of Many Colors*. We'll go row by row, starting with the left side of the room."

Tricia sprang to her feet and moved to station herself behind the table, ready to take each book from those in line, open it to the title page, and hold it for Lauren to sign.

Angelica stepped forward. "Hello, Ms. Barker. Little Sofia here has fallen in love with the Cuddly Chameleon. Could you please—?"

"I'm only signing my signature. No personalization. I suffer from carpal tunnel syndrome," Lauren stated flatly, brandishing the black wrist brace that graced her right hand. Still, she signed the book with a flourish, the signature little more than a scribble. She shoved the book back at Angelica, who looked at her granddaughter in Ginny's arms.

"I wove da cudwee Cammy-le-on," Sofia said, shaking a licensed stuffed toy in the air as though to emphasize her words.

"Thank you." Lauren looked past the toddler. "Next!"

Angelica gave Tricia a chagrined look but then gave Ginny a resigned nod, and they moved aside.

Stella Kraft was the next to present her book for signing. "Lauren Barker, I can't tell you how proud I am of you and your accomplishments. And I'm sure it was *I* who first encouraged you and your thirst to have your voice be heard by your millions of fans."

Lauren cocked her head and studied the older woman's wrinkled face. "Do I know you?"

"Of course! Ms. Kraft. I was your ninth-grade English teacher. You were my star pupil."

Lauren scrunched her face into a scowl. "I don't recall a single Stoneham High teacher *ever* encouraging me. More often, I was sent to detention for some minor infraction or other."

Stella bristled with umbrage. "I never!"

"I'll bet you did—and that's probably why I *don't* remember you. It was probably a conscious decision I made that blocked you out of my memory," Lauren fired back.

Stella's mouth dropped in indignation. "I most certainly did *not* abuse my authority over you—or any of my students—and I resent the implication!"

Suddenly, Tricia was aware that Patti Perkins from the *Stoneham Weekly News* was hovering nearby with her phone out, apparently recording the verbal altercation.

"Ladies, ladies," Tricia implored, but it seemed that Lauren had more ammunition to fire.

"Never once did a teacher in the entire village school system support me in any way," she spat with venom.

"That's not true," Stella insisted. "I still have proof. I have copies of some of your papers."

That revelation seemed only to infuriate Lauren. "That is *my* work. If that's true, then anything you do with them would be copyright infringement, and now that I know about it, you had better turn them over to me, or I will sue you for everything you've got."

This time, Tricia's mouth dropped in shock. She knew that elderly, retired Stella was living on social security and not all that well off.

"How dare you threaten me," Stella proclaimed.

"I've got the law on my side!" Lauren shrilled. "My attorney will be in touch!"

Tricia knew that simply setting words on paper—or an electronic conveyance—did, indeed, cover an author's copyright. And Lauren had the financial means to go after anyone who might exploit her work. Tricia also knew that a successful published author wouldn't want an inferior work to be made public.

David stepped in to separate the women before the tension between them could escalate. "Let's keep the line moving," he said, gesturing for Stella to move along, but the older woman refused to budge. "No, I—"

"Please, ma'am, others are waiting patiently behind you," David implored.

Stella turned her ire back on her former student. "You haven't heard the last of me!"

"I sure as hell hope I have," Lauren muttered.

"Stella, won't you join me for a few refreshments?" Tricia grasped the older woman's arm and led her away. With a quick look over her shoulder, she saw David mouth a silent *Thank you* as he took her place behind the table.

"That ingrate," Stella muttered, a glower souring her expression. "I taught her everything she knows about writing."

Tricia doubted that. She faked a shiver. "Wouldn't a nice cup of coffee be just the thing on this cool October evening?"

Stella leveled an evil glare at Tricia. "Not really. In fact, I don't think I'll stay for the refreshments." She scowled at the book in her hands. "And I don't want to take trash home, either." She dropped the picture book on the floor and pivoted, walking away.

"Stella! Surely you don't mean that."

The retired teacher glanced over her shoulder. "I sure as hell do!"

"What do you want me to do with Lauren's book?"

"Throw it away," Stella grated, but then her features softened. "No, maybe some child here in Stoneham might improve his or her reading skills because of it. But I don't want it. I want nothing to do with Lauren Barker or her work. She's *dead* to me," she practically spat and, with that, stalked out of the library.

After the ruckus caused by Dan Reed and Stella Kraft, the rest of the signing went without incident. Tricia relieved David to hold the books open for signing so that he could again act as the host of the affair.

Once all the books had been signed, the guests mingled among themselves, partaking in the cookies and beverages. The gift-wrapped box still sat on the table. Tricia had noted the beautifully calligraphed tab with a burgundy satin ribbon that was taped under a matching bow.

"Should I have opened this when the crowd was still seated?" Lauren asked.

"Uh, no," David answered. "I don't know where it came from or how it got here. It's been sitting here since just after we set up the chairs."

Lauren's eyes widened. "It's not a gift from the library?"
David shook his head.
Lauren took a step back. "Would you mind opening it?"
David glanced in Tricia's direction. She merely shrugged. He pulled at the ribbon and then carefully slid his index finger under the tape and removed the paper. The nondescript box was plain white with no markings. David raised the lid and pulled aside the pristine-white-and-iridescent-glitter tissue paper.

Lauren gasped and took another step back.

Tricia stepped forward. Inside the box was an uncut peanut butter sandwich on white bread.

"Is this some kind of a sick joke?" Lauren asked.

David looked puzzled. "I'm sorry, I don't know anything about this. What do you want me to do with it?"

"Throw it away!"

"Are you sure—?"

"Yes! Just . . . get rid of it." Lauren seemed pretty shaken by what seemed like an inoffensive lunch offering.

"Of course. Some of the kids might have a peanut allergy, anyway,"

9

David said, picked up the box, and ducked out the room's back entrance.

"Can I get you anything?" Tricia asked, noticing Lauren's sudden pallor. "Perhaps a cup of coffee." With lots of sugar.

"No, no thanks. But I think I might grab one of those cookies. I haven't had dinner yet."

Tricia let her go and turned to see David return.

"I'd better make an appearance at the front of the room where the patrons are gathering. I hope I don't get chewed out too badly," he said.

"It wasn't *that* bad an event."

"It wasn't that good, either." David straightened and put on a brave face before offering Tricia his crooked arm. "May I escort you?"

"I'd be delighted." David had learned a lot from watching old black-and-white movies. He knew how to treat a lady.

Angelica, Ginny, and Sofia had already left the library, and Tricia mingled for a few minutes before noticing Lauren was no longer present. Looking out the room's opened double doors, she saw the children's author standing not far from the checkout desk with a man dressed in jeans and a black leather jacket, with salt-and-pepper hair and a silver-streaked beard. But when she looked again, she saw that both had disappeared.

The crowd had pretty much dispersed when Tricia caught up with David a few minutes later and asked about the author's whereabouts.

"I don't care where she went. I'm just glad she's gone. The contract the library signed said she would do a reading. After all, that's why we were *paying* her to be here. It wasn't a minimal fee, either. She certainly didn't hold up her end of the deal, and I'll call her agent on Monday to see if we can renegotiate the terms."

"I'm sorry your first event wasn't entirely successful, but it seemed like most of the people were satisfied with having their books signed."

Tricia thought about it. "In fact, many of the parents had multiple books for her to sign. Betty Barnes must be very pleased with the sales."

"I wouldn't know. Once the signing was over, she packed up her leftover stock and left the library in a hurry."

Tricia frowned. How odd.

"What do you make of the whole gift-wrapped sandwich?" David asked.

"Someone's idea of a bad joke?" Tricia offered.

"Maybe."

She and David hung around until the last patrons left the library's community room. None of the volunteers had stayed to clean up the refreshments table, so she helped David clear away the mess, fold the chairs, and wash the library's big coffee urn. David even vacuumed the space and finished just after the library closed for the night. He was tasked with locking things up—something he'd done only a couple of times since being hired—and he and Tricia walked along the concrete path to where their cars were parked in the nether regions of the lot.

A lone car sat in the farthest reaches of the lot. "That's weird," David said. "There shouldn't be anyone left here. I wonder if it's another dumped vehicle. Kids steal cars, have a joy ride, and then leave them in our lot. It's happened a couple of times since I started working here. Usually, they're pretty dented up, too."

But the car in question looked to be in pristine condition. Tricia and David exchanged curious glances. "Do you think we should check it out?" he asked.

"It can't hurt."

Hand in hand, the couple walked toward the car. "Thanks for giving us reserved seats in the front of the room. Maybe Angelica will cut you some slack because of it."

"Mark my words—I'm going to win her over. Eventually," David said.

It couldn't come soon enough for Tricia.

Shadows were few in the lot's darkest spot. When they arrived at the vehicle, David tested the door and found it locked. It was too dark to see inside the car, which had tinted windows and sported a sticker from a well-known rental agency on its back window.

"Who'd park their car in the library lot overnight?" Tricia asked.

"People who live in their cars. That's happened a few times in the past month or so, too. I can't imagine how uncomfortable it must be."

"Should we call the police?" Tricia asked.

"Probably not. I mean, if the car is still here tomorrow, I'll give Chief McDonald a call."

But Tricia wasn't sure they should wait that long. Taking out her phone, she hit the flashlight icon. A burst of light illuminated the area, and Tricia placed it against the driver's side window. Her stomach did a flip-flop. Lauren Barker lay slumped against the console, unmoving. Tricia knocked on the window, but there was no response.

"Uh-oh," she muttered.

"What's up?" David asked.

Tricia passed her phone to David, and he peered through the glass, then he, too, knocked on the glass to no effect.

"Are you thinking what I'm thinking?" he asked, his voice taking on an odd tone.

"I don't think you should delay that call to Chief McDonald," Tricia said. "Just in case."

TWO

 Stoneham Police Chief Ian McDonald shook his head sadly. "I'm beginning to understand why you have such an unfortunate reputation."

Tricia knew he was speaking about the nickname some villagers called her behind her back: the village jinx.

"May I remind you that it was David who noticed the car in the parking lot. Not me."

"Yes, but you're always nearby when these things happen," McDonald practically accused, his usually faint Irish accent growing thicker.

Tricia held up a hand to raise a point. "Not *when* they happen. Perhaps soon *after*." She glanced over at Lauren Barker's rental car. The driver's and passenger side doors were now open, although the body and the vehicle's contents had not been disturbed. Investigating the fine details would be up to the county medical examiner. The officers had kept Tricia and David away from what was apparently a crime scene, but it was clear that the woman had struggled with her killer. The flats she'd worn to the book signing were missing from her feet, probably coming loose during the tussle, and no doubt there'd be fingermarks—or some other form of strangulation—marring the skin on her neck.

"And what about you?" McDonald said, looking at David with disdain, as though the younger man was something he might scrape off his shoe.

David shrugged. "I was concerned that one of the library's patrons might have a flat or that the car had been dumped. We've reported a few of those instances in the past. As I was the one to lock up tonight, it's kind of my duty to investigate these kinds of things."

McDonald seemed skeptical of that idea, but Tricia doubted he saw David as a potential suspect.

"So, this woman is a famous author?"

"Surely you saw the ads the library put out in the past couple of issues of the *Stoneham Weekly News*," David said.

McDonald shrugged. "There are a *lot* of ads in that paper every week."

"Lauren Barker has won the Newbery award multiple times. She's hit practically every bestseller list on the planet. Her books have been translated into over twenty languages. We publicized the event and had what was for us a pretty spectacular turnout—more than fifty people," David explained.

McDonald closed his eyes for a moment, suddenly looking exhausted.

"I must point out that at least two-thirds of the audience were children under five," Tricia said. "They can't be considered suspects."

McDonald seemed relieved to hear that. He might not feel that way after what else Tricia had to say.

"However," she began, "there were a couple of incidents this evening."

"Of course there were," McDonald said wearily.

"Yeah, the signing definitely didn't start with a bang," David remarked. "Well," he amended, "I guess that depends on your point of view."

McDonald looked at Tricia to explain.

"Well, first, a number of people were disappointed that Ms. Barker refused to personalize the books when signing."

"Is that a thing?" McDonald asked.

"Most authors who've signed at my store will ask if readers want their books personalized—especially if they're first edition hardbacks. Signed books that're personalized aren't worth as much on the secondary market."

"You mean people get books signed just to sell them off to the highest bidder?" McDonald asked, appalled.

Tricia nodded. "Think of what a first edition copy of Stephen King's *Carrie* might bring with just his signature."

"I have no idea."

"Well, it's a lot more than if it was signed to Debbie, Joan, or Maxine."

"If you say so."

"I do."

"What else?" McDonald asked.

David glanced in Tricia's direction as if to tell her to continue her explanation.

"Unfortunately, Ms. Barker and one of her former teachers had a little sparring match."

"In what way?"

"Stella Kraft, a retired Stoneham High English teacher, seemed to remember Ms. Barker's year in her classroom differently than the author did."

"Sparks flew," David commented, and McDonald raised an eyebrow.

"I'm surprised Patti Perkins from the *Stoneham Weekly News* isn't here now. I can only assume she's turned off her police scanner for the night because she recorded most of the war of words on her cell phone."

"I'll make sure to contact her to ask about it," McDonald said. "Anything else?"

"Dan Reed—"

McDonald held up a hand to stop her. "Caused a scene."

"As usual," Tricia agreed, and explained Dan's beef.

"I'll be sure to speak with him. Is that all?"

"Not quite," Tricia said hesitantly.

McDonald glowered. "Explain."

"Well, I don't know if this means anything, but while the library's patrons were enjoying the refreshments, Ms. Barker left the community room. I saw her outside the room speaking to a man."

"Who?"

Tricia shrugged. "I have no idea."

"What did he look like?" he asked.

Tricia thought about the man. "Nondescript."

"That's not helpful."

"White, male, fiftyish. Salt-and-pepper hair and beard. A black bomber jacket and jeans."

"That's better, but not exactly unique."

McDonald threw a look in David's direction. "What's the library got in the way of CCC?" He was referring to the closed-circuit cameras.

David shrugged. "We only have the checkout desk monitored. It's not like the Board of Selectmen is overly generous with the dollars they allot to the library. We rely on a lot of grants and the funds the Friends of the Library contribute. We'd be lost without them."

"Can you pull the video for me?"

"I can't, but I'm sure someone on our staff can."

McDonald nodded. "Let's get back to this altercation with the teacher," McDonald said. He faced Tricia. "Could this Kraft woman have posed a viable threat to Ms. Barker?"

"I doubt it. I mean, the woman is in her late seventies—maybe early eighties. Although . . ." Tricia let the sentence trail off.

"Yes?" McDonald prompted.

Tricia winced. "After their exchange, Stella did say that Lauren Barker was now dead to her."

McDonald's eyes widened.

"I'm sure it was just a figure of speech. Stella was upset. Lauren— Ms. Barker—practically accused her and every other teacher she encountered in the village of abuse."

McDonald's expression darkened. "What kind of abuse?"

"Of power. She seemed to think the teachers at Stoneham High had picked on her," David volunteered. "She didn't have a kind word to say about any of them."

"Did she name anyone other than this Kraft woman?"

Tricia shook her head.

McDonald looked back toward the rental car sitting in the darkest part of the lot. "So, we have disgruntled patrons, a conspiratorialist, a verbal altercation with a former teacher, and a mysterious man who spoke with Ms. Barker before her death. "Anything else?"

Tricia nodded. "There was the sandwich."

"The what?"

"A peanut butter sandwich."

"No jelly," David pointed out. "It's like sacrilege."

"What about this . . . sandwich?"

"It came in a very pretty wrapped box with a bow and a tag with Ms. Barker's name on it," Tricia said.

"Was it a joke?"

"That's what I thought, but Lauren was pretty upset to see it and told David to throw it away."

"Where's this sandwich and packaging now?" McDonald asked.

"In the employee break room trash. I can dig it out if you want."

"I want," McDonald said firmly. "But I'll have one of my team retrieve it. And what happened when Ms. Barker left the library?"

"The last I saw her, she thanked me for inviting her," David said.

"What was her attitude?"

David shrugged. "Amiable, I guess. She was polite, said thanks. She did mention how much her hand hurt."

McDonald's brow furrowed.

"She said she had carpal tunnel syndrome. That's why she didn't want to personalize the books," Tricia piped up.

"Yeah. She said that Betty Barnes had a huge amount of stock and had asked her to sign all of it earlier in the day," David said.

Tricia and McDonald turned to stare at him.

"A *huge* amount?" Tricia asked.

"So she said," David answered blithely.

"Is that significant?" McDonald asked Tricia.

"Well, now that Ms. Barker is dead . . . yeah. Every book she signed would be twice—maybe even more times—as valuable."

McDonald scowled. "I think I'd better talk to this Barnes woman."

"Oh, you can't think she'd kill an author just to sell her books at an inflated price," Tricia said, defending her fellow bookseller.

"That depends on how many books Ms. Barker signed—and how much they might be worth now that she's dead."

"I can't imagine it was more than twenty or thirty books," Tricia remarked.

"We'll see," McDonald said.

"Are we done here?" David asked.

"I'll need your contact information and who I should talk to about retrieving that video footage."

David cheerfully complied.

Tricia frowned. David didn't seem all that bothered by the death they'd reported. Was he treating this terrible event as though it was just another day in Stoneham? After all, he'd known the village's reputation as the death capital of New Hampshire when he'd first arrived as the Chamber of Commerce's summer intern five months before.

A lot had happened since that time. But one thing Tricia might need to impress upon her young lover was that a death such as Lauren Barker's was a tragedy—not as trivial as the plot of a book or a victim in a video game.

It was times like this that the age chasm between them had the potential to tear them apart.

The thought bothered her. She'd have to talk to him about it, but not now. Not until they were alone with real time to discuss the situation.

Unfortunately, with everything else going on with their lives, Tricia wasn't sure when that time might present itself.

Thanks to Lauren Barker's death, Tricia and David's Friday-night plans had definitely been derailed. They'd planned to order a pizza and for her to spend the night at his apartment in Milford, but following the events of that evening, she was in no mood for romance. After driving to the municipal parking lot, David reluctantly walked her back to Haven't Got a Clue. "Tomorrow night?" he asked hopefully.

Tricia wasn't sure. "We'll see," she said regretfully. For some reason, Lauren Barker's death had seemed to hit her harder than everyone around her. Of course, as far as she knew, only the police and David knew, but she was sure the author's death would be a top headline by morning.

Once David departed, Tricia pulled out her cell phone and did what she always did in times of trouble: she called her sister.

"What's up?" Angelica asked.

"Can I come up?"

"Are you okay? You don't sound so good."

"Break out the whiskey, and I'll tell all," Tricia said.

"Come over right now," Angelica said, and ended the call.

By the time Tricia ascended the stairs to Angelica's apartment over her vintage cookbook and gadget store, the Cookery, her sister was waiting at the top of the stairs to greet her.

"Don't tell me," Angelica deadpanned. "You've found another body."

"*David* and I found another body," Tricia admitted.

Angelica heaved a heavy sigh. "Come in."

Tricia entered the apartment, and Angelica's bichon frise, Sarge, welcomed her by bouncing up and down as though on a trampoline and yipping excitedly. He knew she was good for at least one dog biscuit, and, of course, she obliged by taking one from the crystal jar on Angelica's kitchen island. Sarge took his prize to his bed in the living room, and Tricia wearily settled onto one of the stools before Angelica's kitchen island.

"So, who bought the farm now?" Angelica asked.

There was no way to sugarcoat the truth. "Lauren Barker was killed tonight."

Angelica's expression soured, and she shook her head in dismay. "And, of course, it had to be *you* who found her."

"Technically, it was David who wondered why there was still a car in the library's parking lot."

Angelica's glare was penetrating. She let out a loud sigh. "Do they think her former teacher killed her?"

"It's a little early to come to that conclusion. Besides, Stella is no spring chicken. I don't think she'd have the strength to strangle anyone."

"You'd be surprised how much strength an older person has when riled," Angelica muttered.

Tricia scrutinized her sister. "What do you mean?"

Angelica's gaze dipped. "I speak from experience." At her sister's bewildered expression, she elaborated. "Between husbands three and four, I dated an older gentleman. Sadly, he had a stroke. I visited him at the nursing home a couple of times, and once—the last time I saw him—he got angry. He blamed me for his being confined to the place. Nothing I could say could quell his rage. He lunged at me, wrapped his fingers around my throat, and tried to throttle me."

"Angelica!" Tricia cried.

"If one of the aides hadn't walked by and heard me choking, I wouldn't be here today."

"That's horrible."

"Tell me about it," Angelica said, and paled just telling the tale.

"And you never saw him again?"

Angelica shook her head. "He did recover, and I spoke to him a few times on the phone, but by then I was dating Drew." She looked thoughtful. "I never forgot the sensation of his fingers pressing against my windpipe." To emphasize it, Angelica touched the skin on her throat. "It was one of the scariest moments of my life. There's no way I could ever trust him again."

"But he wasn't well when that happened," Tricia pointed out.

Angelica shook her head. "Once trust is gone, there's no saving a relationship." Angelica's gaze drifted to the floor, and she gave a little shiver before picking up her glass and taking a healthy swig.

There'd been years—almost decades—when the sisters had been estranged and knew nothing about what the other was doing. Tricia amended that thought. *Estranged* was too strong a word. Uninterested? Alienated? Other descriptors could also be applied. That they'd shared so little of each other's lives until both had come to Booktown was just plain sad. And yet . . . Angelica had let Tricia's relationship with David come between them. Not that the couple spent an excessive amount of time together. David had goals. He was determined to finish his degree by taking online classes in the evenings, so they usually got together only on the weekends, along with a few stolen moments throughout the week.

"I suppose you reported the problem to Chief McDonald."

It was pathetic that a woman's death could be explained away as just a *problem*. "Yes. Ian wasn't exactly happy. At least he didn't accuse us of ruining his evening."

"And what are the two of you going to do about poor Lauren Barker's death?"

Tricia shrugged. "I told Ian all I know. It's up to him to figure it out."

"Oh, yeah, and pigs fly." Angelica leveled a dark gaze at her sister. "You know you're going to nose around to try to figure out what happened to that woman."

"I feel bad for her, but I certainly had no loyalty to her. She didn't come across as the most likable person on the planet."

"That never stopped you before," Angelica muttered.

Tricia looked away, and her stomach growled.

"Don't tell me you haven't had dinner."

"Okay, I won't."

"But I thought you and David—"

"There wasn't time."

Angelica shook her head and turned toward the refrigerator. She surveyed the contents. "Would you like an omelet? I've got onions, bell pepper, and some cheddar cheese."

Tricia's stomach again complained about being empty. "That sounds heavenly."

"With sourdough toast?"

"It's escalating into nirvana territory," Tricia admitted.

Angelica nodded and raided the fridge, getting out the ingredients and turning on one of the electric stove's burners to heat up.

Tricia knew that Angelica equated food with love, so making Tricia's meal was the best way she knew to support her sister.

"You're too good to me, Ange."

Angelica turned to study her sister's face and scowled. "I wish I could say it had always been that way."

Tricia didn't know how to react to that statement. Gratitude seemed the best option. "You've made up for it in spades these last few years."

The sisters didn't speak much as Angelica served Tricia a superb comfort meal and plopped grape jelly on the toast. No doubt she kept a jar on hand for Sofia. It tasted divine. She served the meal on a pretty plate with a sprig of parsley pinched from a plant on the counter.

"What happens tomorrow?" Angelica asked as she sipped the last of her whiskey and soda.

Tricia shrugged, contemplating another bite of toast. "I open my store and life goes on."

"For *you*," Angelica said bitterly.

Tricia frowned. "I got the feeling you were annoyed with Lauren when she refused to personalize Sofia's copy of her book."

"Of course I was annoyed. The woman was a prima donna. But that doesn't mean I wished her harm."

"It turns out Betty Barnes expected her to sign an inordinate amount of books. That might be why her hand hurt too much to personalize any books at the library. I once had an author sign at Haven't Got a Clue who dutifully signed everything I had in stock *and* signed and personalized what readers brought in. She grimaced through it, but she did it and afterward told me she'd regret it for a week, but she was so grateful to have fans who valued her work that she thought it was worth it." Tricia scrutinized her sister's face. "And what about you? As a published cookbook author, how do you feel about signing?"

Angelica's mouth trembled. "I'm sad I never finished my third book, but I must confess, except for missing my own bed while on the road, I loved every one of the book signings I did."

"Will you ever finish that third cookbook?" Tricia asked.

"Probably. But I'll probably have to self-publish it. It's been too long since the second one came out, and I only had a two-book contract. Whatever momentum I had is long gone. My editor no longer answers my e-mails. The same with my agent." Angelica's gaze dipped toward the floor, and she looked close to tears. "I feel like such a failure."

Tricia set her fork down with a thunk. "Are you kidding me?"

Angelica looked up. "What do you mean?"

"My goodness. How can you *possibly* think you're a failure with the empire you've built—both as Nigela Ricita and in your own right?"

Angelica wouldn't meet her gaze.

"Ange," Tricia implored. When her sister didn't react, Tricia got up, walked around the island, embraced Angelica, and was filled with compassion when her sister clung to her. Angelica had always presented herself as invincible, and she was 99 percent of the time. At that moment, that 1 percent seemed to need reassurance.

Angelica pulled back and seemed to shake herself. "Never mind," she said, wiping a knuckle against her damp eyes. "We all make choices. It doesn't pay to second-guess ourselves."

No, it didn't.

Tricia squeezed her sister's shoulder and walked back to finish what was left of her dinner.

"What do you think happened to Lauren?" Angelica asked.

"That someone was upset with her. It was probably a spur-of-the-moment thing. She was speaking to a stranger outside the library's reception desk."

"A stranger to you. But was he a stranger to Lauren?"

That was a question Tricia couldn't answer.

"It's all up to Ian to figure this out."

Angelica frowned and squinted at her sister once more. "I repeat. When pigs fly."

THREE

The next morning, Tricia distracted herself from thoughts of murder by going through her usual morning rituals: a long walk, a shower and change, and then baking a batch of thumbprint cookies for her customers all before ten o'clock, when her elderly employee, Mr. Everett, showed up for work on that chilly October Saturday morning. Her assistant manager, Pixie Poe, had the day off—which meant she would work at Angelica's day spa, Booked for Beauty, for a few hours as a nail artist, before heading out to tag or estate sales in search of vintage clothes for herself, and acting as a picker looking for vintage books and other items for Haven't Got a Clue and several other merchants.

Mr. Everett's greeting was subdued, and Tricia had a feeling she knew why.

"Is everything okay?" Tricia asked as she poured coffee from the carafe at the store's beverage station set up for customers and staff.

"I think I should be asking you that question," he said, accepting the cup she handed him.

"You heard what happened after the signing at the library last night."

"Grace saw it online as soon as she logged in to the computer this morning."

Tricia nodded and watched as Mr. Everett added creamer and sugar to his mug.

"I understand it was young David who found the body."

"I was there, too," Tricia admitted.

"So I gathered." Mr. Everett turned toward the reader's nook, where they both took their accustomed seats. "Was the poor lad traumatized?"

"I wouldn't use that descriptor," Tricia admitted, but that was as far as she was willing to attest.

"Are there any viable suspects?" Mr. Everett asked, and sipped his brew.

"Several." Tricia related the events of the previous evening, with Mr. Everett nodding with each revelation.

"It would seem that Chief McDonald has enough to start his investigation."

Tricia nodded but was glad the shop's door opening to admit the day's first customers would keep her from elaborating.

Mr. Everett sprang to his feet with remarkable agility for someone his age and intercepted the man and woman, offering to help them with the selection of a book or books. Tricia took her half-drunk mug of coffee to the store's vintage glass display case that doubled as a cash desk and wondered if she ought to call David. Actually, she was surprised he hadn't called her upon waking. They often chatted before work, and he usually joined her on her Saturday-morning walks. That he hadn't that day was telling. Or was she just looking for a problem where there was none?

It wasn't until after eleven when she finally got a text from David. It simply said: *Lunch?*

Tricia usually had her midday meal with Angelica, but after the events of the evening before, she was pretty sure Angelica would cut her some slack to reconnect with her boyfriend.

*Boy*friend. Tricia always cringed at the word. David was hardly a boy, but sometimes—on days like this—she felt their age difference keenly.

Where? She texted.

Your place?

Time?

1?

Okay.

Tricia hadn't had the opportunity to hit the grocery store that week and wondered what she might have in her larder that she could use to concoct some kind of meal. She could just repeat Angelica's offering the previous evening and make a couple of omelets. She had eggs, some sharp cheddar, and a half loaf of white bread in the freezer that would thaw in seconds in her microwave and easily be transformed into toast. She could set everything up before Mr. Everett took his lunch break and pull it together in minutes, giving them at least a forty-minute window to talk before each had to be back at work.

See you then.

Glancing at the clock, Tricia decided she had better hightail it up to her apartment and kitchen to get things started.

The shop was busy while Mr. Everett was gone. He'd joined his wife for a box lunch at her office across the street at the space they leased for the Everett Foundation, a philanthropic organization they'd founded and she'd managed after Mr. Everett had won big in the state lottery some years before. Thanks to the Bashful Moose craft brewery tasting room that had opened only a few weeks before, autumn weekend traffic in Booktown had picked up. It seemed that beer drinkers were also rabid readers, which suited Tricia and the other bookstore owners—and especially their bottom lines. Years before, tourism had dropped off after Labor Day, resuming at peak leaf-peeping season.

Mr. Everett had returned only a minute or so before David showed up at Haven't Got a Clue's door. The younger man did not look happy.

"I'm going to take my lunch break now," Tricia told her employee.

"I can manage here," Mr. Everett said brightly, and Tricia led David up to her apartment, with Tricia's cat, Miss Marple, scampering up the stairs ahead of them, probably figuring she might finagle a few treats from either of them—knowing what suckers they were for wide eyes and a plaintive cry.

"I'm sorry I haven't got much to offer you," Tricia apologized. "How about a cheese omelet?"

"I'd take bread and water about now," David said sourly as he slumped into one of the stools in front of her kitchen island, looking utterly miserable.

"What's wrong?" Tricia asked, resisting the urge to draw him into an embrace. There was a time and place for such actions. She sensed that this was not the time.

"Oh, just about everything." David's gaze wandered to the cabinet where Tricia kept her liquor. This was also not the time to imbibe.

"Talk to me as I make us lunch," she said.

David leaned his elbows on the marble counter and looked depressed, a state she'd never seen him in.

"Amelia," he began, and Tricia knew he was speaking of his boss, the library's new director, Amelia Doyle, "reamed me a new—"

Tricia held up a hand to stop him. "I get it."

"Yeah, well, she was upset that I didn't immediately call her after the whole situation at the library last night."

"Oh."

"Oh?" he asked.

Tricia paused in breaking eggs into a bowl. "Uh, I just assumed you would have done that as soon as you got home last night."

"Why?"

"Well, because if nothing else, it's got to be a PR nightmare for the library."

David sighed. "I guess. I mean, yeah, it is. But I just wasn't thinking about that last night."

"Because you were traumatized?" Tricia asked, echoing Mr. Everett's thoughts.

David's expression was bland. "Not really. I mean, I'm sad that Lauren was killed, but I don't feel guilty about it. I mean . . . it wasn't my fault so many people seemed to have grudges against her."

No, but maybe if he'd escorted her to her car, she might still be alive. David had spoken to her, and she seemed to have gotten over the sandwich. Then again, Lauren had made herself scarce after the signing. At least, that had been Tricia's perception. Still, the signing had been David's first time in the trenches, and he'd been handed a few wrenches to muck up the signing's works. While Tricia could forgive him for such a transgression, she could understand why his boss might not.

"How deep in trouble are you?" she asked, dreading the answer.

"At least six feet," he said sadly.

"Surely you won't lose your job over this. I mean, it's hardly your fault that Lauren was killed. There was enough drama last evening to cast suspicion on a number of people."

"That's what I tried to tell Amelia. She wasn't buying it."

"Then you ought to suggest she talk to Chief McDonald."

"I didn't get the feeling the guy was in my court, if you catch my drift." And his words made Tricia feel guilty. She and McDonald might have connected if things had worked out differently. Ian was close to her age, and they had a lot in common. But. Those three letters held a lot of baggage.

"Anyway, the chief showed up at the library before we even opened, wanting to see the footage taken at the circulation desk."

"And?" Tricia asked hopefully.

"It caught Lauren, but not the person she was speaking to. Looks like you're the only eyewitness."

"Is Amelia going to punish you?" Good grief—now Tricia sounded like a stern schoolmarm.

David nodded. "I'm to present all my programs to her to approve before I can implement them—including every book I order. Amelia apparently agrees with Dan Reed that a creature who changes color might be too subversive for young minds."

A flood of anger roiled through Tricia. "The biological functions of a chameleon are subversive?"

David nodded.

Tricia broke the eggs into a glass bowl and beat them, probably with unnecessary force, before speaking again. "Is your job in danger?"

"Kind of. Amelia has extended my probation period by another six months. That means I won't be eligible for a raise until I've been on the job for a full year."

It seemed awfully unfair to punish David for circumstances beyond his control, and she said so.

"Yeah, well . . . I've got a year's lease and not enough experience under my belt to look elsewhere for a job. Yet."

Tricia's stomach did a bit of a flip-flop. Would David scrap what they shared to find less restrictive employment? He said he was devoted to her, and yet they'd only been together for less than two months. Two glorious months. Young as he was, David not only made her feel desirable, but they could talk for hours on just about any subject. Even her late ex-husband, Christopher, whom she'd previously considered her best match, had been bored to tears by the subject of vintage mysteries. However, David had embraced her love of those tomes and was making his way through her personal library of favorites. And now he could not only talk to her about the genre, but he made a point to speak to Mr. Everett and Pixie, too. She didn't want that to end.

David watched as she placed the egg mixture into the hot, buttered pan. "Should I get some toast going?"

"Yes, thanks."

He knew where she kept the bread—and the toaster. Within minutes, they sat kitty-corner at the kitchen island, eating their lunches. Miss Marple sat between them, staring up at Tricia and looking hopeful.

"You still have crunchies in your bowl," Tricia admonished the cat.

"She wants cheese, don't you, Miss?" David asked.

Miss Marple turned her attention to their guest, momentarily closed her eyes as though in agreement, and answered him with a soft "*Yow.*"

It pleased Tricia that her cat had readily accepted David's addition to her life. Miss Marple had been fond of Christopher but had acted aloof with Tricia's other male companions.

David cut a small cheesy piece from his omelet and offered it to the cat, who thoroughly sniffed it before swallowing it whole.

Tricia sighed. "I've asked you *not* to feed her people food."

"I've never met a cat who considered cheese as strictly a human food. And, honestly, what harm does it really do to give your little princess a treat?"

That schoolmarm persona seemed to swoop over Tricia like a smothering cloth, but she held her tongue and watched as her cat rubbed her body against David's legs. How could she complain when his small act had given her cat such pleasure?

All too soon, they'd finished their meals, and it was time for David to return to work.

"Will I see you tonight?" he asked.

"After—"

"Yeah, yeah—after you have dinner with Angelica. I wish we could have more meals together," he muttered. "It seems like too often the time we spend together is stolen."

"Would you like to have dinner with us?"

He shook his head and she knew why. The few times she'd invited him, times when she'd been the hostess, Angelica had acted cool toward him, even though they got along quite well when left on their own. Angelica was definitely jealous of the time Tricia spent with her new love, but she had no trouble blowing Tricia off when an opportunity arose to spend more time with her grandchildren.

Hmmm. Perhaps she ought to speak to Ginny about arranging more such time. New moms needed downtime from their little bundles of joy, and doting grandmothers often were eager to take on such tasks. And if nothing else, Angelica was a doting nonna.

"We can get together afterward," Tricia said. She nodded toward the ceiling and her bedroom above. "My place or yours?"

David's gaze strayed to the cat, still rubbing her cheek along his pants leg, marking him as her own. "I always feel guilty when you leave little Miss alone overnight. People say that cats aren't as devoted as dogs, but I know from experience that isn't true. This little girl needs you." He glanced down at the cat. "Don't you, little Miss?"

As though understanding, Miss Marple answered, *"Yow!"*

Tricia nodded. "My place it is."

"I'll bring the fixings for breakfast," David said.

"You don't have to," Tricia protested.

David leveled a stern look in her direction. "Tricia, my love, your cupboard is bare."

He was right.

"Okay. What do you have planned?"

He gave her a sly smile. "It'll be a surprise."

She rewarded him with a grin. "I'll look forward to it."

She gave him a kiss that hinted at things to come, and reluctantly said good-bye. And once he'd left, it felt like all the life had been leached from her home.

Feeling just a little down, Tricia washed the dishes, tidied her kitchen, and looked forward to the evening to come.

Knowing David's financial situation, Tricia always felt guilty when he insisted on paying for meals or treats. At her stage of life, she was in a much better position to pay for such things, but she let him do so to spare his feelings. That said, he was right; her cupboards were pretty bare.

Mr. Everett was fine with handling Haven't Got a Clue's customers while she headed to the nearest grocery store to replenish her supplies. She first aimed for the produce department. David wasn't a food snob, but he was into eating fresh. The farmer's market had already shut down for the day, so the grocery store's products were as good as she was going to get. And, honestly, lemons, avocados, and out-of-season berries were all going to be trucked or flown from farms much farther than ten miles away.

Moving on from Veggieland, Tricia pushed her cart in the direction of the store's bakery department, thinking she might pick up a sweet treat to enjoy with David along with a glass of wine or two since she didn't have time to concoct a home-baked delicacy. However, her mission was diverted when she saw Stella Kraft loading her cart with a quarter sheet cake, a cardboard carton filled with a dozen doughnuts, and several plastic containers filled with pink-frosted sugar cookies.

"Stella?" Tricia called.

The woman froze at the sound of her name. Slowly, she turned. "Tricia?"

Tricia advanced and stopped her much smaller cart next to Stella's. "Hey, are you okay?"

Stella's brown eyes widened with indignation. "Of course I am! Why wouldn't I be?" she answered sharply.

Tricia took a step back. "I thought that after learning of Lauren Barker's death, you might—"

"What? Be responsible?" Stella's voice kept rising. "Was it *you* who turned the cops onto me?" she shrilled.

Perhaps.

Tricia dodged the question. "The reporter from the *Stoneham Weekly News* caught your conversation with Laura on her cell phone."

Stella looked horrified. "I didn't know." Looking panicked, she broke open one of the plastic containers, grabbed a cookie, and practically shoved it whole into her mouth, chewing violently.

Again, Tricia asked, "Are you okay?"

Stella swallowed and coughed. "No, I'm not! This morning, that new chief of police grilled me for over an hour, wanting to know what my relationship was with Lauren and whether I felt any animosity toward her. I told him I did not—and in no uncertain terms!"

That was a bald-faced lie, and Patti Perkins's recording of the altercation would prove the lie.

Stella grabbed another cookie, taking a monster-sized bite from it. Tricia's gaze again dipped to the retired teacher's cart, and she hoped the woman wasn't a diabetic. Consuming all that sugar could bring on a diabetic coma.

As though sensing Tricia's concern, Stella blurted, "I'm a stress eater, and after what I was put through this morning I can verify I'm acutely stressed!"

"Is there anything I can do to help?"

"Yes! Your reputation precedes you. Find out who killed Lauren and get Chief McDonald off my back."

"Well, I—"

"Don't tell me you can't do anything to help me. You've been integral in solving every murder that's occurred since you moved to Stoneham. Some people think it's *your* fault, but not me. Too often, people—and why don't I just come right out and say it—*men* aren't as capable as they think they are. If women ran the world, there'd be food, education, health care, and, most of all, peace for all. No one will ever convince me otherwise."

It was a pretty cynical point of view, even if Tricia might agree . . . for the most part. Still, it was Chief McDonald's job to investigate every avenue open to him. And Stella's antagonistic responses the night before had certainly spotlighted her as a suspect. But when she thought about it, Tricia immediately discounted Stella as a suspect. Lauren could have allowed her killer to enter the passenger side of her car. After the sparks that had flown during her conversation with Stella, Tricia doubted Lauren would have deigned to speak to her former teacher in close proximity.

Stella's dark eyes were moist with unshed tears. "Do you honestly think I could have killed Lauren?"

"No, I don't."

Stella's relief was palpable. "Thank you. Now, what will you do to prove me innocent?"

"I can give the chief a character reference."

"That's not enough," Stella said. "If McDonald pins this murder on me, we're talking about the end of my life. Promise me you'll try to find out who killed Lauren and prove me innocent?"

"Oh, Stella, you know I can't do that."

"I'm only asking you to try. Try and do your best. As the voice of reason in this burg, it's kind of your duty."

Tricia's thoughts were instantly whisked back to her childhood interactions with the Girl Scouts. She'd pledged to do her duty, to do her best. Looking at Stella's worried, creased face, her heart felt heavy, but she didn't quibble. "I'll do my best," she promised.

Stella's mouth quivered, and, for a moment, Tricia thought she might burst into tears, but then the older woman straightened. "Would you like one of my cookies?"

Tricia stifled a laugh. Should she consider the offer a bribe? "No, but thank you."

"Will you keep in touch with me?" Stella asked earnestly.

"Yes, I will. Would you like me to phone you?"

"You can text me," Stella said, and Tricia was surprised—but only for a moment. Stella was a teacher. Learning new things—and technologies—was in her blood. Stella recited her number, and Tricia dutifully entered it into her phone's contact list. On the other hand, it was with reluctance that she gave out her own number. Would Stella hound her?

Stella crimped the edges of the cookie receptacle closed, signaling she probably wouldn't eat another while still in the store. "Thank you. I look forward to hearing from you in the coming days."

Tricia reached out a hand to clasp the older woman's shoulder.

"I know it'll be hard, but try not to let this consume your life. I'll do my best to find out what happened."

Stella nodded, apparently not noticing that Tricia hadn't promised to try to prove her innocence. She had way too much to learn before she could do that.

FOUR

 The rest of the day passed quickly. After putting away her groceries, Tricia rejoined Mr. Everett, and they enjoyed an afternoon of brisk sales. Thanks to the bright fall foliage and customers visiting the Bashful Moose's tasting room, sales were at least 10 percent higher than they'd been the year before. Sadly, Tricia was becoming increasingly dependent on selling reprints of classic mysteries as vintage editions were getting harder and harder to find. But the store's accounts were in the black, which was the most important factor.

Closing time rolled around, and Mr. Everett hung up his hunter green apron and returned to the front of the shop. "The weatherman says rain tomorrow."

That probably meant they'd have fewer customers, but then they could catch up on paperwork and assess inventory. And Tricia hoped Pixie would have good luck at the estate sales she attended. Tricia always felt more than a little guilty about acquiring books that way.

Someone had to die to keep her shelves filled with product. But then, as Pixie assured her, buying those tomes kept them from landfills and entertained even more readers. Pixie was wise that way.

"The end of another fine workday," Mr. Everett intoned as he zipped his jacket.

"Any plans for the evening?" Tricia inquired.

"Just to sit before the fire with Grace and the kitties and chill."

"Chill?" Tricia asked, amused.

"It's my night to make dinner. I may play some classic rock tunes as I chop the veggies for the salad."

"Classic rock? You?" Tricia asked, surprised.

"Of course. What kind of music did you think I listened to?"

Tricia shrugged. "I don't know. Frank Sinatra?"

Mr. Everett frowned. "Is that because I'm *old*?" he challenged.

"No!" Tricia insisted, not quite truthfully.

"My *parents* listened to Sinatra," Mr. Everett said with emphasis. "I was—and still am—into progressive rock. The Who, Yes, Rush, to name a few."

Tricia knew at least one song by each of those groups. She just hadn't pictured staid, quiet Mr. Everett as a fan of such loud, often raucous music. He must be bored silly by the music he was forced to listen to while working at Haven't Got a Clue—music *she* preferred. Sometimes, Tricia let Pixie choose the music. Pixie, younger than Mr. Everett by at least two decades, was enthralled with the likes of Sinatra and the big bands from the 1930s and '40s.

"When Grace was sentenced to that nursing home before you worked so hard to free her," Mr. Everett continued, "she said the music sing-alongs were painful to endure. They kept pushing songs from her childhood when what she wanted to hear was ABBA, Madonna, Billy Joel, and Fleetwood Mac."

"Really?" Tricia asked.

"No lie." Mr. Everett's expression softened into a wistful smile. "I wish you could see my beautiful Grace dance in the kitchen as she cooks our breakfasts and dinners. My Alice did the same. There's something magical about the power of music."

Tricia sighed. "Yes, there is."

Mr. Everett seemed to shake himself. "Well, I'm off. And to quote Yes, 'I'll be the roundabout.'"

Tricia wasn't quite sure what he meant, but called, "Good night," as Mr. Everett passed through the shop's door with a wave over his shoulder.

It took only a few minutes for Tricia to close shop for the day before she was off to Angelica's for happy hour and dinner, glad it hadn't been her turn to make a meal for the two of them. She tended to make the same meals over and over again, mostly due to time constraints, but if Angelica didn't have time, she'd have Tommy at Booked for Lunch pull something together and, on rarer occasions, had the Brookview Inn or the Dog-Eared Page deliver something. Angelica owned Booked for Lunch outright. The other two establishments were—again—part of the Nigela Ricita brand, although not many realized the extent of Angelica's holdings—especially in her Nigela persona.

Sarge met Tricia at the door, greeting her as though it had been years instead of a day since he'd last seen her. "Oh, hush!" Angelica ordered not unkindly, and the dog instantly silenced, or at least stopped barking. His little squeals of joy continued until Tricia gave him a couple of biscuits so he could calm down and enjoy his treats in his little bed.

As usual, the sweating glass pitcher of martinis sat on the counter, along with the chilled glasses, and Angelica poured as Tricia set her jacket on the back of one of the kitchen stools.

"Brrr! The Cookery is only a few steps from my store, but there's a decided chill in the air."

"October happens that way every year," Angelica said blithely.

Tricia noticed the plate of what looked like cheese squares wrapped in prosciutto on the counter. "Shall I carry these into the living room?"

"Yes, please," Angelica said as she piled the glasses with their garnishes and the pitcher of stirred martinis onto a polished silver tray.

Tricia led the way, taking her usual chair, with Angelica taking her accustomed seat on the big sectional. Angelica poured the drinks and handed Tricia one of the stemmed glasses before raising her own. "Here's to Lauren Barker. May she rest in peace."

They clinked glasses, and Tricia picked up one of the cheese squares before settling back in her chair. She sipped her drink and then took a bite. Extra sharp cheddar! "Mmm. These *are* good."

"Of course," Angelica said, taking one for herself. She'd no doubt tasted them before filling the plate. "So, how was your day?" she asked. By her tone, she seemed to expect the worst.

"Not bad. Sales were good at the store."

"I meant in the aftermath of Lauren Barker's death. The Internet has been very active with tributes and diatribes."

"Really? I haven't been online since early this morning. What's the scuttlebutt?"

"Just what you'd expect. The trolls are out there spouting conspiracy theories—no doubt egged on by the likes of Dan Reed. But it seems children—and adults—are heartbroken as there'll be no more Cuddly Chameleon books."

"Is Sofia among them?"

"You don't think Ginny would tell her about Lauren's death, do you?" Angelica asked, aghast.

"You're right," Tricia said contritely. "I'm sorry I mentioned it."

"Yes, well, Sofia is too young to ask if there'll be more books in the series. She loves having all of them read to her over and over again.

She's already memorized some parts of the books. That girl will be a genius—just like her nonna."

Angelica, a genius? Well, when it came to having business savvy, she was the smartest woman Tricia had ever known, but she wasn't going to give her sister the satisfaction of agreeing with her.

"I did run into Stella Kraft at the grocery store in Milford," Tricia said as a distraction.

Angelica looked down her nose at her sister. "And?"

"Apparently, Patti Perkins turned over the cell phone video she took last night of the spat between Stella and Lauren to Chief McDonald."

"Without selling it to one of the major networks first? Hmm. Antonio might just have to have a word with her. We might have gotten some national attention from it." The *Stoneham Weekly News* was also a part of the Nigela Ricita brand. Tricia frowned. Was her sister looking to profit off Lauren's death? She asked.

Angelica sighed. "You're right. But you know the old saying, 'There's no such thing as bad publicity.' And Patti should probably get a bonus for helping law enforcement with their investigation. I'll speak to Antonio about it." She shook her head. "Poor Stella. I assume she's now scared spitless."

"I honestly don't think she has anything to worry about. But, yes, until the real killer is revealed, Stella looks like the most likely suspect."

"And you don't think so?"

"No." And Tricia told her sister the same theory she'd shared with Stella earlier that day.

Angelica nodded. "You've got a point. So, who do you think *did* kill the woman?"

Tricia stared into the contents of her glass. "I have no idea."

Angelica looked thoughtful. "How about Dan Reed? I could see his sticky fingers all over a situation like this. And after the stink he caused last night . . ."

"Maybe," Tricia remarked, but she couldn't really see him as a likely suspect. At least not yet. He'd voiced his objections about Lauren's chosen subject matter, but that hardly seemed worth killing someone over. And she didn't think Dan was quite *that* crazy.

"What I didn't have a chance to tell you was that I saw Lauren speaking to a strange man after the signing while everyone else was pigging out on cookies and punch."

"I was *not* pigging out," Angelica declared.

"Okay, while *some* were pigging out."

"And what was so peculiar about the man?"

"Perhaps 'stranger' is a better term. I certainly didn't recognize him, but obviously Lauren did."

"Did she seem upset?"

Tricia thought about it. "No." And she wondered why McDonald hadn't asked her the same question. Maybe he would when she came into the station to give her official statement. Then again, she wondered why his office hadn't already badgered her to do so. Maybe she'd drop by his office in the morning. Despite it being a Sunday, she knew the village's top cop didn't have much of a social life and could often be found behind his desk on his days off. Then again, his apartment was so small that maybe he just felt claustrophobic when there during his off-hours. Tricia had been instrumental in helping him find the furnished place and making it his own. Again, she thought about what her life might have been like if she and McDonald had connected. But then she thought about David and how happy he made her.

Angelica leaned forward. "What are you smiling for?"

Tricia shook her head. "Oh, just thinking about . . ." But then she didn't finish the sentence.

"David?"

Tricia's eyes narrowed. "I don't know why you resent my being with him."

"He's too young for you," Angelica snapped.

"And you're jealous."

Angelica's eyes widened. "I am not."

Oh, yes, she was.

"May I bring him to dinner tomorrow night?"

"I've already ordered everything from the Brookview Inn. It would be a *real* inconvenience for the kitchen to amend the menu this late."

"There're always leftovers. No one would starve with an extra person at the table. And I can always bring an extra side or two to pad things out."

"When would you have time to make them?"

"I could *make* time. Mr. Everett says it's going to rain. Rain means we'll have fewer customers."

Angelica looked chagrined. "I suppose you can bring him. If you feel you must."

"I'll invite him. It'll be up to him to accept."

"And why wouldn't he?" Angelica asked, taking umbrage.

"Well, you haven't exactly thrown out the welcome mat for him."

"Lies—all lies," Angelica said, and sniffed.

"And what have you ordered for tomorrow?"

"It's a surprise," Angelica said firmly.

Tricia didn't believe her. She'd bet Angelica hadn't yet ordered their meal for the following day.

"What if he decides *not* to come?" Angelica badgered.

"Then we have leftovers. Ginny has never turned down any leftovers if it means less cooking for her after a hard day at work."

"You make it sound like I've sentenced her to a chain gang in her position as NR Associates' marketing manager."

Tricia sighed. "I just meant that as a working mom, she juggles a lot of balls."

"Are you saying I don't help my son and daughter-in-law enough?" Angelica asked sharply.

"Not at all." Tricia let out a breath. "Why are you so crabby tonight, anyway?"

"I'm not crabby. I'm *never* crabby," Angelica griped.

It was Tricia's turn to look down her nose at her sister. After long seconds of silence, she decided to change the subject. "Before he left this evening, I discussed music with Mr. Everett."

"And?"

"I always thought of him as . . ." Tricia hated to say it, "well, old."

"He's been around the block a few times," Angelica agreed.

"Yes, but his favorite music is progressive rock. It's just such a weird thing to contemplate. He loves wild, loud, raucous music, and David, who's at least a half-century younger, identifies more with the big band music Pixie enjoys. And even she's twenty years younger than Mr. Everett."

Angelica's eyes widened, and she looked just a little startled. "Yes, I'd say that's weird."

"So, do you think I should play some of Mr. Everett's music in the shop? I mean, many of my customers are—" She didn't want to say elderly. "In Mr. Everett's age group."

"And a lot aren't," Angelica pointed out with a slight edge to her voice.

"Anyway," Tricia continued, "I've heard songs from some of the groups he mentioned. I suppose I could download a few greatest hits albums from that era to play in the shop. I mean, if other older people love those tunes, perhaps they might be encouraged to buy more books."

"Anything's possible," Angelica remarked. "Why not ask him for a recommendation?"

"Good idea. I'll do that tomorrow. Thanks." Tricia sniffed the air. "I don't smell anything in the oven. What are we having tonight?"

"I thought we could do something simple. We're splitting a sub sandwich. I can open a can of tomato soup if you want."

Tricia had hoped for something a little more interesting, but she didn't mind, either. Soup and a sandwich went down fast, and she was eager to return home and spend time with David. She'd been aching all *day* to spend quality time with him. She drained her glass. "Are we having chips with that?"

"We can," Angelica said, and rose from her chair. "Shall we have our second drink while we eat?"

"Sounds good to me," Tricia said, and got up to gather the rest of the appetizers and her glass, and followed her sister to the kitchen, taking a seat at the kitchen island.

The rest of their conversation was mundane. Angelica thought she might like to change the Brookview Inn's holiday decorations—something she should have started planning months before. But Tricia thought there was something else going on that Angelica wasn't yet ready to share. And as Tricia gazed at Angelica's kitchen clock, she didn't want to probe for the answer just yet. She didn't want to spoil the rest of the evening with David.

Again, she found herself grinning. Angelica looked up from placing sub halves on plates and noticed. Tricia wiped the smile from her lips, but that didn't quell the anticipation growing within her.

Angelica didn't have that much power over her.

Tricia returned to her apartment mere minutes before David texted her and asked if the coast was clear. The idea that he had to ask gave her pause. Angelica had never been as possessive when Tricia had dated others. There had to be some way Tricia could convince her sister that what she had with David was a good thing, even knowing it might be fleeting. That thought alone caused her to doubt the future. But then she shook herself. Life was fleeting, and she was determined to live it fully.

She unlocked the door to Haven't Got a Clue and David followed her up to her apartment, carrying a reusable shopping bag. Tricia could tell by the worry lines on his young face that something was terribly wrong.

After Miss Marple had been properly greeted by their guest, and the breakfast food David brought had been put away, Tricia offered her new love a glass of wine, and they settled on her couch, sitting close enough that their elbows touched.

"Something's wrong," Tricia stated.

David sighed. "Oh, yeah."

"Bad day at the library?"

He nodded. "That and being summoned by Chief McDonald to make an official statement. I had to take time off from work to see him, which didn't sit well with Amelia. She said she was going to dock me for the hours I spent at the police station."

"That's not fair. Lauren Barker died on library property. It's your duty as a good citizen—and a witness—to be available to help law enforcement solve the crime. Especially as it happened on library property."

"You'd think," David said, staring into his balloon glass of Cabernet.

Poor David. Until the evening before, he'd *loved* his job, and now . . .

"I sure wish Lois hadn't retired," he said, sipping his wine, staring into the distance. Lois Kerr had hired David as one of her last acts before leaving the job she'd held for decades.

As though sensing David's melancholy, Miss Marple jumped onto the couch, settling herself against David's thigh. He reached out a hand and absently petted the cat, who began to purr just loud enough for Tricia to hear.

Tricia studied her lover's face. "What is it you're not saying?"

David's head dipped lower. "I don't want to sound crass, but . . . did you have a relationship with Chief McDonald before I came onto the scene?"

Tricia shook her head. "Okay, I once thought there *might* be chemistry between us, but we never seemed to gel." Once again, she told David about how she and McDonald met on the *Celtic Lady* cruise ship and McDonald's subsequent move to Stoneham. "I like to think we're friends. And if he's being hard on you because nothing ever developed between us, well, that's just wrong. Would you like me to speak to him?"

David looked up, alarmed. "Absolutely not! I can handle the situation. I just wanted to know where I stood."

Tricia reached out to touch his arm. "Pretty high, in my estimation. But I feel bad that this experience might sour you on our village and the job you love doing."

"Yeah, well, it doesn't help that the woman who hired me retired, and the woman who took her place doesn't feel my position is necessary."

Would he like to hear Tricia's opinion on the subject? She took a chance. "Then you'll just have to prove to Amelia that Lois was right. That you *are* the right person for the job. That you *can* change the lives of children in Stoneham by bringing them the very best books and experiences so that they develop a lifelong love of reading. You *have* to push boundaries; you *have* to prove her wrong."

David didn't look up to face her, but she could see the corners of his lips turn up ever so slightly. "I like to hear you say that." Then he did look up. Did look her in the eyes. Did lean closer to kiss her, his lips warm on hers.

When she pulled back, she looked him in the eyes. "This will all work out."

"You promise?" he asked, sounding unsure.

"Yes."

He leaned forward, brushing another quick kiss against her lips. "Then I believe you."

Tricia smiled. But inside, her gut squirmed.

What if she couldn't fulfill that promise?

What if petty resentments ruled the day? It was something she knew might keep her awake at night.

She reached out and clasped David's hand and gave him what she hoped was an encouraging smile.

Unfortunately, she didn't feel at all sure she was right.

FIVE

David spent the night. Despite what some villagers thought, the hours weren't spent making passionate love. Instead, they'd settled into Tricia's king-sized bed, and he'd nestled close to her, wrapping his arm around her, making her feel safe . . . cherished. Miss Marple settled at the bottom of the bed and all was right with the world.

Come morning, Tricia got up early and tiptoed to the kitchen to prepare breakfast from the fixings David had provided the night before: batter for waffles, a carafe of OJ from frozen concentrate, and half a pound of bacon. She set the table, using cloth napkins David had bought her—freshly washed and ironed—as well as her best dishes. David liked a pretty table. By the time he appeared in her kitchen, dressed in a robe, with his wild, untamed curls hanging around his head like a halo, she had the waffle maker up to speed and had ladled in the batter. She poured him a cup of tea from the pretty floral teapot she'd had for years but had only recently started to use.

He leaned forward and rewarded her with a kiss as she pressed a mug into his hand.

"Did you sleep well?" Tricia asked, setting the plate of crispy bacon on the island.

"Like a baby," he said, capturing one of the kitchen island's stools. "How about you?"

"The same." Tricia placed a jug of warm maple syrup in front of his place setting. Sensing David's good mood, she decided to push her luck. "It's family dinner night at Antonio and Ginny's house. I'd love for you to come."

David's mug thunked against the counter. "Please don't make me go," he said, his tone weary.

"Angelica swears she'll be on her best behavior."

David frowned. "She always treats me well when we're one-on-one, but when you're in the room, she acts like a lioness protecting her cub. I really don't need that kind of negativity. Especially now."

"I understand," Tricia said sadly. She turned away to pour herself a cup of tea in a floral bone china mug David had gifted her. She turned back and watched as David placed a couple of pieces of bacon on his plate.

"What do you enjoy most about those dinners?" he asked.

Tricia took a moment to think about it. "I told you about my issues with food and the anxiety I felt at every meal in my mother's house." Did he note she didn't call it home? "That anxiety is now gone. I love that we have three generations coming together. I love that Grace and Mr. Everett are now a part of my chosen family. I love Antonio, Ginny, and the little ones. I'm too old to have a family of my own, so . . ." She didn't elaborate. David was so young. No doubt he might one day decide he was ready to settle down and have a family . . . but it wouldn't be with her.

Still, she'd entered this relationship knowing it was an aberration. Because of that, she decided it was best to live for the moment . . . not knowing how long that moment might last.

"Anyway," Tricia continued, "these dinners—those people—are dear to me. I love them, and I hope you won't judge me harshly because of that."

David's expression softened. "Not at all." He let out a breath. "If it means that much to you, I'm willing to give Angelica another chance."

Tricia restrained herself from leaping over the island to kiss him. Reining in her pleasure, she merely said, "Thank you. And we always have a lovely meal," she said as an added inducement.

"At least I won't have to fend for myself for supper. Everyone else is always nice to me, and I love to see Sofia play with Sarge. It makes me homesick for our family dog."

Tricia knew about Cuddles, the pit bull David's parents had obtained from a rescue organization. The dog was now elderly but beloved by the entire Price family, and David had spoken fondly of the dog on numerous occasions.

"Have you thought about getting a pet?"

"Definitely." But he shook his head as he stabbed the piece of bacon he'd been toying with and popped it into his mouth. "I don't spend enough time at my apartment to warrant having one. I mean, between work and the time I spend with you, it wouldn't be fair to the dog or cat." He looked around the living room and caught sight of Miss Marple. "But I can commune with your cat on a regular basis, so I do get to enjoy some pet vibes."

Tricia caught a whiff of scorched waffle and found the batter she'd poured onto the griddle minutes before was now black. She pried off the overcooked waffle, sprayed the griddle with vegetable oil, and started another.

"Sorry about that," she apologized. "Now your bacon is cold."

"Are you kidding? I could eat bacon hot, cold, or anywhere in between."

Tricia smiled. "What are your plans for the day?"

"Fred"—Pixie's husband—"wants to watch the Patriots game, so Pixie and I are going to four estate sales this afternoon."

"And what's on your list of things to find?" Tricia asked.

David smiled. "Vintage Halloween, hell, even current decorations. I'm looking forward to the big night. It'll be the first time I've ever given out candy. I'm already planning my costume."

As a child, Tricia had never gone trick-or-treating. As an adult, she'd never lived in a place where she could easily give out candy. Except for parties at school and decorating her shop with pumpkins and other autumn fare, the holiday had never been important to her.

"Sounds like fun."

David's expression soured. "Yeah. Pixie and I always have a good time. It'll be a good distraction. And she said she'll show me where to get the best chowder in the area."

Tricia knew the place well.

"Is there anything you want me to look for?"

"Just the usual."

Tricia realized the waffle had been cooking for a while and quickly checked on it. It was crisp, but as that's how David liked them, she'd made the save in time. She served it to him on a pretty floral plate he'd gifted to her from one of the sales he'd attended. She was getting quite the collection of vintage, mismatched dishes and was beginning to enjoy using each . . . but not when Angelica came for dinner. Which reminded her, she needed to text her sister to let her know about their additional dinner guest. It felt like taking the coward's way out to text instead of calling, but at that moment, Tricia wasn't feeling all that brave.

*   *   *

David had things to do (ugh—laundry), so he headed for home, and Tricia walked him to his car before taking off on her morning constitutional. She found herself watching her feet take one step at a time instead of paying attention to her surroundings. So she was surprised at how quickly she'd arrived at Maple Avenue. She turned south and realized Stoneham's former librarian—the woman who'd hired David—lived on the street.

Sure enough, Tricia found Lois Kerr vigorously raking the fallen maple leaves on the lawn in front of her white-painted Cape Cod house. The leaves were the only blight on the home's pristine appearance. Everything else was prim and proper and decorated for the season, as evidenced by the plump pumpkin that sat on the concrete stoop and the corn shocks that encased the lamppost near the front of the house.

"Lois!" Tricia called, and the older woman stopped raking to look up.

"Tricia Miles! My, it's good to see you," she said, and stopped working.

Tricia left the sidewalk and approached the Stoneham Library's former director. "How's retirement treating you?"

Lois's mouth drooped, but only for a moment before she brandished what seemed to be a forced smile. "Everything's just dandy."

Tricia frowned. Lois's words were perfectly fine, but something in her tone was definitely off.

Lois leaned against her rake as though it was a crutch. "How are things in your world?"

"Pretty good," Tricia said.

"And with your young man?" Lois asked with a raised brow.

Tricia bit her lower lip. She was getting tired of people intimating that she was robbing the cradle. Men, from all walks of life, often took on much younger women as paramours, but older women with younger lovers seemed to be viewed as pariahs.

"We're fine," Tricia said, her tone clipped.

Louis seemed to understand her faux pas. "I'm sorry. I didn't mean to sound judgmental. Maybe I'm just a little jealous," she said, and laughed nervously.

"David and I have a lot in common," Tricia said mildly. "Foremost, a love of the written word."

"Yes, of course," Lois said. "I was very impressed by young David and his passion for his work. That's why I hired him as the children's librarian. It was my last act to improve our library's standing. I fought the Board of Selectmen hard to add the position." Lois's expression soured. "It was a ten-year battle to get that funding."

"Sadly, because of what happened Friday night, it's possible his job might be eliminated."

"What?" Lois practically squawked.

Tricia nodded. "It seems his arranging for Lauren Barker's appearance at the library has ruffled the feathers of some village members who are already petitioning for his removal."

Lois's expression darkened. "Why am I only now hearing of this?"

Tricia shrugged. "I'm not sure. Perhaps the library board doesn't want it known—at least until they cave and it's a done deal."

Dark pink spots appeared on Lois's withered cheeks. "Not on my watch!"

That was the thing. Lois was no longer in a position of power at the library. Amelia Doyle now called the shots, and she was definitely not in David's court.

"I'm sure David would appreciate the support. Until this incident, he was very happy with his job."

Lois nodded. "I visit the library at least once a week—as a patron, you understand," she clarified. "And I've paid attention to how David's been building the children's collection and the programming he's introduced. He's done exactly what I hired him to do—and more."

"It's too bad Amelia doesn't appreciate his talents," Tricia said.

Lois nodded, her expression sour, and Tricia had a feeling the former head of the library would be making her feelings known to those on the institute's board.

"I swear, that woman is trying to undo just about everything I accomplished during my thirty-five years at the library."

"Oh?"

"Did you know she wants the bees to be removed?"

Tricia frowned. "Bees?"

"Yes. There're a couple of hives up on the roof. Larry Harvick has several of them set up on roofs around the village. It's to encourage the survival of the species. It's good for the village, it's good for the Harvicks, and it's good for the bees."

"Why does Amelia want to get rid of them?"

"She says they're a safety hazard. Ha! Not one person has been stung since they arrived more than a year ago. The bees keep to themselves, and the Harvicks donate part of the proceeds from the honey to the library. It's a win-win situation."

"I'm for that." Tricia glanced at her watch. "I'd best be on my way. My store opens pretty soon. It was lovely to speak to you, Lois. Perhaps we could get together for lunch someday soon."

"I'd like that," Lois said, looking wistful. "I hoped I might connect with some of my former co-workers now and then, but it hasn't happened." She looked back to her immaculate house, and Tricia did not doubt that Lois had been filling her time with cleaning and yard work. And also that the poor woman was bored to tears without the job she'd loved and done so well for so many years.

"We'll talk soon," Tricia promised.

"I'll look forward to it," Lois said.

Tricia smiled and waved before she set off again. As she traveled her usual route, she wondered if Lois would follow through with her vow to look out for David. Of course, Tricia had a selfish reason for hoping the former librarian would be true to her word, but she wondered what might happen if Amelia Doyle terminated David's job. He was tied to a lease on his apartment until the following September, although his landlady seemed a reasonable type. She *might* let David out of his lease. He also had student loan payments hanging over his head. Stoneham was a tourist town, and most of the available jobs were minimum wage, which probably wouldn't cover his rent and certainly nothing more.

Of course Tricia had more than enough money to support herself, her cat, her store, and David, too, but she knew he wouldn't want that. He was proud of what he'd accomplished, and she was pretty sure he'd (reluctantly) rather rely on his parents for support than her. She respected that in him, but she also suspected she was in a better financial state than Mr. and Mrs. Price. They insisted she call them Ed and Trudy, and she did, but felt just a little uncomfortable. They'd been pleasant toward her but she'd seen Trudy's tight smile and Ed's grimace when David talked about his future. Sadly, it seemed David's future in Stoneham might be short-lived.

Well, if he had to leave, Tricia would just have to accept it. She'd had worse things happen. But she couldn't help but feel real anger toward whoever killed Lauren Barker. That person had taken one life but had potentially ruined at least two others. David's . . . and perhaps Tricia's.

As she walked toward her shop, Tricia opted not to think the worst and decided not to dwell on it lest she invoke a self-fulfilling prophecy.

With almost an hour to go before her store opened, Tricia decided to cross the street to see what cookies were on offer that she might put out for her patrons.

Upon entering the Coffee Bean, Alexa Kozlov greeted Tricia with a smile. "And what can I do for you today?" the Russian immigrant asked.

Tricia examined the cookies in the shop's big glass display case. "Two dozen butter cookies."

"Coming right up," Alexa said, and with a plastic-gloved hand, scooped out the star-shaped goodness and deposited them into a white bakery bag. "And how are you this not-so-fine day?"

"Just dandy," Tricia lied, sounding just as dishonest as Lois Kerr had been not long before.

Alexa rang up the sale, and Tricia reached into her slacks pocket for the money clip she kept there for just such occasions. "So, dere was a murder at the library Friday night," Alexa said in her accented English, adding a *tsk tsk*.

Tricia handed Alexa a ten-dollar bill. "I'm afraid so."

"Boris and I used to like to take a valk at night, but ve vouldn't tink to do so dese days. Is much too dangerous."

Tricia didn't venture out farther than the Dog-Eared Page alone at night, either, but she didn't feel afraid to do so during daylight hours. At least . . . not yet.

"Da voman who vas kilt came into our shop Friday afternoon," Alexa said as she made change and handed it and the paper bag to Tricia.

"Oh?"

"She vas vit a man."

Could it have been the same guy who'd shown up at the library and had been in deep conversation with Lauren before she was found dead in her car?

"I think you should talk to Chief McDonald about that. She was seen talking with a man at the library not long before she was killed. It could be important."

As always, Alexa balked at the idea of speaking to law enforcement, memories of being a Russian citizen and wary of authority seemed to haunt her and her husband.

"I vould not begin such a conversation," Alexa said warily.

"Would you mind if I mentioned it to the chief?"

Alexa seemed to think it over for long seconds. "I suppose you could."

"Thank you. You're a good citizen."

Alexa shrugged. "Is easy to be good citizen in this country. Not so much in Mother Russia."

"I'm very glad you're here—and if you can help solve Lauren's murder, you'd be doing a great service to our community."

Alexa looked thoughtful. Perhaps she hadn't thought of that perspective in the past. And while Alexa and Boris hadn't exactly integrated into Stoneham society, neither had many (any?) of the other merchants who'd been recruited to resurrect the village. Keeping their businesses afloat, and especially when the tourists were few and far between, was a continual struggle. That so many had made it past the five-year mark was a wonder.

"I'll call Chief McDonald and ask him to come visit you, shall I?" Tricia asked.

Alexa shrugged. "I guess dat vould be okay."

"Great." She proffered the bag in her hand. "I'm sure my customers—and especially Mr. Everett—will love these cookies."

"Dey are made vit love," Alexa said, and Tricia did not doubt it.

"I'll talk to you soon," Tricia said, echoing what she'd so recently told Lois Kerr, and headed out the door.

With her purchase—and conversation—complete, Tricia crossed the road. She unlocked the door to Haven't Got a Clue and was greeted by Miss Marple, who'd been waiting for her return. *"Yow!"* she scolded.

Tricia couldn't help but smile. "Would you like a kitty snack?"

Miss Marple *never* said no, and Tricia rewarded her pet with a handful of crunchies.

She picked up the monumentally heavy receiver of the vintage telephone and called the number she knew by heart.

"Stoneham Police Department. This is Polly. How may I direct your call?"

The PD's secretary must have been working overtime yet again. "Hi, Polly. It's Tricia Miles." She waited a beat. Polly had taken a dislike to Tricia under the former chief's tenure, but after being told by McDonald to treat *all* citizens with respect, Polly had complied, but her saccharine-sweet voice didn't fool Tricia. And as long as she was polite, Tricia didn't care. "Would you pass on a message for me to Chief McDonald, as I would hate to bother him?"

"Of course," Polly said, and Tricia could envision the woman gritting her teeth.

"He might want to talk to Alexa at the Coffee Bean, who served Lauren Barker in her store Friday afternoon before her death and was accompanied by a man who may have been seen talking with her at the library just before her death."

"I'll be sure to tell the chief," Polly said.

"Thank you. Have a good rest of your weekend," Tricia added cheerfully.

"And you, too," Polly said, although Tricia didn't for a moment believe the good wish.

Tricia put down the receiver. Was that her good deed for the day?

She wasn't sure.

Certain tasks needed to be completed before Haven't Got a Clue opened for the day, and Tricia happily did them. She hoped that the rest of the day might present other hopeful circumstances.

Unfortunately, she'd just have to wait and see.

SIX

 Mr. Everett arrived two minutes before opening, which was fine as Tricia didn't anticipate a crowd to immediately descend upon Haven't Got a Clue.

"And how are you this cloudy day?" Mr. Everett asked as he donned his apron with the shop's name embroidered along the top in gold and his name beneath.

The sky had clouded over since Tricia's return from the Coffee Bean, but the beverage station had been set up and she and her employee/friend had doctored their mugs of coffee and taken two each of the butter cookies placed on napkins before retreating to the reader's nook.

"Things are okay," Tricia lied.

Mr. Everett raised an eyebrow. He wasn't easily taken in.

"Well, things could be better," Tricia admitted.

"Young David and what happened Friday night?" he asked.

Tricia nodded.

Mr. Everett let out a breath, looking troubled. "I'm not one to convey gossip," he began, "but Grace, as you know, is on the Stoneham Library's board of directors. She says David's job *could* be in jeopardy."

Tricia closed her eyes and bit her lip so as not to comment, upset to hear her fears were justified.

"As she feels she has somewhat of a personal interest—because of you—Grace has been following David's work at the library, which she feels is exemplary. She's quite upset at the mere notion he could be blamed for what happened to Ms. Barker, as am I."

Tricia's gaze dipped to the cookie-laden napkin that rested on her thigh. The idea of food and drink had suddenly become repugnant. Still, she said nothing.

"Would you like Grace to speak to you about it at our family dinner this evening?"

"Maybe not," Tricia said. "You see, David will be joining us."

"Oh," Mr. Everett said flatly.

"Perhaps Grace could mention her support for David before dinner is served."

Mr. Everett's expression darkened. "I'm not sure that would be appropriate."

He was probably right. Still, knowing Grace was in David's corner was of some—albeit small—comfort. Tricia dipped one of her butter cookies into her coffee, saturating it, and shoved it into her mouth where it promptly disintegrated. She swallowed and did the same with the other cookie. After that, she chugged a few swallows of coffee before she stood. "Well, I've got things to do in the office. Can you handle things up here for a while?"

Mr. Everett looked confused, but chirped, "Of course."

"Great," Tricia said brightly. "See you in a little bit."

Tricia took her mug of cooling coffee with her to the store's basement office, but when she got there, she simply sat down in front of her computer. She had no work to catch up on, as Mr. Everett well knew. She needed some time to think. Easier said than done. David's predicament could very well have a negative impact on not only his life but hers, too.

Tricia sipped her coffee, which had by now gone cold, and frowned. She set the cup down on the desk and grimaced. Why—*why*—whenever it looked like she might grasp the brass ring of happiness it was always snatched out from under her fingers?

Tricia let out a breath and fought the urge to cry. Well, as she'd heard before, "fate is a fickle bitch who dotes on irony." Irony seemed to hang around her like a black cloud. Would she ever catch a break?

Mr. Everett's rain held off for most of the day, appearing as Pixie arrived at Haven't Got a Clue just before closing, with David in tow. "And what have you brought me today?" Tricia asked in anticipation.

"Don't get excited," Pixie warned as she opened the trunk of her car. "The pickings were slim."

"Not for me," David said with enthusiasm.

"Why? What did you get?"

"Some incredible prints to hang in my living room. Landscapes, mostly, but I only spent about twenty bucks and got six pieces."

"Congratulations. And for me?" Tricia asked hopefully.

"Some not-so-crummy paperback reprints. Mostly Travis McGee and Agatha Raisin novels, with a few other titles thrown in for good measure. If nothing else, they'll help fill the shelves," Pixie said, and was about to haul out a carton when David swooped in to take it from her.

"I got it," he said.

Pixie closed the car's hatchback and turned to face Tricia. "We can settle up tomorrow. Have a good one," she said with a wave as she eased back behind the wheel of her car.

Tricia waved but saw that David's arms were straining under the weight of the paperbacks.

"I'll get the door," she said, and held it while he entered and deposited the box on the top of the glass display case.

He glanced at the old analog clock on the wall. "Looks like it's suppertime."

Mr. Everett emerged from the back of the shop. He'd retired his apron and once again donned his jacket.

"Hello, David."

"Hey, Mr. E."

"Whose car are we going in?" Mr. Everett asked.

"Mine!" Tricia and David said at once. They laughed.

"How about we take your car and I'll drive," David volunteered.

"Or we could go in separate cars—in case you want to make a quick escape."

David shook his head. "Nope. Good, bad, or indifferent, I'm in for the long haul, or at least until the dinner plates are scraped." He looked thoughtful. "What's on the menu?"

"No idea," Tricia remarked.

He nodded. Angelica wouldn't punish the rest of the crowd with something just to annoy David's palate. After all, he actually *enjoyed* liver and onions.

Tricia broke out the umbrellas—a big golf one for David and her and a smaller one for Mr. Everett—and they walked through the rain to the municipal parking lot.

It was a good thing they were taking Tricia's car, as it was more comfortable than David's Jeep. Tricia handed over the keys, letting David take the wheel, with Mr. Everett riding shotgun.

The Barberos' home was only a three-minute drive from the village center and David pulled the Lexus next to Grace's little white Kia. Despite his claim to the contrary, if they had to make a quick escape, they could.

As they exited the car, David paused. "Should we have brought something? Like dessert or a bottle of wine?"

Oops. Tricia had forgotten to ask. "Uh, I'm sure everything will be taken care of," she said, wondering if she'd get a tongue-lashing from Angelica. It didn't happen often, but when it did it was unexpected.

The trio walked up the drive to the home's front door, with Tricia leading the way. She opened the door and the men followed. "We're here!" she called.

Sofia was the first to greet them. "Papa! Twisha!" she cried happily until she saw David and stopped in her tracks. It had been several weeks since she first met Tricia's friend, as he'd been introduced to her.

Mr. Everett bent down and scooped up his little munchkin, as he called her. Sofia giggled, already forgetting about the stranger in the doorway.

"Hey, glad to see you, David," Ginny called from the living room. "Hang up your coats and then come sit down," Ginny encouraged. They did so, soon entering the living room.

"What can I get you guys to drink?" Ginny asked.

"I can take care of that," Antonio said, rounding the corner from the kitchen. Angelica was nowhere in sight. She was probably in the kitchen grousing.

"Can I help?" Tricia asked.

"Not at all. Sit down. Relax. Be our guest." And then Antonio broke into song, which delighted Sofia, who demanded that Mr. Everett set her down on the floor so that she could twirl in circles to the familiar tune. Grace, Mr. Everett, and even David broke into smiles at the sight, but Tricia's gaze traveled in the direction of the kitchen, where Angelica was either busy preparing or reheating their meal, or had hidden herself so she wouldn't have to interact with David.

Or maybe Tricia was just being paranoid.

After telling Antonio their drink preferences, Tricia, David, and Mr. Everett settled down on the living room's comfortable seating. For some reason, David chose to sit as far away from Tricia as possible, probably to placate Angelica. It burned Tricia.

Sofia sucked up all the oxygen in the room by entertaining the quartet of guests with songs and interpretative dances, which were funny and sweet but couldn't dispel the underlying tension that was still quite palpable.

Ginny arrived with baby Will, handing him over to Mr. Everett, which was a good distraction, and returned to the kitchen. She was soon back, holding a tray of puffy orange appetizers, offering them to Grace, who took one.

"Ooh, what are these?" Grace asked.

"Pumpkin cheese puffs. Certainly seasonal," Ginny said, and laughed. "David?"

"Don't mind if I do," he said, selecting a puff and popping it into his mouth and chewing, giving Ginny a thumbs-up before she moved on to offer the tray to Mr. Everett.

"David," Grace said with cheer coloring her tone. "I'm so happy you could make it today. I've missed speaking to you."

"Thanks," David said self-consciously.

"So, how's the new job going?" Grace asked.

David's gaze dropped to the carpeted floor. "Before Friday night, I would have said fantastic."

"Yes," Grace acknowledged. "But I want you to know that while Amelia Doyle is the library director, she does *not* have the final word on what affects the library and its personnel. When push comes to shove, the board makes the final decision on what happens."

Tricia was pleased to hear Grace's proclamation but had to remind herself that the board consisted of eight individuals and Grace was only one person. Tricia had no idea how the other seven individuals might feel.

"Thanks, Mrs. Harris-Everett," David said.

Grace positively tittered. "Oh, please call me Grace—I insist."

"Thanks, Grace," David said, and smiled. Then he turned his gaze toward Tricia, his expression seeming to implore her to *please change the subject*. But Tricia didn't have the opportunity to do so before Antonio arrived with their drinks and Ginny brought out a second tray of appetizers, this time cream-cheese-and-pepper-stuffed tortilla pinwheels.

"What's on the menu tonight? Tricia asked as she selected one of the delectable bites.

"Shrimp scampi on linguine. It smells heavenly."

Tricia shot a look in David's direction. His gaze merely returned to the carpet. Angelica knew full well that David had a shrimp intolerance. Tricia had mentioned it to Angelica more than once—and yet Angelica had decided to prepare a dish knowing at least one of her guests could not ingest the meal without unfortunate consequences.

Tricia opened her mouth to say something, but a look at her "friend" made her pause. David shook his head. Tricia knew there'd be salad and bread that David could fill up on, but that wasn't the point. She pursed her lips. She'd have it out with her sister, but not at the family event. And in her mind's eye, Tricia was already preparing a menu that she and David might share on the following Sunday. Alone. Without the family. Sometimes, when family ignores the choices one makes, it shouldn't be a surprise for one to distance themselves from said family.

But that wasn't fair to the others. Antonio and Ginny, and Grace and Mr. Everett, had always been welcoming toward David. Only Angelica insisted on being a pill.

"We've hardly seen Angelica," Grace observed. "Will she be joining us for our pre-dinner chat?"

"She is like a madwoman in the kitchen—or perhaps more like a circus performer juggling many balls. She does not *have* to cook for us all, but she insists. She has a glass of wine and is happy in her work," Antonio said.

"Does she need help in the kitchen?" Tricia asked, hoping no one would discern her rapidly deteriorating mood.

"No, she insists she's fine and reminds me she has been in charge of Booked for Lunch when Tommy has gone on vacation or called in sick."

Excuses, excuses, Tricia thought, and downed the rest of her wine in one great gulp.

Grace changed the subject and turned her attention toward Ginny. "Has your team moved into the Morrison Mansion offices?"

Ginny's smile immediately soured. "Apparently, that isn't going to happen."

Tricia looked up sharply. "What?"

Ginny glared in her husband's direction.

"Uh . . . Nigela Ricita has decided that the mansion should not be used as office space," Antonio explained.

"Why the change?" Tricia asked, once again furious at her sister—this time for keeping such information from her.

"The fire," Antonio said matter-of-factly. "After the blaze this summer—and the stolen architectural details—Ms. Ricita has decided the mansion should be used for other purposes."

"Such as?" Tricia pushed.

"Er . . . another business purpose. Perhaps a high-end bed-and-breakfast."

It was true the village could use more of that kind of accommodation, but why hadn't Angelica discussed the plans with her own sister? The siblings might just be destined for a knock-down, drag-out fight, albeit with words instead of fists.

"When was this decision made?" Grace asked.

"Last month," Ginny said through gritted teeth. She shot another glare at her husband, the face of NR Associates. "I was only told this past week!"

"Yes," Antonio said in a placating tone. "Our marketing team will be moving to a suite of offices in a professional building in Milford until we can find permanent accommodations."

"How do you feel about that, Ginny?" David asked.

Ginny frowned. "I have to admit, the new offices are in a nice building within walking distance of a couple of restaurants. My team is actually excited to relocate during the first week in November. Some of them weren't exactly excited to be moving into a historic building."

"And how about you?" Tricia asked.

"I just want to feel settled. The idea that we might have to relocate in another year or so means more upheaval. I just want some peace."

Tricia could relate to that.

"Antonio! Ginny," came Angelica's voice from the kitchen. "Could you help me dish up?"

"Excuse us," Antonio said, and offered his hand to escort Ginny to the kitchen.

"Perhaps the rest of us should move to the dining room," Grace suggested, and rose from her seat. Mr. Everett followed, offering his hand to Sofia, who happily took it.

"I'm sorry," Tricia whispered to David once the Everetts were out of earshot.

David merely shrugged. "It is what it is."

Tricia wasn't fond of that phrase, which seemed like surrendering to bad behavior. Still, she rose and offered her hand, which David took, and they headed for the dining room. Silver champagne buckets held more pedestrian wines and the table had been graced with name cards in front of each seat, which was not in keeping with past dinners. Had Angelica plotted this, too? It turned out that David was set to sit beside Angelica. Was that so she could berate or mock him?

Tricia's fury rose once again.

"Would you mind if we changed the seating?" Tricia asked Mr. Everett.

"Why—"

"No," David said firmly. "Our hosts thought this was the most congenial seating arrangement, we should probably just go with it."

"Are you sure?" Tricia asked.

David nodded and took his seat.

Seconds later, Antonio entered the room with a large salad bowl. The table was already laden with glass cruets containing various dressings, each bearing a label describing the contents: Italian, blue cheese, and ranch. Then Ginny appeared with a large tray that contained sliced Italian bread stacked on platters, two butter dishes, and another two small bowls of olive oil studded with minced garlic.

Finally, Angelica appeared with a gigantic ceramic bowl that presumably held the scampi. She set it on the table and said, *"Mangia, mangia!"*

Before anyone could say a word, she pivoted and headed back to the kitchen as Antonio uncorked the vino and began to pour.

David took a slice of bread and reached for the butter, his expression bland.

Antonio began serving the guests and at last, Angelica swooped in with another bowl in hand.

"Dear David," she began, "I know you're unable to eat shrimp, so I made you a special chicken and sun-dried tomato sauce to put over the linguine. I hope you like it," she said, plopped the bowl in front of him, and sat down, reaching for the new glass of wine that awaited her.

"Thank you, Angelica," David said quietly as Antonio heaped a pile of pasta onto his plate. David served himself from the bowl prepared especially for him. Upon taking a bite, he smiled, something different from what Tricia had seen during the few short months they'd been together. "Wow. This is . . . amazing," he said. "Thank you."

Angelica blushed. "Just something I concocted. I wonder if it is something we ought to offer at Booked for Lunch. I should talk to Tommy about it."

"Would it be impertinent of me to ask for a bite?" Mr. Everett asked.

"Not at all," David said, and pushed the bowl across the table.

Tricia locked eyes with her sister. Angelica shrugged and took a sip of her wine.

Thank you, Tricia silently mouthed.

Angelica didn't acknowledge the gesture.

Soon, everyone was digging into their meals, while little Will sat strapped in his high chair with a rattle in hand to gnaw upon.

Tricia suppressed the urge to cry with happiness. Perhaps Angelica hadn't completely accepted David's presence in her life, but it felt like a start. A *good* start.

Only time would tell.

SEVEN

The rain had stopped by the time Tricia and David returned to Stoneham's Main Street. "I wish you could stay," Tricia said wistfully as David walked her back to Haven't Got a Clue after the family dinner. They progressed slowly along Main Street's sidewalk to draw out the evening just a little bit longer.

"If I'm going to finish my degree by next May, I need to keep up my grades."

"I'm so proud of you," Tricia said, meaning it. She'd sacrificed her social life to finish her degree, too. But then, she wasn't exactly the most extroverted person in her class. Not when she'd retreated to her dorm room to reward herself for studying by reading a vintage mystery—the subject of her thesis. It was her minor in business administration that had served her in her professional career—until she'd arrived in Booktown.

They ducked inside the shop for a couple of clandestine kisses before David reluctantly pulled away. "I'll see you soon," he said.

"Tomorrow?"

"I'll try. It depends on Amelia and . . ."

Tricia held out a hand to stave off a further explanation.

"I'll text you in the morning," David promised.

"I'll look forward to it," Tricia said, and gave him one last quick kiss before she shut the door after him. Her heart always ached just a little when they parted.

Upon entering her apartment, and giving Miss Marple her goodnight treat, Tricia texted her sister.

> *Thanks for making that amazing dish for David. I really appreciate it.*

Although she checked her phone several times that evening, Angelica didn't acknowledge the message. They were on for lunch the next day. Tricia would speak to Angelica about it then.

Tricia changed into her nightgown and climbed into bed, wondering why she'd ever purchased a king-sized version—especially as she'd lived alone since her divorce. A double was far too small for two—at least in her opinion—and David's queen-sized bed was far superior for a cuddle before drifting off to la-la land.

As promised, David texted Tricia the next morning, only to tell her he'd overslept since studying far into the night and couldn't join her on her morning walk. Tricia frowned, disappointed, but it wasn't the end of the world, either.

Tricia started off and made it her goal to walk past the old Morrison Mansion that Angelica was still renovating, but apparently now in an effort to restore it to its former glory, something she'd said she wasn't yet prepared to do back in June. She'd hired a new contractor and Tricia paused to take in the building's facade. It didn't look much different than it had the last time she'd walked past. Nothing had been done to the landscape, and from the front of the property, one couldn't see if the gardens of the past were in the process of being restored. Now that she knew Angelica's plans for the building, Tricia decided it could be a subject of discussion at their usual lunch gathering. Boy, did they have a *lot* to discuss.

In fact, if she hurried, Tricia could probably catch Angelica at home before she started her workday. She texted her sister to ask if she could drop by, received an affirmative answer, and quickened her pace.

Tricia let herself in to the Cookery, and hurried up the steps to Angelica's apartment. No barking greeted her, and when she arrived she found Sarge asleep on the job.

"It's just as well. I don't need the hysteria this early in the day," Angelica remarked. "Coffee?"

"Sure," Tricia said, accepting the cup her sister offered.

Angelica leaned against the counter and sighed. "There's so much going on at the old Morrison Mansion . . . I don't know how I'm going to wedge all those decisions I need to make into my busy schedule."

"How come you didn't tell me you were renovating it as a bed-and-breakfast?"

"Didn't I?" Angelica asked, wide-eyed.

"You know darn well you didn't."

"Oh. Sorry. Yes. After the fire and the aftermath, I just couldn't bear to defile that poor building for another second. It needs to be reverted to the stately home it once was—even if I won't be living there."

"So, what's the plan? To have an innkeeper on site?"

"It's worked well at the Sheer Comfort Inn. I don't see why it can't work there. And the carriage house would be perfect as the innkeeper's cottage."

"I guess so," Tricia said coolly. "And the garden restoration?"

"Without the need for a large parking lot, that can happen, too."

Though Tricia wasn't a gardener, the news made her heart soar, sparking a new idea. "Have you thought about adding an aviary?"

"Why would I do that?"

"It would be period appropriate, and did you know Larry Harvick has beehives scattered around the village?"

"Really? What for?"

"Honey. Wax. There's a hive on the library's roof in exchange for a donation from the proceeds from the honey. If you're restoring the mansion's gardens, that might be a great place for a hive or two."

"But wouldn't it be dangerous for my guests?" Angelica asked.

"Not unless they upset the bees. Lois Kerr said no one at the library had been stung."

Angelica looked intrigued. "I'll have to think about it—and talk to Larry, of course."

Tricia sipped her coffee before changing the subject. "Thank you for treating David so kindly last night."

Angelica shrugged, her expression bland. "It's my way."

Most of the time, but not always.

"Well, I appreciate it. Does this mean you're going to be nice to him from now on?"

Angelica leveled an icy glare in Tricia's direction. "I am *always* nice."

Tricia didn't want to spoil Angelica's somewhat benevolent feelings toward David by refuting that statement. Luckily, Angelica changed the subject. "Anything else going on?"

"I Googled information on Lauren Barker's death, but there doesn't seem to be anything new."

"Why are you relying on the Internet?" Angelica asked, sounding perturbed.

Tricia frowned. That was a good question. Was it because her relationship with David had distracted her? It was a distinct possibility.

"What is it about her death that seems suspicious to you?" Angelica asked. "Despite the fact she was strangled, of course."

Tricia thought back to what she'd learned three days before. "Well, it seemed odd to me that Betty Barnes had Lauren sign so many books."

"Signed books by a dead author could be worth a whole lot more," Angelica said.

"You can't possibly believe Betty would kill Lauren to make a mint on signed books."

"People have been killed for lesser things," Angelica pointed out.

Tricia nodded. "I think I'll pay Betty a visit this afternoon."

"I'm surprised you haven't done so already," Angelica said, picked up her cup, and sipped her coffee. "Are you losing your touch?"

Was Tricia losing her investigative mojo? She didn't answer the question.

"So, what's your game plan?" Angelica asked, plowing on ahead.

"Sorry?"

"Besides talking to Betty Barnes. You haven't mentioned talking to Chief McDonald. Shouldn't you—and David—have gone to his office to make an official statement?"

That was an oversight on both Tricia's—*and* Chief McDonald's— part. Yes, she would have to talk to Ian as well. "David's already given a statement. I'll make sure I do the same—maybe later this morning."

"Maybe?"

"Probably."

Tricia's phone pinged. She retrieved it from her pocket, glanced at the screen, and grimaced.

"Bad news?" Angelica asked.

Tricia sighed. "No. Just a text from Stella Kraft. I knew it was a mistake giving her my cell number."

"Why's that?"

"She made me promise to help clear her name."

"Oh, Tricia," Angelica admonished her.

"I know," Tricia lamented.

"What are you going to tell her?"

"Nothing new to report—because there *is* nothing."

"You have the option to block her," Angelica pointed out.

"I can't. At least, not until or if she becomes obnoxious."

"And how long do you think that will take?"

Tricia's heart sank. She had a feeling the time could come sooner rather than later.

Tricia made it back to Haven't Got a Clue with time for a quick shower before heading down to the store and setting up the beverage station before her assistant manager, Pixie, arrived.

Pixie's outfit that day was a long-sleeved vintage shirtwaist dress with a black background and large—and loud—yellow cabbage roses. It should have been hideous, but somehow Pixie was able to carry it off.

"So what happened over the weekend?" Pixie asked as she and Tricia took seats in the reader's nook some twenty minutes before the store's official opening for the day.

Besides the obvious, Tricia thought back over the events of the previous two days. "Did you know that Mr. Everett is a classic rock fan?"

"Of course! We talk about it all the time. Fred is also a huge Rush fan—we especially like their live stuff. Oh my God, until you watch their live *Rush in Rio* DVD you have not *lived*," she gushed.

Tricia blinked. "If you say so."

"I do."

"Do you think we should play that kind of music for our patrons?"

Pixie shrugged. "I wouldn't mind something different. Uh, you haven't bought the shop any new music in a *long* time."

Oh, dear. Was it that obvious?

"Is there anything else you might want to discuss?" Pixie asked, blinking rapidly.

Tricia wasn't fooled by Pixie's innocent routine. "Well, of course, you know that author Lauren Barker was killed on Friday night in the library's parking lot."

"That old news stinks like a dead fish," Pixie commented, and took a sip of her coffee. "Any idea who's responsible?"

"I haven't got a clue," Tricia said, mimicking the name of her store, which made Pixie laugh, although the author's death wasn't the least bit funny.

"Lauren Barker was all anyone could talk about at Booked for Beauty on Saturday," Pixie said.

"And what was the consensus?" Tricia asked, knowing Pixie eagerly listened to gossip but was reluctant to spread it.

"A few of the ladies knew the victim years ago." And that's where Pixie drew the line when it came to repeating what she knew. "Did Sofia have a good time at the signing?" Pixie asked.

"Honestly, I don't think *anyone* did, including Lauren. She wore a wrist splint, intimating that her hand was too sore to do more than sign an illegible signature on the books the guests bought. She also refused to read her work to the audience."

Pixie nodded solemnly. "So I heard." She was quiet for long moments, her gaze wandering to the floor. "Was it . . . awful?"

"You mean finding Lauren?"

Pixie nodded.

Tricia sighed. "More so for poor David." She didn't want to elaborate.

Again, Pixie nodded. "You never forget finding a dead person . . . it becomes a wound on your soul that never quite heals."

To Tricia's knowledge, Pixie had had only one such experience. That was the thing; *to her knowledge*. During Pixie's sordid past of prostitution and drugs, she might have witnessed other such tragedies. Tragedies that had obviously scarred her.

It was time to bring up a happier topic. "Did you have a good time thrifting with David yesterday?"

Pixie instantly brightened. "Did we! That kid has a nose for picking," Pixie said, laughing at her own joke. "He's almost as good as me, and that's sayin' something." Pixie ducked her head and gave Tricia a sly smile. "You got yourself one cool dude, lady."

Tricia tried not to grin. "Don't I know it."

The day's first customer entered the shop and it was time for the women to start work for the day. Unfortunately, the man was just browsing and soon left, and Tricia was reminded of other things.

"I have a couple of errands to run. Are you okay with that?" Tricia asked.

"Sure thing, boss," Pixie said, smiling.

Tricia grabbed her coat. "I might be gone an hour or so. I need to check something out, and then I have to stop by the police station."

Pixie grimaced. "I'm glad it's not me going there." She'd seen the inside of far too many cop shops.

"I'll be back soon," Tricia promised, and hurried out the door.

Pixie was quick to close it behind her.

Tricia had visited Barney's Book Barn on several occasions when buying books for Sofia—including a number of the Cuddly Chameleon editions. But on that day, a somber mood encapsulated the store. Black crepe streamers surrounded a life-sized cutout of Lauren Barker, whose expression was unsmiling and looking somewhat sinister. Was that the look Betty Barnes really wanted to convey to her young readers?

The store had two customers milling about, neither of them under the age of fifty, and they seemed to be loitering around a large display of the dead author's books and other promotional swag: bookmarks, pins, hats, stuffed toys, coffee mugs, T-shirts, and more, all featuring the Cuddly Chameleon or covers of the many books that chronicled its adventures.

"Tricia," Betty called, sounding positively jovial. "What brings you to Barney's fabulous Book Barn?" Was she about to change the name of her store?

Tricia whipped up a quick lie. "I was wondering how you were doing."

"Me?" Betty asked, sounding surprised.

"Yes, well, I understand you spent a lot of time with Lauren Barker the afternoon before she was so cruelly taken from this earth."

Betty's jovial demeanor instantly plummeted, and her gaze dipped to the plank floor beneath her feet. "Yes, it was a terrible, terrible shock."

Was it?

"I spent six or seven hours with Lauren on Friday while she signed stock for me."

Six or seven hours? No wonder poor Lauren's hand ached and she was in a foul mood.

"Yes, she mentioned as much," Tricia said gravely.

Betty looked up, her gaze narrowing. "Chief McDonald has visited me twice to talk about it. I wonder who mentioned that to him," she said, looking at Tricia with suspicion.

"You were there. You heard Lauren speak about it at her library signing. It could have been anyone," Tricia said, not mentioning her own admission to the chief.

"Yes, well, it's all very sad. But I'm sure Lauren would have wanted us to soldier on."

Would she?

Tricia's gaze strayed to the life-sized cutout once more. "Had you scheduled a signing for Lauren at your store?"

"Uh, no," Betty answered succinctly. "Our deal was for her to just sign books."

"And you arranged this in conjunction with the library?"

"Of course," Betty answered, sounding just a bit annoyed.

Tricia glanced at the table heaped with books. "Why so many?"

Betty's expression soured. "Those books are evergreen sellers. When was I going to get a Newbery-winning author to visit my store again?"

It was true. Big-name authors like Stephen King or John Grisham seldom—okay, *never*—visited Haven't Got a Clue, but plenty of mid-list authors were grateful to sign books and speak to readers—staying in the village, or the cheaper motels out on the highway—on their own nickels just to connect with their readers. David had mentioned that the library had footed the bill for a two-night stay at the Sheer Comfort Inn for Lauren, who'd never made it to the inn for her second night of accommodation. Had the police searched and collected her belongings?

Hmm. If Tricia could convince Angelica to ask her current inn-keeper about Lauren, perhaps Tricia could be present when it happened. It would be something she'd bring up.

Betty looked back to the customers crowding around the table examining the stock on offer. "I have a feeling this is going to be my *best* Christmas season ever," Betty boasted.

"Really?"

"Oh, yes," Betty gushed, an avaricious gleam entering her gaze. "But I'll be holding back a bit of the stock Lauren signed to sell on Etsy or eBay. I could potentially make a mint off the books."

It seemed unusual that a general bookstore such as Barney's Book Barn would have so much author-specific licensed merchandise. Tricia asked about it.

"Once I learned Lauren had died, I ordered everything Cuddly Chameleon I could find and had it drop-shipped overnight. I should make out like a bandit," she gushed.

"Betty!" Tricia scolded.

"Well, wouldn't you do the same?"

No, Tricia would not.

Betty scowled. And she seemed relieved when a customer arrived at the cash desk, her arms loaded with Cuddly Chameleon swag, and ready to surrender her credit card for the stuff.

"Excuse me," Betty said pointedly, leveling a hard glare in Tricia's direction, "but I have customers to attend to."

"We'll talk again soon," Tricia said.

"I hope not," Betty muttered without moving her lips and turned all her attention to ringing up the sale.

Tricia gave the shop one last look, shook her head, and left the premises. She had other avenues of investigation to pursue, but first, she needed to stop at the police station to check in with Chief McDonald. It bugged her that he hadn't sought her out to file a witness report when he'd been adamant that David do so, and he'd grilled Stella, as well as Betty.

Could Ian McDonald be deliberately avoiding Tricia? And if so, why?

EIGHT

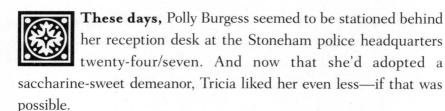**These days,** Polly Burgess seemed to be stationed behind her reception desk at the Stoneham police headquarters twenty-four/seven. And now that she'd adopted a saccharine-sweet demeanor, Tricia liked her even less—if that was possible.

"Tricia!" Polly greeted. "How are you, my friend?"

Friend? The woman had never and *would* never be Tricia's friend.

"I'm well. And you?" Tricia asked warily.

"Fine as a fiddlehead fern. What can I do for you?"

"I've come to make my statement concerning Lauren Barker's death. Do I need to see Chief McDonald or can you help me with that?"

"I sure can." Polly turned to access one of the drawers in her desk, selecting a form and clamping it onto an old wooden clipboard. She handed it and a pen to Tricia. "Take a seat and fill it out. I'll make sure the chief adds it to his case file."

"Thanks," Tricia said, and took one of the uncomfortable plastic chairs in the waiting area.

After composing her thoughts, Tricia began to write in her best penmanship—albeit printing in case someone to whom cursive was a foreign language might have to read it. She and Angelica—and everyone else who attended the Warrington School for Young Ladies—learned to dot their i's and cross their t's with a flourish that was no longer appreciated.

When she'd filled out a page and a half of prose, Tricia returned the form and clipboard to Polly. Did she dare ask why Ian seemed so distracted the last few times she'd spoken to him? She decided not to. She didn't trust Polly, who might misinterpret why Tricia might make such an inquiry.

"Thank you," Polly said sweetly, but the strained muscles around her lips betrayed her, or at least the animosity behind the smile. Tricia decided she'd text the chief to let him know she'd rendered her statement . . . just in case Polly *forgot* about it.

"Thanks, Polly. I appreciate your dedication."

Polly's expression softened. "Thank you for noticing," she said softly, and for a moment Tricia thought the older woman might cry.

"Is everything okay?" Tricia asked.

Polly straightened in her seat, her lips pursing. "Of course it is. Why shouldn't it be?"

Tricia shrugged. "I just thought . . ." But then she didn't elaborate. Still, the next time she spoke to McDonald she decided she'd ask a few questions about the department's white-haired receptionist. Maybe there was a story to be told about her, although Tricia had a feeling Polly might be too embarrassed—or ashamed—to disclose it. Still, the next time she spoke to McDonald she decided she'd ask a few questions about the department's white-haired receptionist.

And when would that be?

Tricia offered a warm smile as she approached the exit. Polly reciprocated in kind . . . for a few seconds, before her facial features dissolved into a sour frown.

Tricia made sure to check out the Stoneham PD parking lot before driving back to the municipal parking lot. The chief's car had been missing. His car wasn't in the municipal lot, either, which meant he was off to who knew where, most likely job-related. Tricia decided she'd text his personal number later so as not to intrude on his workday. But then . . . what she needed to speak to him about *was* work-related. Once she returned to Haven't Got a Clue, Tricia decided to wait to text the chief. After all, nothing she had to say or ask was related to Lauren's murder. But then she reconsidered. Tricia thought of Ian as a friend. Okay, more like an acquaintance, but what was wrong with trying to cultivate a friendship? She guessed that depended on one's motive. Hers were pure . . . at least, that's what she told herself.

"Oh, good. You're back," Pixie said in greeting as Tricia reentered Haven't Got a Clue.

"Anything happen while I was gone?"

"Only that Angelica came by looking for you."

Tricia retrieved her phone and found no text message or missed call. "What did she want?"

"To see if you wanted to go with her to the Sheer Comfort Inn. She didn't say why."

Tricia knew full well why. "I'll give her a call." She retreated to the back of the shop for some privacy before tapping the call icon. "You rang?"

"No, I didn't," Angelica said sharply. "I stopped by your store."

"So Pixie said. I was going to call and ask you about it. When do you want to hit the inn?"

"I've been ready for at least half an hour."

"You *did* encourage me to visit Betty Barnes," Tricia said in self-defense.

"Yes, well, Marina"—the inn's manager—"wants to discuss what to do with Lauren Barker's belongings."

"I'd love to eavesdrop . . . and maybe a little more."

"I figured as much. If you're available now—let's go."

"Meet me on the sidewalk outside the Cookery in a minute."

"Will do," Angelica said, and the connection was broken.

Tricia returned to the front of her shop. "I've got to pop out for another errand."

"Don't worry. We're not so busy I can't handle things here while you're gone," Pixie said.

Tricia forced a smile. "Thanks."

"Good luck," Pixie called.

Luck for what? To find a clue in Lauren's belongings that the police had missed? She doubted that. Ian McDonald was sharp, as were his investigative skills. Still, Tricia also had a keen eye—and mind—and she'd bet the force's only woman officer hadn't been invited to go through Lauren's belongings. The force definitely needed to employ a woman's perspective when it came to digging for answers. Tricia was sure even Polly could be helpful in that regard. And if Tricia found anything of note the police had missed, she'd press upon Ian to think about asking for such a view when it came to future investigations. The man wasn't a misogynist jerk . . . although he might be a little obtuse.

Tricia left her shop and waited just half a minute before Angelica exited the Cookery.

"Shall we walk to the inn?" Tricia asked hopefully. It was only about eight blocks away.

"Not on your life," Angelica answered.

It bothered Tricia that Angelica seemed averse to exercise but she said nothing and the sisters started toward the municipal parking lot, a block away, where they got into Angelica's car and drove to the big Victorian home just off Main Street's beaten path, parking in front of the inn. The engine died and Angelica yanked the key from the ignition, looking up at the looming building before them. She shook her head as though in wonderment. "I love this place, and I know I'll love the old Morrison Mansion just as much when I return it to its former glory."

"I want to know all your plans. Everything. Don't skip a thing."

"Yes, well, that'll happen but not right now. Let's see what Lauren left behind and what we're going to do to return it to her heirs."

The sisters exited the vehicle and walked up the concrete path and onto the big veranda. Angelica didn't bother to knock and stepped right inside.

The entryway was just as Tricia remembered on the day of Pixie's bridal shower. On that day, the front parlor had been transformed in homage to the 1950s—Pixie's favorite decade, not that she'd been alive during that time. It had been a fun afternoon. The task before them now wasn't joyful but possibly grim.

"Marina!" Angelica called. The sisters waited less than a minute before Marina Costas descended the lovely oak staircase. Marina was an olive-skinned beauty, a proudly first-generation American of Greek extraction. Dressed in jeans, a Cookery sweatshirt, and sensible shoes, her dark curls tumbled over her shoulders. "Angelica," she said in greeting. "Hey, Tricia."

"Hi."

"So, where are the goods?" Angelica asked without preamble.

"I had to move them to the storeroom. The room is booked every night for the next week." It was peak leaf peeping season in New Hampshire, and the Milford pumpkin festival would be held on the upcoming weekend.

"That's perfectly fine," Angelica said.

"Did you see anything of note?" Tricia asked.

"Although Ms. Barker had already been with us for a night, she hadn't really unpacked. I just gathered up her toiletries from the bathroom and stuck them in her suitcase. Come on," Marina encouraged.

Tricia followed her sister and the innkeeper to the small storeroom that had once been the home's butler's pantry, but now also housed the inn's washer and dryer as well as shelves for food staples.

A black, hard-body suitcase lay on its side on a fold-down table on hinges. Marina gestured toward it.

"I assume the police have already gone through it," Tricia said.

Marina nodded. "Chief McDonald had a look through it on Saturday. I left a message with the receptionist asking for information on next of kin, but at the time she said they hadn't yet located anyone."

Was that correct or had Polly been derelict in her duty once more? In the past, she'd failed to pass on Tricia's messages. Was Tricia looking to disparage the woman or had Ian so far failed to find a next of kin? Tricia would find out.

"Did anything out of the ordinary occur?"

"Well, there was one odd thing."

"Oh?" Tricia asked.

"Yes. A take-out order was delivered just before Ms. Barker arrived."

Uh-oh.

"What was it?" Angelica asked.

"A peanut butter sandwich. No jelly."

Tricia's heart froze.

"How do you know that?"

"A plain brown bag was delivered by the Eat Lunch food truck. I put it in Ms. Barker's room. I assumed she'd ordered it."

"Did you tell Chief McDonald about it?" Tricia asked.

Marina shook her head. "No. It didn't seem important."

Tricia and Angelica exchanged glances. Someone was going to have to tell him.

"What happened to the sandwich?" Tricia asked.

"I assume Ms. Barker took it with her to the library. It wasn't in the room when Chief McDonald searched it."

Angelica nodded toward the suitcase. "Would you like the honors?"

Tricia caught sight of the innkeeper's panicked expression. "Uh, if you don't mind, I need to finish cleaning the bathroom up in the top-floor suite. Text or call me if you need anything."

"Sure thing," Angelica said. "We'll only be a few minutes and then we'll be on our way." Marina nodded and quickly escaped. Was she afraid she might get in trouble for sharing the contents of Lauren's belongings? Angelica was (technically) half owner of the inn, in partnership with Nigela Ricita Associates, which she also owned. And unless asked to testify, who was going to ask if Lauren's personal items had been examined by a third party?

The case was unlocked, and Tricia flipped the catches and raised the lid. The case's contents looked like they'd been stirred with a big wooden spoon. After the cops had gone through Lauren's belongings, they'd apparently been tossed in with no regard for order. Only the toiletries Marina had gathered were safely secured in a gallon-sized plastic bag. Conditioning shampoo, deodorant, toothbrush and paste, a bottle of pills—Tricia wasn't familiar with the drug name—hairbrush, foundation, lipstick, and mascara.

Tricia hefted the little prescription bottle filled with oblong tablets. "I wonder what these are?"

"Thyroid pills. Drew"—Angelica's fourth ex-husband—"took them. They're pretty common. In fact, it seems like half the world is on these pills. Makes you wonder what's missing from our food chain, doesn't it?"

Tricia had never considered the idea. Setting the plastic bag aside, Tricia began unloading the clothes from the case, neatly folding them and setting them on the table. There weren't many—just enough for a couple of days' travel. "I haven't done much research on Lauren. Any idea where she lived?"

Angelica scowled. "You really are out of touch on this one. I Googled her Wikipedia page. She's originally from Ohio, grew up here in Stoneham, but had been living in our home state for the past decade."

Connecticut. It was relatively close to the publishing capital of the world—Manhattan—and, depending on where one claimed a stake, a pretty nice place to live.

At the bottom of the case was an e-reader along with a charging cord. Tricia pressed the on switch and the device flashed to life. The list of the latest downloaded books appeared. The titles meant nothing to Tricia, most of them appearing to be true crime or memoirs, which seemed strange reading for a children's book author. Then again, she'd met several current mystery authors who preferred not to read books in their own genre lest they be "tainted" by absorbing the plotlines of their peers. She had to admit that those authors often had the most unique perspectives when it came to the modern mystery.

Tricia withdrew her phone from her slacks pocket and took a picture of the ten titles on the reader's first screen. Perhaps one of them might give her a clue as to why Lauren was killed—if not . . . well, maybe she'd gain some insight into the author's state of mind before her death by her choice of reading material. It was a long shot. And perhaps she'd just be entertained by what another person chose as reading material.

"Do you really think that's important?" Angelica said.

Tricia shrugged. "One never knows."

Angelica looked doubtful. "I wonder why she had an e-reader? Don't most people read on their phones these days?"

"Only if they have good vision. I prefer the printed word, but I also have an e-reader that I keep charged—just in case."

"You dog, you," Angelica quipped. But then she sobered. "So, there's nothing of real interest here? Nothing to lead you to whoever killed Lauren?"

Tricia shook her head and began to repack the case. "I don't think so." She paused. "It's sad, really. The person who killed Lauren was probably at the signing on Friday night. And though Lauren wasn't as nice as she could have been, perhaps she was just having a bad day."

"I'm glad you're considering that possibility."

"There's always the unknown man who spoke to her near the circulation desk the night she was killed."

"And what was his demeanor, since apparently you were the only one who witnessed the encounter?" Angelica asked.

Tricia thought back. "I didn't get a sense that there was conflict between them." She thought about what she'd seen. "In fact, Lauren's expression was pretty neutral. And she nodded as she listened to whatever the man was telling her."

Again Angelica shrugged. "If only we knew what she was saying to him."

Tricia frowned. "I wonder . . ." she said, and pursed her lips as she thought about it.

"Yes?" Angelica prodded.

"I wonder if someone adept at lipreading should look at the library's tape."

"Surely these things are no longer on tape."

"Tape—digital—who cares. Someone with such a skill should

view that video if only to see if Lauren said anything that could lead to the identity of her killer."

"So, bring it up to Chief McDonald just in case he hasn't thought of it himself."

Tricia nodded. "I think I will."

"I *know* you will," Angelica said. She heaved a sigh. "Let's go. We'll learn nothing more about Lauren Barker here."

"You're probably right. But perhaps you should flex your authority to find out who to return Lauren's personal effects to, if for no other reason than to get them out of the inn and off Marina's shoulders. And, of course, find out who ordered the peanut butter sandwich to be delivered to Lauren, and then report it to the chief."

"Anything else?" Angelica grated.

"That'll do."

Angelica shook her head. "I'll do it as soon as I get back to my home base." Angelica pulled out her phone to text Marina to let her know they were leaving and that she'd be in touch, then the sisters left the inn.

"What's next on your agenda?" Angelica asked as she steered them back toward the municipal parking lot.

"I'm not sure," Tricia said. Should she confide her fears that David might lose his job and leave her bereft? Angelica had gone out of her way to make David welcome the evening before. Even so, Tricia didn't want to push her luck. She didn't want to admit to her unlucky-in-love sister just how incredibly happy she felt in David's presence. How she hadn't felt that way with most of her former partners. David took such delight in just about everything. He hadn't (yet) been beaten down by his job and life in general. They laughed together. They cooked together. That he was a pet person who cared about Miss Marple's happiness over his own made Tricia's heart swell with affection. She'd really lucked out . . . so far.

Angelica pulled the car into a parking space and killed the engine. "Back to work." She pulled out her phone and glanced at the time. "Hmm. I've lost too much of the morning. I'll grab some takeout from Booked for Lunch at my place."

"Sure . . . unless you have things you need to get done."

"I can get some work done before lunch rolls around," she said.

The sisters exited the car and hit the sidewalk, which was more crowded than when they'd left half an hour before. They walked south toward their places of business.

"See you later," Angelica called as she thumbed the Cookery's door latch and entered.

"Back at you," Tricia said, and continued to Haven't Got a Clue. Despite what the sisters had learned at the Sheer Comfort Inn, Tricia had to admit that when it came to figuring out who'd killed Lauren Barker . . . she didn't have a clue.

NINE

 Tricia entered her store, which seemed to be stuffed with customers, glanced at the cash register, and saw that Pixie, who was usually unflappable, seemed to be overwhelmed.

"Help!" Pixie called, and Tricia quickly circled the big glass display case that was piled with paperback editions of classic mysteries, shoving books into the store's logo-emblazoned paper bags with handles.

"A bus arrived right after you left," Pixie explained between customers.

"That's good."

"It's better that David and I came up with so much new inventory over the weekend," Pixie said before greeting yet another customer. It was total chaos for the next hour until the crowd had to return to the bus.

"Whew! That was a successful morning," Pixie exclaimed as she flopped onto her favorite chair in the reader's nook. Tricia joined her.

"Thanks for your hard work."

Pixie eyed her critically. "We have a serious problem."

"Oh?" Tricia asked.

"Inventory. I think it might be time for us to admit that we aren't a vintage mystery store anymore."

Tricia averted her gaze, turning it to the carpeted floor that could use a good clean—a testament to the thousands of customers who'd walked upon it over years of inclement weather. "Go on."

"Let's face it, these days, our oldest stock is Nancy Drew and Hardy Boys novels. As for classic adult mysteries, we're only finding mass-market paperbacks from the 1980s forward, and most of them aren't anywhere near pristine condition."

Tricia heaved a sigh. "I know."

"My suggestion—and I know you didn't ask for it," Pixie began, "is to concentrate on new reprints and new titles. We could still sell the vintage Nancy Drew, Trixie Belden, and Hardy Boys titles that I find at yard and estate sales, but anything of any real worth should be sold on auction sites where they'll bring in the most money."

For someone who'd never even graduated high school, Pixie's knowledge and experience in retail sales were worth her weight in gold.

Tricia contemplated her reply for long seconds. "I don't like what you've just said."

Pixie's eyes widened in what could only be described as horror.

"But," Tricia began, "you've voiced what I've been trying to deny for quite some time."

Pixie let out a breath and sank deeper into her seat. "Thanks," she whispered.

Tricia laughed. "Did you think I would fire you for voicing an honest opinion?"

"No, but . . ."

Maybe she had.

"Why don't we go through the most recent publisher catalogs and make lists? And we'll ask Mr. Everett for his input, too." He was a lot more hip than Tricia had given him credit for.

"I'm not saying we can't still sell used books," Pixie said. "It's just that we should only sell stock in near-pristine condition. Otherwise . . ."

Tricia knew what Pixie meant. She'd often shopped in used bookstores whose owners dumpster-dived their stock from mainstream stores that had stripped the covers from books in lieu of returns, receiving credit from the publishers. And those "stolen" books that were resold cheated both authors—many of whom couldn't pay their mortgages on their writing incomes—and publishers, who paid advances to authors, money they might never recoup, making them less likely to buy another book from said author and curtailing many promising careers. It was a vicious cycle.

"Do you want to go through the catalogs now?" Tricia asked.

Pixie shook her head. "After the last couple of hours, my brain is scrod."

Fish? Tricia didn't ask.

"I'd be glad to take a couple of them home and go through them tonight while Fred watches football. That way, we can spend time together and both be happy."

"Thanks," Tricia said, gratefully.

"Not a problem." Pixie glanced at the clock and winced. "I'm a little late for lunch."

"That's okay. I'm meeting Angelica at her place instead of Booked for Lunch. We're both too pressed for time today to sit back and be waited on."

Pixie nodded, grabbed her coat and purse, and left the store. She soon returned with a white paper bakery bag from the Coffee Bean.

"There's no buses in sight. I thought I might eat my lunch at the cash desk and peruse some of those catalogs. Why don't you hit the trail for Angelica's?"

"Are you sure?" Tricia asked.

"Positive. Just let me hang up my coat."

Less than a minute later, Tricia flew out the door.

Unlike earlier in the day, Sarge was ecstatic to see Tricia. How she wished she could feel as joyful as that playful pup. Everything he encountered brought him immense happiness. If only his human counterparts could experience that level of glee.

After she tossed him a couple of dog biscuits, Sarge retreated to his comfy bed and Tricia faced her sister. "Did you get some work done?" she asked.

Angelica glared at her sister. "Not really."

"Why?"

Angelica heaved a theatrical sigh worthy of a Barrymore. "I got a call from Becca Chandler. It seems she hired Lauren Barker in some capacity back in her early days as"—Angelica struck a pose—"a tennis star."

"Why did she call you?"

Angelica shrugged. "A fishing expedition, although I'm not really sure what she was fishing for." She frowned as she wiped the counter. "You have a better connection with Becca than me. I thought *you* might want to follow up on that."

Did she ever!

"I'll give her a call tomorrow," Tricia said. She'd do so early. Perhaps the two of them could talk over lunch at the Brookview Inn. It was possible Becca might—and only *might*—spill her guts to Tricia. That said, the woman *had* reached out—albeit to Angelica and not Tricia, with whom she had a closer relationship. And why was that?

Probably because the Chamber membership still saw Angelica as a leader and Tricia as a follower, thanks to her previous volunteer position in the organization. But Becca hadn't even been a member during that time. It irked Tricia, but not enough that she wouldn't grill Becca for what she knew about the newly departed.

"On second thought, I think I'll text her and ask her to lunch tomorrow—if she can pencil me in. I'll let you know how it goes."

"Good." Angelica looked wistfully toward the balcony and shook her head. Mid-October in New Hampshire was just a little too chilly for sitting outside without a fire pit and a lap robe.

"What's for lunch?" Tricia asked.

It seemed like Angelica had forgotten the reason for Tricia's visit. "Oh, I got a couple of orders of the quiche of the day and soup," she said. Tricia could smell the tomato soup that was simmering on the stove.

"And the quiche?"

"Broccoli and cheese."

Tricia sighed. Wasn't it *always* broccoli and cheese?

Angelica took out two plates from the fridge, and placed one in the microwave to heat. "Marina called. She still hasn't heard from Chief McDonald about Lauren's next of kin. You'd think after nearly four days *someone* would have contacted him about her belongings." Angelica looked thoughtful. "The national media covered the news of her death. I wonder if anyone has stepped forward to claim her body—if not a relative, even a lawyer."

"That we know of," Tricia pointed out.

Angelica shook her head and took two bowls from the cupboard, ladling soup into each. "It seems odd. Someone as beloved to the nation's children ought to get at least some kind of send-off."

"Sadly, her death is yesterday's—or at least last Friday's—news. The media's moved on."

Angelica carried the bowls to the kitchen island, and then grabbed a couple of spoons. "What do you want to drink?"

"Water's fine."

Angelica poured two glasses and set them on the island just as the microwave chimed.

Tricia raised her glass. "To Thursday's Chamber meeting."

Angelica looked stricken and turned to retrieve the first of the plates. "Oh, no! I completely forgot about it."

How could she forget such an important event? But then Angelica was juggling far too many balls in the air.

"We have leftover business from last month's meeting," Tricia pointed out, trying to decide if she should try the soup or quiche first.

"Oh, don't remind me," Angelica said, and took a healthy gulp of her water.

"It's your turn to chair the meeting, which is why I brought it up."

Angelica sighed theatrically. "Why did we ever volunteer to take the job?"

"Because Russ Smith destroyed everything you did to build the Chamber—and in so little time."

"That's the thing," Angelica said. "We could build it back up and the next person to take to the job could destroy it again."

"That's true," Tricia reluctantly admitted. "But . . . we're helping every member of the Chamber with tips to maximize their business's potential. We're two smart women with a lot of business sense we can pass on to others. Together, our members are making this out-of-the-way burg into a destination point. People enjoy visiting Booktown, and now we've ventured past that moniker. We're luring in a more diverse demographic with businesses like the Bee's Knees and the Bashful Moose tasting room. And when Becca's tennis club finally opens, it'll bring in even more people."

"You're right," Angelica said, and raised her glass. "To us. And to all the Chamber members who subscribe to our philosophy of working together for the greater good."

"Hear, hear," Tricia said. Too bad government didn't always work that way.

A sharp ping pierced the space between them. Tricia looked at her cell phone to see a text from her sort-of friend, Becca.

We need to talk.

Tricia glanced at Angelica. "It's Becca. Do you mind if I reply to this text?"

"Go ahead."

Busy right now. Can I call you later tonight or tomorrow?

Not really.

Tricia could almost hear the disdain in Becca's voice—had the woman said the words aloud.

"She wants to talk."

"Good grief," Angelica muttered. "You may as well get it over with."

"You don't mind?"

"I'd mind more if it was me who had to speak to her *again*!"

Tricia tapped her phone's contact icon, found Becca's entry, and hit the call button. Becca picked up right away.

"Hey, Becca. It's Tricia. What's up?"

"I dunno. I just thought I'd call you for a little girl talk."

Tricia couldn't help but roll her eyes, grateful the woman on the other end of the connection couldn't see her reaction. When Becca Dickson-Chandler, former world champion tennis player, called to chat, she usually had some kind of agenda.

"On what subject?" Tricia asked blithely.

"Well, I thought you might be interested to know that I had lunch with Lauren Barker last Friday."

Tricia's mouth dropped. Suddenly, Becca commanded all of Tricia's attention. "Uh, I'm having my lunch right now. Do you mind if I put you on speaker?"

Angelica nodded vigorously.

"As long as you're not in a public place," Becca agreed.

"Oh, I'm not. So tell me more."

"Lauren worked as my admin for a couple of years before chasing fame and fortune as a children's author." She sighed. "To be candid, I think she was writing those books on *my* time, but that's another story for another day. Anyway, we had *quite* a lot to talk about," Becca teased.

"Anything that might help the authorities solve her murder?" Tricia asked anxiously.

"I don't know about *that*. . . ." Becca's voice trailed off. She didn't seem all that broken up by the death of a former employee.

"I'm sorry for the loss of your friend," Tricia said sincerely.

"Oh, Lauren and I were *never* friends," Becca proclaimed.

"Then why did you meet for lunch?"

"Believe me, I didn't seek *her* out. She sought *me*."

"And why was that?"

A long silence greeted that question before Becca answered. "Let's just say she asked my advice about security."

"Her own?"

"That and other things." Becca let the sentence hang.

"So, what have you got to tell me?" Tricia asked, dipping her spoon into her soup.

As suspected, Becca wasn't about to immediately drop her bombshell. Instead, she launched into a lengthy recitation about the obstacles she'd encountered with the Board of Selectmen and the county's zoning entity on what she could and couldn't do with the major tennis complex she intended to build on the village's outskirts.

"It's been so much harder than I ever thought it would be," Becca wailed dramatically.

Becca, O she of fame and fortune, expected results at the snap of her fingers. Perhaps it might have happened at the height of her fame, but now some might call her a has-been.

"I'm sorry it's taking so much longer than you anticipated," Tricia said solicitously, "but I'm sure it'll be worth the wait."

"It had better be," Becca grated.

Tricia took the conversational lead. "So, you mentioned Lauren Barker was interested in obtaining some kind of personal security."

"She seemed to think she was in danger."

"In what way?"

"A cyberstalker. Someone sent her a number of threatening e-mails of late."

"What kind of threat?"

"I will *kill* you," Becca said, enunciating each word.

Tricia's eyes widened. "Have you told Chief McDonald about that conversation?"

"Why would I?" Becca asked blankly.

Was the woman crazy? "Because whoever sent the threat obviously went through with their plan and strangled the poor woman!"

"You don't know that," Becca exclaimed. "I've been receiving death threats for decades, and *I'm* still here."

"Yes, because *you* had a security force."

Becca didn't dignify Tricia's protest with a remark.

"When was the last time someone threatened you?" Tricia demanded.

Becca sighed dramatically. "A couple of years ago. I have a much lower profile these days."

The word *has-been* again echoed in Tricia's mind.

"But once my tennis clubs take off, I'm sure some resentful tennis wannabe I've never met will decide I've deprived them of fame and fortune and will come after me."

Angelica rolled her eyes and polished off the last of her soup.

Tricia frowned. Just because Becca hadn't succumbed to a crazed fan didn't mean it hadn't happened to other celebrities in the past. Rabid fans often evolved into stalkers if they felt the object of their devotion had dissed them in some way. Some people just didn't get that individuals with public personas deserved to keep some—often the largest—parts of their lives private.

"You need to tell Chief McDonald about your conversation with Lauren."

Becca didn't comment.

"If you don't," Tricia continued, "I *will*."

Becca hesitated before speaking. "Do you have to be so . . . so bitchy?"

Tricia's mouth dropped. "A woman died. She voiced she'd been threatened. How can you be so complacent?"

The silence lengthened before Becca sighed. "I suppose you're right. Perhaps I *should* have taken Lauren's concerns a little more seriously."

"Perhaps?" Tricia had to bite her lip so as not to let loose the volley of vitriol that threatened to explode from within her. Tricia picked up her fork and took a bite of quiche. It had gone cold. She got up and placed the plate in the microwave again, knowing another thirty or forty seconds in it would reduce the once-soft pie to a rubbery mass. "So, when are you going to call Chief McDonald?" Tricia asked.

"When I get a chance." Becca seemed distinctly annoyed by the question.

"Today," Tricia said firmly.

Again, Becca sighed theatrically. Perhaps instead of playing tennis, she should have become a thespian. "If you insist."

"I do. It's the right thing to do."

The microwave pinged once again and Tricia retrieved her plate, taking it back to her seat at the island.

"So, how are you and your *little* boyfriend getting on?" Becca finally said, as though remembering that conversations were supposed to be a two-way street.

Tricia wasn't about to react to Becca's slur. "Quite happily."

Becca's eyes narrowed. "And?"

"We have a lot in common."

"*And?*" Becca pressed.

Angelica leaned in, paying close attention.

"What do you want me to say?"

Becca laughed. "That the sex is great. That you're happier than you've ever been."

"Well," Tricia said, cutting another bite of quiche with her fork. "There is that."

Another long silence fell between them. Tricia guessed Becca might be just a tad jealous. As far as she knew, Becca had no one in her life to depend on, to make her days better . . . to love her. And for that, she felt pity for the woman. Still, she wasn't about to divulge anything more about her relationship with David—or anyone else. Instead, Tricia asked for more details about the upcoming tennis club. If nothing else, she could use the information for a short update in the Chamber's newsletter's next issue.

Angelica got up and began clearing their places.

After Becca yammered on for another five minutes, Tricia interrupted her. "I hate to cut this short," Tricia lied, "but I need to get back to my shop."

"Ah, yes. How tedious it must be to be a working stiff. Well, it was *so* good to talk to you, Tricia," Becca said without sincerity. "We'll have to do this again soon." And with that, she ended the call.

Tricia fought against but succumbed to the urge to stick out her tongue at the phone before she shoved it away.

Angelica returned to the island. "Well, that was quite the conversation."

"Yeah," Tricia agreed. "Tomorrow, I'll follow up with Ian McDonald, because I'm not sure Becca will do the right thing and tell him about Lauren's concerns and how they might be why she was killed."

Angelica said nothing and instead regarded the nails on her left hand.

Tricia's brows furrowed. "What?"

Angelica shook her head. "You could have couched your threat in much softer language."

"Threat?" Tricia asked, feeling heat rise from her neck to color her cheeks.

"Yes, a threat. I understand your passion—and I agree that the chief should be told about Lauren's concerns—but you could have encouraged Becca to report what she knows without being confrontational."

Tricia clutched her glass. Had she been too forceful when speaking with Becca? Possibly. "You know, this isn't the first time I've had to encourage Becca to do the right thing."

"What a bitch," Angelica muttered, frowning.

"That's what Becca accused me of when I said I'd speak to Ian."

Angelica shrugged, and then her gaze narrowed. "So, the sex is great, huh?"

Tricia glowered at her sister.

TEN

As Tricia left the Cookery, she saw Larry Harvick of the Bee's Knees unloading stock for the store from the back of his car. "Larry!" she called and waved, hurrying past her store to meet the man at his.

Harvick turned at the sound of her voice. "Tricia. Good to see you."

Tricia soon joined him on the sidewalk. "Hey, I heard about the hives you've got scattered around the village, and what a great success they are."

Harvick practically beamed. "So far, so good." Then his expression darkened. "Well, mostly."

Tricia knew the problem. "I understand Amelia Doyle isn't happy about the bees atop the library's roof."

"She says she's allergic to beestings," he said with chagrin.

"You don't believe her?"

"Oh, I do. But my bees keep pretty much to themselves—unless provoked. There's not much chance of that happening when they're on the roof, but I promised the Board of Selectmen that I'd remove a hive if there were a complaint. So, I'll bring them home in the next few days."

"Can I help with that?" Tricia asked eagerly.

Harvick scrutinized her face. "You're not afraid of getting stung?"

"I've been stung before with no bad results, although I think they were wasps, not bees. I'm rather fascinated by the whole idea. I mean, I've been following the news stories about bee colony collapse disorder for the past couple of years and I now know how important they are to our food chain."

"Unless riled, they're really quite gentle creatures. I often work with them without protection. You just have to know how to handle them."

"I'd love to at least observe you in action."

"That can *be* arranged—no pun intended," he said, smiling.

Tricia returned the grin. "That sounds great. When would be a good time?"

"I'll check with the wife on our schedule and get back to you later today."

"Wonderful. Thanks." Tricia smiled and nodded in the direction of her store. "I guess I'd better get back to work."

"Time is money," Harvick said, agreeing and grinning. "And for me, time is also honey."

"Talk to you soon." Tricia gave him a nod and continued on her way. She felt pretty good until she remembered her recent conversation with Becca.

Again, Tricia put the woman out of her mind and instead glanced at her watch, calculating how many hours it would be until she could again connect with David.

Until then, she had a store to run.

* * *

Upon returning to Haven't Got a Clue, Tricia found it empty of customers. Pixie sat behind the cash desk while Ella Fitzgerald's voice bathed the air like a jar of the Harvicks' warmed honey.

"Pretty boring around here," Pixie proclaimed, and pushed aside the catalogs she'd been flipping through.

"Is it my imagination, or has this been the longest day of my life?" Tricia asked.

"Mine, too. I wonder what Mr. E is doing on his day off. I'll sure be glad when he returns tomorrow."

"Anything happen while I was gone?" Tricia asked.

"We had a few customers, but nothing very interesting." Before Tricia could ask, Pixie said, "I got a call from Ginger over at the *Stoneham Weekly News* giving me a heads-up on an estate sale outside of Milford. It starts Thursday, which is a day before their next issue comes out. Apparently, the poor dead guy was quite the reader, and they're advertising a lot of books. Depending on what the old boy was interested in, I could make a killing for half the booksellers in the village—maybe buy out the whole place."

"Do you think you should go on the first day of the sale?" Usually Pixie visited estate and tag sales on the last day, when the sellers were ready to make deals.

"It wouldn't hurt."

"Okay, then let's plan on it."

"It starts at eight, so I wouldn't even have to miss work."

"Yes, but that means you'll be standing in line for at least an hour before the sale even starts."

"You know me well," Pixie said, cracking a smile.

"You can leave early that afternoon to make up for your time."

"You're the best! And I figure I can always go back on Sunday and pick up the dregs—if they're worth having."

Tricia nodded, and her smile returned. For the past couple of years, and as a side hustle, Pixie had been employed to buy books from estate and tag sales for a number of used bookstores on Main Street. "You really do provide a wonderful service for the booksellers in the village."

"Eh, not everybody," Pixie muttered. "'I picked up books for Barney's Book Barn a few times. Kids either destroy them or never touch 'em, and you can often find 'em in mint condition. But after she stiffed me twice, I stopped looking for stuff for Ms. Barnes."

"She didn't pay you?" Tricia asked, aghast.

"Nope. Looked me straight in the eye and insisted she had—plus had written me a receipt—which was another big fat lie."

"What did you say to her?"

"Nothin'—literally. She called and left messages and texted me a few times, begging me to keep picking for her, but I blocked her. She always seems to be staring out her big display window, so I don't go past her store when I walk home from work, either. I don't need her badgering me in person."

"I'm sorry she treated you so badly," Tricia said sincerely.

Pixie shrugged. "Stuff like that happens to people like me all the time. Cuz we've got a record, crappy people think they can take advantage of us cuz they know we won't call the cops. Who's gonna make a fuss over ten or twenty bucks?"

Betty had never been Tricia's favorite person, but it said a lot about her character that she would cheat someone with little opportunity to demand justice.

"I'm so sorry," Tricia apologized once again. "That should've never happened. I wish you'd told me sooner so we could have done something about it."

Pixie shook her head. "Like I said, she'd get the benefit of the doubt—not me."

What Pixie said was true. Upon their first meeting, Tricia had expected the worst from Pixie, and she now felt ashamed. Pixie had never lied to her, and Tricia trusted her to make bank deposits and handle the store's cash sales. And the till had never been short while Pixie was on the job.

After the excitement of the bus earlier that morning, the afternoon trade was practically nonexistent. Tricia and Pixie decided to move one of the stand-alone shelves, rearrange the stock, and bring up a box of books on the building's dumbwaiter.

The store's phone rang and Tricia crossed the expanse of carpet to pick up the receiver. "Haven't Got a Clue—"

"Hey, Tricia, it's Larry Harvick."

Wow—that was fast.

"I've got to be at the old homestead tomorrow afternoon. Could you come over around three o'clock?"

"Sounds perfect. Where do I show up?"

He gave her the address, which she dutifully committed to memory.

"Great, I'll see you then."

Tricia put the phone down, unable to suppress the smile that curved her lips.

"Well, don't you look happy?" Pixie said as Tricia returned to the shelves.

"I'm going to visit the Harvicks' beehives tomorrow."

Pixie grimaced. "Why would you want to do that? Aren't you afraid of getting stung?"

"If necessary, I assume Larry will provide me with protective gear. I'm curious, but I don't want to be stung, either."

"A wise move," Pixie agreed.

"You know," Tricia said as they continued their work, "I was thinking . . . What do we want to do to decorate the shop for the holiday season?" Pixie latched on to the new topic, and they spent a happy ten minutes discussing their past decorations and how to incorporate them with new ideas. By the time the workday ended, they had a list of wonderful ideas, and Tricia's and Pixie's spirits had been raised.

"Time for you to go home."

Pixie didn't argue, hung up her apron, and donned her coat.

"One of us can inventory the new stock tomorrow," Tricia said.

"One of Mr. E's favorite jobs," Pixie agreed, grabbing her keys from her purse. "Hitting the trail!"

"See you in the morning," Tricia called, and closed the shop's door and got ready to go to her sister's, feeling more than ready for a happy hour martini and the last meal of the day. And then her cell phone rang. She looked at the screen and saw it was Angelica calling.

"What's up?" Tricia answered.

"Do you mind if we don't have dinner tonight? I was going to order something for us but I'm absolutely exhausted."

"Yeah, me, too," Tricia lamented.

"How was the rest of your day?" Angelica asked.

"Long," Tricia replied. "Don't worry, I can rustle up something for myself." And maybe see if David was free to stop by earlier. He knew better than to intrude on Angelica's happy hour/dinnertime with Tricia. This way, he wouldn't have to.

"Hey, Pixie's going to a book-heavy estate sale on Thursday morning to scope things out and maybe pick up the best of the books she finds. Then if it's worth going back, she'll buy whatever's left the last day."

"I can always use more vintage copies of *The Good Housekeeping Cook Book* and *The Joy of Cooking*. And speaking of acquiring books reminds me that the big library sale is coming up in January, which the Chamber is co-sponsoring," Angelica said offhandedly. "We need to coordinate the publicity for the event."

"I hate to say it, but I get some of my best bargains there," Tricia lamented. "It's sad how many books the library purges from their shelves every year."

"If people don't check them out, it makes sense to trade them out for newer stock, and their loss—pennies on the dollar—is your gain," Angelica said pragmatically.

"Yours, too."

"So, would you like to spearhead the PR effort on the Chamber's behalf?" Angelica asked.

Tricia sighed. "Sure."

"Good."

That would mean Tricia would most likely have to work with Amelia Doyle. Tricia had met the woman only once at a Friends of the Library sale two weeks before, where Tricia purchased almost a hundred dollars' worth of books, mostly paperbacks and book club editions, that had been collected from local patrons. The books weren't exceptional, but they were mysteries by authors such as Sue Grafton, Elizabeth Peters, and John Mortimer. Not vintage, but with recommendations from herself and her staff, these books would help keep the shop in the black. Amelia had seemed like a perfectly nice person. David was giving her some bad press—and she believed every word—but she also knew that there were two sides to every story. She was more than willing to give Amelia the benefit of the doubt.

Angelica's tone changed. "Did you get the invitation?"

Tricia frowned, confused. "To what?"

"Lauren Barker's memorial service."

Tricia's frown deepened. "How?"

"It *was* an e-mail, which I found rather gauche," Angelica confided, and Tricia could imagine she'd accompanied the words with an eye roll. "But I suppose these days it's better than a text message."

"I haven't checked my inbox in a couple of hours. Who sent it?"

"Betty Barnes."

"*She's* hosting the service?" Tricia said, incredulous. "Why?"

"I suppose because she had a recent connection with Lauren. Perhaps the family will have one in another place, but Betty couched this as a local tribute to one of our own," Angelica said.

"Except Betty was recruited to open a store here, just like us and, also like Lauren, isn't a native to New Hampshire," Tricia pointed out.

"Whatever," Angelica said carelessly. "Do you want to go?"

"Of course—if only to see who else shows up."

"Do you think her killer will be there?" Angelica asked.

"It's not without precedent in these situations."

Angelica sounded unconvinced. "I suppose."

"So when is this service—and where?" Tricia asked.

"Betty has booked the Stoneham High School auditorium."

"I wasn't aware they did such things."

"Apparently, it's a done deal."

"And when is the memorial?" Tricia asked.

"Saturday morning at ten. Will you go?"

That was opening time for Haven't Got a Clue and all the other shops on Main Street, but Tricia blurted, "I wouldn't miss it for the world—invitation or not."

"I thought you'd say that. What do you think it will entail? I mean, from what I understand, Lauren left the village right after graduating from high school. I'm not sure she has any family left here in Stoneham. And she made an enemy of her high school English teacher the night she died."

"And?" Tricia quizzed her sister.

"Well, I don't like to think *bad* of people, but I also wonder if Betty might have an ulterior motive for hosting the affair."

"Such as?"

"To sell that load of books she had Lauren sign before she died."

"Angelica!" Tricia admonished.

"I've been watching Betty's eBay and Etsy shop listings, and the prices have dropped on the offerings for Lauren's books."

"Isn't it rather soon for her to do that?" Tricia asked.

Angelica shrugged. "Perhaps she thought they'd bring in big bucks fast and was disappointed when she didn't immediately get a lot of bites." Betty had certainly been bragging about it earlier in the day.

"Perhaps. I imagine her credit card bill for the books will be due fairly soon."

"My thoughts exactly," Angelica agreed.

Did that fact make Betty a strong suspect in the case? Murder for profit wasn't unheard of. But signing Lauren up for the event had been a very recent occurrence. David had been on the job for only a little over a month. Had Lauren been hungry for such an appearance? And the library (or at least David) had probably connected Barney's Book Barn and Lauren to collaborate on the project. That wasn't much time for a nefarious plot to be designed by either Lauren or Betty. Still . . .

"I'm going to make myself a cocktail, kick off my shoes, and read a good cookbook," Angelica declared.

"Yeah, maybe I'll do the same," Tricia said. "Well, have a good evening. We'll talk tomorrow."

"Sleep well."

Maybe Tricia would and maybe she wouldn't. But as soon as she disconnected, Tricia immediately powered up her laptop with a curious Miss Marple monitoring the situation. Sure enough, upon checking her e-mail, Tricia found the invitation to Lauren Barker's memorial service that had been cc'd to every member of the Stoneham Chamber of Commerce.

Tricia hit reply—and not reply all—to let Betty know she would indeed be at the service. Would she ever! Tricia hit the send button and sat back in her chair.

Then, Tricia's phone pinged. A text message from Ginny.

Thought you might want to see this.

A link accompanied the sentence. Tricia tapped it and was taken to a website where she found the video Patti Perkins had taken the night of Lauren's signing. She watched in discomfort to again witness the ugly exchange between the elderly woman and the person she'd thought of as a sort of protégé. It bothered Tricia that there was no context to ground the clip. How on earth had Ginny found it?

She asked.

Antonio saw it on his newsfeed.

Tricia answered, *Thanks.*

Tricia Googled and soon found that a national news service had picked up the clip and posted it on their website, which was probably where the social media outlet had picked it up. The story didn't accuse Stella of the murder, but it didn't do much to debunk the theory, either.

Poor Stella. Tricia envisioned the poor old lady stuck in her home, afraid to open her door in case a bunch of reporters decided to camp on her front lawn hoping to get a quote. *No comment* was more likely, if Stella even deigned to utter those two words.

Tricia tried to call Stella but was rewarded with the message that the customer's voice mail box was full. Tricia sent a text and wasn't surprised to receive no reply.

Miss Marple sat at Tricia's feet, looking expectant. It was too early for her dinner, but most pets were ever hopeful.

"Except for your perpetually empty belly, you don't have a care in the world, do you?" Tricia asked.

Miss Marple said, *"Yow!"*

ELEVEN

After powering down her laptop, Tricia immediately texted David, who was more than happy to join her for a makeshift dinner. After a cursory glance in the fridge, Tricia closed the door and frowned. It hadn't crossed her mind before, but everything in it was either packed in or covered in plastic. It *had* occurred to her lately that there was entirely too much plastic in her life. There had to be a better alternative. Since she had a few minutes, Tricia pulled out her phone and went online to check out kitchen containers and organizers. Ten minutes later, she had just enough time to light a few candles and set the ambience for what was beginning to seem like a stolen evening.

David texted her when he arrived at Haven't Got a Clue's door. They hadn't yet reached the point where they shared keys to their respective homes. It just seemed too soon. After letting him in, David followed Tricia to her apartment, which he was already thoroughly acquainted with.

"Would you like something to drink?" Tricia asked.

"Just a beer."

"Coming right up." Tricia wasn't a beer drinker but learned she could tolerate the taste on an unbearably hot day to quench her rabid thirst. David said his taste in beer had apparently improved since he'd first sampled the Bashful Moose's pale ale.

Tricia poured a glass of chardonnay for herself, mainly for something to hold on to as they settled on the couch, their knees knocking. It brought a smile to Tricia's face.

"How was work today?" she asked.

David took a long slug of his beer. She was pleased he preferred it in a glass, not the bottle. "Brutal. The way Amelia acts, you'd think *I* killed Lauren Barker."

"Nobody else thinks that," Tricia protested.

"Are you sure?" he asked, his expression darkening.

"Ninety-nine and forty-four one-hundredths percent sure."

David looked puzzled by the reference. Tricia explained about the soap ad campaign decades before he was born. Tricia's grandmother had used the product and used to recite the tagline every time she washed her hands. David's lack of recognition was a reminder of the gap in their ages.

Tricia put that thought out of her mind.

"Anything new on Lauren's murder?" David asked.

Tricia brought him up to speed. It didn't seem to brighten his mood.

"Would you like an omelet? Or I've got some turkey sausage patties and English muffins. I could make you a pretty good facsimile of a Sausage McMuffin."

"You eat at McDonald's?" he asked skeptically.

"Don't forget, I have a great-niece who thinks McNuggets are *haute cuisine*."

"Okay. Sounds great," David said eagerly as they abandoned the living room for the kitchen, with Miss Marple following.

David settled at the kitchen island and sipped his beer while Tricia puttered around the kitchen, assembling the ingredients for their breakfast sandwiches. "Amelia's got you on edge, but what about the job itself?"

David let out a sigh. "I've been feeling kind of bad about it since Amelia took over, which was obviously even before Lauren Barker's death," he admitted, watching Tricia take a sausage patty and English muffin from the freezer. "But this morning, a little girl, dressed in a black leotard, a pink tutu, and sneakers that flashed when she walked, marched into the library's children's section and announced, 'I'm here! Show me what you've got.'"

Tricia laughed. "And did you show her?"

"You bet. She didn't want books on princesses or dinosaurs. She wanted to know about trucks. She confided that one day she might like to drive a garbage truck or maybe work an excavator. But then, she thought she might also like to be a pastry chef and make cupcakes for the rest of her life."

Tricia grinned. "Don't you love that kind of enthusiasm?"

"Totally," he said, returning her smile. "So, we found books on trucks and other heavy machinery and a cookbook for kids with over a dozen cupcake recipes she can work on with her grown-up."

"And?" Tricia prompted, hauling out the toaster.

"It made my day. In the short time I've held the job, I've had twenty or thirty of these encounters, and it never gets old. Getting boys and girls enthused about reading gives me hope for the future." His smile dimmed. "Even if I might not get to interact with those kids at the library ever again."

His words—the threat that he might have to leave Stoneham—were like knife thrusts in Tricia's heart. She didn't know what to say, so she said nothing. Instead, she retrieved the butter from the fridge.

Luckily, David changed the subject. "By the way, I got a call from Angelica this afternoon. She asked me to take her around to the local antique shops."

"She what?" Tricia asked, startled.

"I know. I was shocked, too."

"And what did you say?" she asked, putting the sliced muffin into the toaster.

"'Yeah. Say when.'"

"Well," Tricia said, her voice filled with uncertainty, "that's a good sign. It means she's accepting our relationship. That she values your opinion." Tricia paused. "What does she want your advice about?"

"Antique furnishings and china. Why would she need those things?"

Tricia had to think fast. "Oh, didn't you know? Angelica is a partner with NR Associates at the Sheer Comfort Inn. She pretty much handled the revamp before they reopened. She's been involved in the Morrison Mansion's renovation—and now restoration—since the very beginning."

"So, she's a consultant?" David asked.

"That's exactly it," Tricia hurriedly agreed.

David nodded, looking thoughtful. "I've often wondered why she's known as Nonna to the Barbero children."

Tricia's stomach tensed. She hated to lie—it was a wonder that her nose didn't grow an inch every time she fibbed—and of course, a fib wasn't as bad as an outright lie. If only Angelica hadn't sworn her to secrecy about her alter ego. "Grace Harris-Everett is also Nonna to the kids. She's not a blood relative." Tricia stopped herself from adding the word *either*.

"So what's Angelica's connection to the Barberos?" David pressed.

"As you know, Ginny originally had Pixie's job at Haven't Got a Clue. We all came to love her, even when she left my employ and took the job as manager of the Happy Domestic."

David frowned. "That still doesn't explain why Angelica is considered the grandmother to those kids instead of you," he said.

Tricia grappled for an explanation. "Uh, kismet?"

David didn't look convinced. "If you're so close to Ginny, shouldn't you be the one thought of as their honorary grandma?"

Tricia gave a nervous laugh. "I'm not old enough to be a grandmother."

"Angelica is only five years older than you," he pointed out.

It wasn't a subject Tricia wanted to pursue. "I'm having lunch with Ginny on Thursday. It's going to be a busy day, what with the Chamber meeting in the morning. I believe Amelia is going to speak to the group."

David scowled. Perhaps bringing up the topic of his boss wasn't such a good idea, but at least the subject of Angelica and the kids had been shoved off the table.

The muffin popped up from the toaster, and Tricia buttered each half before placing the patty on top. "There you are," she said, and presented it to him. "Oh, dear. A McMuffin and a beer. Is that a good combination?"

"I'm fine with it," he said.

"Is one going to be enough?"

"Well . . ."

Tricia took out another muffin and patty from the freezer and began the process again. "Would you like cheese on it?"

"I wouldn't say no."

"Sorry, I only have cheddar or Swiss. No processed American."

"I'm sure I can choke it down," David said, and grinned before taking another bite. He chewed and swallowed. "This is really *good*."

"Maybe we can go on a date to Mickey D's?" Tricia suggested.

"Why go to that trouble when yours tastes just as good?"

"I *am* a gourmand," she told him, straight-faced.

He laughed.

"What do you want to do this evening?" Tricia asked.

"You mean *before* we go to bed?" he asked with wide eyes.

"Uh-huh."

"We could just skip the middleman and go straight to the highlight of the evening." He waggled his eyebrows suggestively.

Tricia eyed him for long seconds.

"Or—" he began, "we could snuggle in front of your computer and log in to Pinterest."

"Pinterest?" Tricia echoed, somewhat shocked.

"Sure, Angelica gave me a hint about what she's looking for. I thought I might create a board or two. I can invite her to look at them, and she can let me know what she likes. She *is* into Pinterest, right?"

"Oh, yeah. She made a ton of boards when she—" Tricia stopped. She'd been about to say when Angelica had designed most of the Barberos' new home, both inside and out. "When she worked on decorating the Sheer Comfort Inn and Booked for Beauty." Whew! She'd dodged telling another lie.

After his second sandwich, David dusted the crumbs off his fingers and onto the plate before getting up, rinsing the dish in the sink, and placing it into the dishwasher. His mama raised him well.

"Let's go down to your office. That computer has a bigger monitor. I want to see all those beautiful pictures on a big screen."

"How about I snag more wine and pour you another beer before we go?" Tricia said.

David's grin reappeared. "I like the way you think."

And so they spent a happy hour and more scrolling through hundreds of beautiful pictures. And not another word about Angelica's relationship with Tricia's and her chosen family was spoken. But Tricia also knew it wasn't the end of the conversation and that it was something that would have to be addressed . . . and soon.

He changed the subject. "What's been happening in your world?" David asked as Tricia led him back up to her apartment. Tricia knew it wasn't just a flippant question. David really seemed to care.

"I've been thinking about all the plastic in my life," Tricia said, putting away the last of the dinner prep.

"And?" David prompted, his eyes widening with interest.

"I'm not happy about it. Everything I buy seems to be wrapped in plastic, from fruits and vegetables to the packaging material from everything I order online."

"So, do something about it," he said matter-of-factly.

"How can I when just about everything I buy is covered in the stuff?"

"Everything?" David asked.

"Okay, most things. And all of my food storage containers are plastic, too."

David shrugged. "So, change them."

"I've thought about that. I even went online to look at options, but most glass containers have plastic lids."

"Yeah," David agreed.

"So . . . do you have a solution?" she asked.

"I do. And it's something you could easily adopt."

Tricia's eyes widened. "Do tell."

"Next time you buy a jar of pickles, save the glass jar and lid. You could store all kinds of stuff in it."

Tricia frowned. "Like what?"

David shrugged. "Pasta. Sugar. Flour. Rice. And you could use smaller jars, like the ones for jams and jellies, for leftovers. Then, you wouldn't be contributing to the plastic overload our planet is experiencing and you'd be keeping microplastic out of your body. I noticed you've only got plastic cutting boards, right?"

Tricia nodded. "They're so easy to clean. I just pop them into the dishwasher."

"Yeah, and every time you cut a fruit or vegetable, you add microscopic bits of plastic to the food you ingest. I hate to think how much plastic is circulating in your body."

The idea horrified Tricia. "And your suggestion to avoid that?"

"Wooden cutting boards. At least they're organic. Ingesting plastic is bad. Ingesting cellulose . . . not so bad. It's your choice."

Tricia frowned, contemplating his words. For decades the world had been sold on the benefits of plastics. Only now, everyone was learning their terrible drawbacks.

"If you want, Pixie and I could look for vintage glass refrigerator containers and wooden cutting boards on the weekends," David volunteered.

"Or I could go online and just buy replacements," Tricia asserted.

"You're missing the point," David said, perturbed.

Again, Tricia frowned.

"There's already so much stuff in thrift shops and estate and yard sales. Why should we support the idea that everything old has to be disposed of, especially if it's still useful?"

He had a valid argument. Still . . .

"Not everything fits in a pickle jar," Tricia countered.

"You're right. But I know you've got a little, almost-empty honey jar in your cupboard that, once finished, could hold a small amount of leftovers. You could reuse it a thousand times and never ingest a molecule of plastic."

Tricia had always banished such containers to the recycle bin, but what David said made a lot of sense. "But what would people think?"

David's brow furrowed in consternation. "Who cares? I mean,

you're not going to serve guests your leftovers, are you? And even if you did, you'd never tell them. Am I right?"

He was right about that. But often, Angelica sent leftovers in plastic bags or containers home with Tricia. She guessed she could bring her own glass containers and not feel guilty about plastic waste . . . but then it might seem like she was being presumptuous by not only expecting to be fed, but carting off what was left. And yet, that was precisely her expectation.

"You're right. And you've given me a lot to think about."

David's lips curved into a grin. "I love that we learn so much from each other."

Tricia was beginning to think she and her former pupil had reversed roles, and now *he* was the teacher. She wasn't sure she felt comfortable about the situation.

"What are you thinking?" David asked.

Tricia allowed herself a grin. "That we get so little time together and how I want to concentrate my attention on you and only you," she said, and stepped closer so that she could rest a hand on his shoulder.

And then David did the unthinkable. He pulled out his phone and turned it off. Tricia took hers out of her pocket and did the same. "There, now we won't have any distractions. In fact, let's do this every time we're together."

Tricia smiled. "I like the way you think."

David offered a sly grin. "Would you like to know what I'm thinking right now?"

Tricia laughed. "I'm a mind reader."

She offered her hand, which he clasped. He rose from the kitchen stool, pulled her close, and nodded toward the stairs and her bedroom suite. "Shall we?"

Tricia positively grinned. "We shall."

* * *

Upon waking to gloom the next morning, Tricia reflected that it seemed an age since Friday evening, when she and David found Lauren Barker's lifeless body in the library's parking lot.

Why did it have to be me? she lamented, but in reality, David had pushed to figure out why the lone car was still in the lot when everyone else had gone.

It bothered Tricia that thoughts of the author she'd barely known kept shadowing her thoughts. It was because of David—the bright light that had so recently lifted her soul from the depths of depression after the deaths of three of her former lovers. Maybe she *was* nothing more than a black widow. She hadn't *caused* their deaths, but she was the link in the chain of misfortune for them.

Putting such dark thoughts aside, Tricia threw back the covers and leapt out of bed. She got dressed, fed her cat, and began preparing a breakfast feast of thawed-and-toasted everything bagels slathered with butter, and coffee made from arabica beans Tricia ground from a vintage grinder David had gifted her from one of the estate sales he'd visited with Pixie. David joined her, and they had a peaceful meal, again with their cell phones off.

He had to go to work earlier than she did, so together they started north on the sidewalk. They briefly kissed when they came to the Stoneham Library, and Tricia continued on her morning walk. That alone time always helped her to clear or focus her thoughts, depending on her mood on any given day.

It was too early for Barney's Book Barn to be open, but just as Pixie had mentioned, Betty was stationed behind her shop's big plate glass window. She waved, and Tricia smiled in return before she looked away and quickened her pace. She was in no hurry to speak to Betty again.

All was quiet as she followed her route through the village, which had changed since the fire at the Morrison Mansion. As she arrived at the stately old home, she stopped to admire the work done to the facade, as well as the first steps in the plan to restore the landscape and gardens. Angelica's vision to return the mansion to its former glory was well under way. Although she'd never really been interested in historic homes, this one intrigued Tricia. When completed, she knew the mansion would be yet another jewel in Angelica's proverbial crown. It pleased her, and Tricia continued her walk with a sense of joy.

Upon returning to Haven't Got a Clue, Tricia headed upstairs to her apartment, where she showered and dressed for work, but wondered what she ought to wear to inspect Larry Harvick's beehives later in the day. Jeans, sturdy shoes, and a denim jacket would probably do. She'd change into those clothes later, and donned her usual dark slacks and sweater set—that day a vibrant red.

Looking at the clock, Tricia gauged she had just enough time to bake a batch of chocolate-chip cookies from dough she'd frozen weeks before. The apartment practically hummed thanks to the heartwarming aroma as Tricia left her abode with a domed cake plate heaped with cookies.

She'd just put out the pots of coffee and hot water for tea or cocoa when the door to Haven't Got a Clue opened to admit Pixie and Mr. Everett, who'd arrived together to begin their workday. Their coffee klatch went with the usual recap of the day before to bring Mr. Everett up to speed, and between customers, there was enough busywork to keep the three of them occupied until the lunch hour and Tricia's employees departed for their midday meals. For Tricia, that hour alone operating the shop was the most demanding part of the day. Not because it was particularly challenging, but she missed the company of her two employees. She was glad the three of them got along so well.

Finally, Pixie and Mr. Everett returned, and it was Tricia's turn for lunch.

She arrived at Booked for Lunch to—as usual—find Angelica already seated at their regular booth. The sisters chatted about possible entrées before Tricia got to the big topic on her mind.

"David says you want him to take you to all his favorite antique shops in the area."

"Yes, I do," Angelica freely admitted.

When her sister didn't elaborate, Tricia asked, "Why?"

"Isn't it obvious? The guy knows his antiques—and in particular, china patterns. I want the Morrison Mansion's furniture, decorations, glassware, and dishes to be period appropriate. I need the advice of someone who can knowledgeably pick out the suitable accoutrements."

Tricia nodded, leaned in, and whispered, "Do you intend to tell him you're Nigela?"

Angelica shook her head. "There's no need . . . until—or unless—you two become serious."

Tricia's heart had already spoken—telling her she *was* serious about the relationship. She'd thought David was as committed until the prospect of losing his dream job at the library had become a possibility.

"He already asked me why we're so close to Antonio and Ginny and why the kids call you their nonna."

Angelica's expression darkened. "Oh, dear. I hadn't thought of that. What did you tell him?"

"I changed the subject. You might want to come up with an explanation in advance . . . just in case he asks."

"It would be rude of him to do so," Angelica said tartly.

"So, will you tell him it's none of his business and possibly alienate him? I wouldn't want that to happen. I love you both."

Angelica's eyes widened. "You *love* him?"

Tricia swallowed before answering. "Yeah. I think I do."

"You've only just met!" Angelica protested in a harsh whisper.

"I've known him for four months," Tricia countered.

"And have been dating him for only weeks. That's not nearly enough time to fall in love with someone. Ask me. I've been married four times. I know from experience how rushing into a relationship can have disastrous consequences."

"What are you saying?" Tricia asked.

Angelica leaned closer and lowered her voice. "Let's face it: you've been extremely unlucky when it comes to love."

"No more than you," Tricia protested.

"Exactly. Only you were smarter than me because you only married once." Angelica's eyes suddenly filled with tears. "I know I would have been happy with Alesandro"—Antonio's father—"for the rest of my life, but I didn't get that opportunity. Everyone who came after him was an also-ran—*not* a winner." Angelica came up with a tissue, blew her nose, and dabbed at the corners of her eyes.

Tricia waited while her sister took a few moments to regain control of her emotions. "I don't like lying to David," she stated finally.

"And if he loses his job at the library he'll probably leave you like all my husbands left me," Angelica countered angrily.

Tricia couldn't refute that statement because she felt the same way. Was she just a passing fancy for David? Would he even understand the clichéd phrase?

Luckily, Tricia didn't have to ponder that question in depth because Molly, the server, arrived to take their orders. Feeling nervous about the upcoming visit to the Harvicks' aviary, Tricia ordered a salad, while Angelia went for the pasta special. She asked for extra garlic bread, too—not a good sign.

The sisters sat in silence for long moments after Molly's retreat.

What would happen if Angelica was with someone? Tricia knew the answer to that as Angelica had spent much of her off-the-clock time with her former significant other, Bob Kelly, while Tricia spent many an evening alone. Once they'd broken up, the sisters had developed the habit of spending happy hours and dinners together, mostly at Angelica's home and apparently that was the way Angelica wanted to keep it. Tricia was willing to go along with what her sister preferred because—and especially in light of current events—she didn't want to totally trash the comfortable routine she and Angelica had fallen into, in case David had to abandon his new life in Stoneham.

Tricia stared into her cooling cup of coffee. Sometimes things that seemed too good to be true were just that.

TWELVE

When she returned to Haven't Got a Clue, it was time for Tricia's visit with Larry Harvick's bees—what she'd been waiting for all day. She changed her clothes and flew out the door, not wishing to be late for her appointment.

Tricia texted Harvick upon arriving at his home, a white-painted colonial structure with black-painted shutters that was set on several acres outside the nearby town of Litchfield. He directed her to meet him behind the house. Conveniently, a gravel path led around the front of the home to the back, which housed a red-painted barn and several smaller, tidy outbuildings. She saw Larry at the farthest end of the property, heading toward her.

"Glad you could make it," he called, sounding jovial.

"Glad to be here. So, tell me about your operation. I'm eager to learn."

Larry looked back to the stacks of white boxes behind them. "Right now, we've got twenty-two hives here and throughout the village. The rule of thumb is twelve hives per acre. Technically, we could manage as many as thirty-six hives, but we're comfortable with what we've got right now."

"It sounds like a lot."

"Not really. You're not considered a viable commercial enterprise until you have about three hundred hives, but that's the keyword: *commercial*. We're more of a specialty operation. Between the two of us—and sometimes our kids helping out—we've got about all we can handle, especially now that we own the retail shop in Booktown."

Tricia glanced toward the hives, which sat near a copse of maples. The leaves were at peak color, and quite a few were already littering the lawn. "I suppose your hives will soon be winding down for the winter."

"Already started. Honeybees don't go dormant like others of their species. They cluster together to keep warm during the winter, ensuring their queen will survive the cold weather. Our recent heat wave has kept them foraging longer than usual, as there are still some flowers around."

"When do you harvest the honey and wax?"

"We did that back in August and September," Harvick said with a wave of his hand.

Tricia couldn't help but feel disappointed. She thought she was going to get to see some real bee action. Even so, she did want to learn more about the bees. "I'm curious: Why did you want to put hives in the village proper?"

"Surprisingly enough, bees do very well in suburban and especially in urban areas."

"Yes, I've heard about hives in places like Manhattan being very successful."

"It's great for biodiversity. Like the bees in our village hives, most urban hives consist of *Apis mellifera ligustica* honeybees, which are pretty docile. There's not a lot of stinging involved."

"Then why is Amelia Doyle so freaked?" Tricia asked.

Harvick shrugged. "A lot of people just hate bugs."

"And you don't consider a bee a bug?"

"Hell, no. They're my business partners," Harvick said. Tricia wasn't sure if he was joking.

Harvick showed Tricia around the couple's outbuildings, one of which was dedicated to retrieving the honey from the combs with a centrifuge called an extractor. Another building was devoted to molding the beeswax into candles. Production for these products was in full force for the upcoming holiday season.

While Tricia was a little disappointed she didn't get to actually interact with the bees, she thoroughly enjoyed learning about the Harvicks' business.

"Thanks for the tour. I feel like I've learned a lot about your operation. If you're interested, I'd love to feature it in an upcoming issue of the Chamber's newsletter. We send copies to area news outlets. I'll cross my fingers that one of them will pick it up and give you more publicity."

"We'll take anything we can get," Larry said appreciatively.

"I'll work something up in the next week or so and send it to you for comments and corrections."

"All right."

Harvick walked Tricia to her car.

"So, what do you know about the village's latest murder?" Harvick asked. As a former sheriff's deputy, he was interested in such things.

"Not much," Tricia said, her euphoria of moments before quickly evaporating. She wasn't about to mention how Lauren's murder might affect David's employment status.

"An awful lot of people have met their end these last couple of years in good old Booktown."

Tricia sighed, hoping Harvick wasn't about to pin her with the jinx label.

"Yes, well . . . I suppose these things are bound to happen as a village grows in prosperity."

Harvick nodded but looked unconvinced. "I haven't heard much about the investigation. That Irish guy who's the Stoneham PD's new chief doesn't seem to share much with the press."

"Or with the Sheriff's Department?" Tricia queried.

"Not that I've heard."

"Ian's good at his job. I'm sure he's got everything under control." And to make sure, Tricia was determined to find out if, as reluctantly promised, Becca had spoken to the village's top cop.

That was next on her list of things to do.

It was after four thirty when Tricia arrived back at the municipal parking lot. Before returning to Haven't Got a Clue, she backtracked a block or so to the Stoneham Police Department and was once again addressed with another saccharine greeting from Polly Burgess. "And what brings you here on this fine afternoon, *dear* Tricia?"

Tricia refrained from wincing at the insincere words. "Is Chief McDonald available? I'd love to speak to him."

"About the Barker murder?" Polly asked sweetly.

"Um . . . perhaps. Is he in?"

"I'll see if he's available." Polly tapped the intercom button. "Chief, Tricia Miles is here if you've got a minute to give her."

"A minute," came McDonald's tinny reply.

"I'll just see myself in," Tricia said.

"You do that, *dear.*"

Tricia appreciated that Polly's change in attitude helped her keep her job, but she also thought she preferred the more honest—old sourpuss—Polly instead.

Tricia knocked on the chief's office door before turning the handle. "Ian?"

McDonald rose from his chair. "Tricia, come in. Sit," he said, gesturing to one of the chairs in front of his desk. "What can I do for you today?"

Tricia took a seat and got straight down to business.

"Have you spoken to Becca Dickson-Chandler about her lunch meeting with Lauren Barker on the day Lauren died?"

McDonald frowned. "No. Was I supposed to?"

Tricia sighed in exasperation. "Becca told me she'd talk to you."

"Well, she didn't. Just what did they chat about?"

Tricia conveyed everything Becca had told her days before about Lauren's security concerns.

McDonald's frown deepened, and he let out a sigh of frustration. "Sometimes I wonder why I don't just hire you as a detective for our force."

She knew he was joking. "I'd have to be an anonymous member. As it is, I sometimes feel like an informant. People tell me things, but I insist it not be in confidence because crime—murder, in particular—is too important, too final, not to give the victim a shot at justice."

McDonald nodded. "I'll pay Ms. Dickson-Chandler a visit."

"Perhaps you'll get more from her than I did—something that could lead to Lauren's killer."

"Perhaps," McDonald agreed, but somehow he didn't look at all convinced.

"Were you able to track down the mystery man I saw Lauren speaking to?"

"Your description was pretty vague. I spoke to Lauren's editor at the publishing house and her agent, but they weren't very helpful. Apparently, Ms. Barker kept her relationships with them on a business level only. Most of their interactions were conducted via e-mail."

Tricia nodded. And she remembered her conversation with Marina Costas about Lauren's personal effects taking up space at the Sheer Comfort Inn and Angelica's promise to contact the village's top cop.

"Has my sister spoken with you concerning Lauren's suitcases?"

"No. And no one's come forward. No attorney has contacted my department to volunteer information relevant to Ms. Barker's estate. But sometimes, these things take time. It could be weeks or months before someone steps forward to claim an inheritance or represent an estate."

"That's too bad," Tricia lamented. "Shouldn't the Stoneham Police Department take possession of Lauren's things? Surely you don't expect the inn to store them indefinitely."

"Of course. I'll make sure my team secures Ms. Barker's personal effects while we try to find an heir."

"Did you find anything of interest when going through her things?" Tricia asked.

"Just a copy of her high school yearbook—the year she graduated."

Tricia's eyes widened with interest. "And?"

McDonald shrugged. "I read through the messages from her former classmates, but it meant nothing to me or anyone in my staff."

Of course, because none of them knew Lauren. Why hadn't he shown the book to someone like Stella Kraft, who not only knew Lauren but had probably taught other members of Lauren's graduating class? She suggested he do so.

Again, McDonald shrugged. "Will do. Have you got anything else?"

Wasn't it enough that she'd given him several venues to investigate?

She told him about the sandwich delivered to the inn and suggested he again speak with Marina. "If I come up with anything else, I'll let you know," she promised. And with that, Tricia rose from her seat. "I need to get back to my store to shut things down for the day."

"Thanks for stopping by," McDonald said sincerely.

"I always strive to be helpful."

"Yes, you do. And I appreciate it."

Those were words seldom (ever?) uttered by McDonald's predecessors. She didn't care to know whether it was a genuine sentiment.

"We'll talk again soon," McDonald promised.

Tricia nodded and left his office, closing the door behind her. As she exited the building, Polly called out sweetly, "Have a nice evening."

Tricia paused long enough to look over her shoulder and replied, "You, too!" And then she was off, heading back to Haven't Got a Clue.

The shadows were already lengthening. The night crept over the landscape ever faster these days. Between that and the chill in the air, Tricia thought about the winter ahead. She longed to spend a week on some tropical beach, come January or February, with David massaging sunscreen on her back. He might be gone by then, she thought, and if he wasn't, as a new employee he wouldn't have earned any vacation by then, either.

George Harrison said it well when singing about a "long, cold, lonely winter."

Tricia only hoped that wouldn't be her fate.

THIRTEEN

Tricia, Pixie, and Mr. Everett closed down Haven't Got a Clue for the day, and it had been a pretty good one, too. The lean days between leaf peeping and the holiday season lurked, but for now they celebrated the seasonal crowds.

Once her employees had left for the day, Tricia trundled over to Angelica's place, feeling more than a little guilty that she welcomed her sister into her home far fewer times than Angelica played hostess to her. She also knew that Angelica was a bit of a control freak and that being in charge had been a part of her nature since Tricia was born, and Angelica had become the big sister.

"How was your day?" Angelica asked once the sisters had retreated to the living room to enjoy their happy hour martinis and a snack, which on that day was a couple of bowls of potato chips.

"Pretty good," Tricia said, and related her conversation with Chief McDonald. "I thought you were going to tell him about the sandwich delivered to the inn."

"Oh, yeah," Angelica said. "Well, I did talk to Ray, who runs Eat Lunch, and he said it was a teenage boy who paid him for the order. He'd never seen the kid before and didn't know how to find him."

"Ian is going to contact you, so you'd better be prepared."

"Right," Angelica said, but she didn't sound happy.

"Are you prepared for the fallout of reporting Becca's lapse?" Angelica asked wryly. Was Angelica thinking along those lines, too?

"There shouldn't be much as I warned Becca that if she didn't talk to the chief, I would. But I'd much rather tell you about my visit to the Harvicks' apiary." Which she did. In detail.

"I'll look forward to reading your article. And, in the spirit of cooperation, I think I'll visit the Bee's Knees. I'm almost out of their wonderful honey."

"As am I," Tricia remarked, remembering David's suggestion for how to reuse the glass jars.

"Let's make it a point to do so soon. Or if you go first, buy some honey for me. I wouldn't say no to a few beeswax candles, too."

"Will do," Tricia said. "And vice versa."

Angelica nodded.

Tricia's ringtone sounded, and she glanced at her cell phone's screen. She winced. "Oh, gee. It's Becca."

"Did I mention fallout?" Angelica said, and got up, grabbing Tricia's empty glass and her own, and headed for the kitchen to give Tricia some privacy for her call.

In truth, Tricia wasn't surprised to hear from Becca just ninety minutes after she'd spoken to Chief McDonald. She answered the call, but didn't have an opportunity to say hello before Becca spoke. "Why did you sic Chief McDonald on me?" the ex–tennis champ demanded.

Tricia took a breath, determined not to be intimidated by Becca's strident tone. "I told you if *you* didn't speak to him, *I* would," Tricia said firmly. She paused, thinking about what she should say next. "Look, if you'd wanted what you know about Lauren's state of mind before her death to be secret, you wouldn't have mentioned it to me." Or possibly anyone else. "You're a good person at heart. I know you want Lauren's killer to be caught and punished."

"A good person *at heart*?" Becca repeated, aghast. "Are you insinuating that I'm only a good person *part* of the time?"

Oh, boy.

"Not at all. I think you wanted to test the waters, trying to figure out if what Lauren told you was pertinent. I just confirmed what you already knew. I don't understand why you were so reluctant to share that with Chief McDonald."

A lengthy silence followed Tricia's words.

"I don't know," Becca finally admitted, her voice subdued. "I guess . . ." She hesitated. "Lauren was my second murder victim." Becca's ex-husband had been the first. It was something the women had in common. "Nobody should have to be acquainted with that kind of pain once, let alone twice."

So, despite her claims to the contrary, Becca had had some feelings—if only pity—for Lauren. Perhaps she'd even given her sound advice regarding Lauren's security problems. It wasn't something Becca would be willing to admit. Someone who'd had to face the worldwide savage press after a significant tennis loss had probably hardened her vulnerable heart—at least to the outside world. That didn't mean Becca was immune to feelings of loss and regret. And, once again, Tricia considered that Becca's life might be filled with loneliness, for it sure didn't seem like she had anyone close to rely on. That thought only made Tricia feel even more grateful for the people in her life.

"So, what did the chief say?"

"That he wished I'd come to see him instead of speaking to you.

Actually," Becca said, her tone softening, "he was quite nice. He was soft-spoken and very polite. He didn't pull a guilt trip on me and said he hoped that if anything ever came up again, I should feel free to call him."

"That doesn't mean he'd fix a parking ticket for you," Tricia pointed out.

"So you say," Becca replied, sounding bored. A long silence followed. "I'd best be going," Becca said. "Plans for expanding my empire take a lot of time. We'll talk again soon."

Was that a promise or a threat?

Tricia wasn't sure she wanted to know.

FOURTEEN

Over dinner the previous evening, Tricia and Angelica had agreed to head for the Brookview Inn and the monthly Chamber of Commerce meeting in Angelica's car. And so they met outside the Cookery at exactly 7:40. That gave them time to get to the inn and make sure everything was ready and to grab a cup of coffee, and maybe a sweet roll during the breakfast-and-networking portion of the meeting.

The Chamber was well represented on that brisk October morning. The Brookview Inn's parking lot was full, and the line for complimentary coffee and pastries was long in the inn's function room. Besides the usual Main Street merchants, quite a few members who ran businesses off the village's main drag were also in attendance.

Among the missing was Ginny, but then Tricia would see her for lunch and she could fill her in on anything earth-shattering. Also missing was Becca, who usually showed up at the meetings if only to grouse about how slow the zoning board was to approve the plans for her proposed tennis club on the village's outskirts. And lastly, the local face of Nigela Ricita Associates: Antonio.

Tricia briefly said hello and chatted with several members before sitting at the table closest to the podium. It was Angelica's turn to chair the meeting, which gave Tricia time to eat her continental breakfast—something that was never guaranteed.

Having already perused the agenda, which was quite full, Tricia hoped Angelica could muster through it with her usual speed and efficiency.

As the clock ticked toward eight thirty, Angelica stepped up to the podium, positioned the microphone, and tested it before speaking. "Welcome, members, to the monthly Stoneham Chamber of Commerce meeting. We've got a full docket, so let's get started.

"First on the agenda is the upcoming food drive the Chamber is sponsoring in conjunction with the Stoneham Library."

Angelica had taken the lead on that project, and she and Tricia had barely spoken about it during their happy hour discussions.

"In case you haven't yet met the library's new director, let me introduce her now." Angelica waved a hand, gesturing for Amelia Doyle to join her. Tricia had been so busy mingling with others that she hadn't even noticed the woman's presence.

"Why don't you tell us about our joint project?" Angelica encouraged, and then stepped aside, letting Amelia take her place in front of the microphone.

"Good morning," Amelia began. "I'm Amelia Doyle, and as Angelica said, I'm the library's new director, replacing retired Lois Kerr just four weeks ago. I have a master's degree in business administration and a doctorate in library science."

Impressive, Tricia thought.

"My interest in food scarcity goes back to my childhood. I lived in a single-parent home with three siblings, and sometimes, there wasn't enough for all of us to eat. My father often went to bed hungry. That made an impression on me, and, like Scarlett O'Hara, I vowed never to be hungry again—and to make sure others wouldn't, either. That's why I reached out to the Chamber to see if we could work together on such a project."

"We already have the Stoneham Food Shelf that Libby Hirt runs," Terry McDonald, owner of All Heroes Comics, pointed out. He didn't sound annoyed . . . just curious.

"That's true," Amelia agreed. "But her organization has asked that we concentrate on holiday meals while they concentrate on the day-to-day needs of her clientele. We'll be collecting money and doing a food drive for shelf staples, holiday turkeys, and canned hams. The library will be a drop-off point. Families can register for holiday baskets with the Stoneham Food Shelf, and we will do our best to fulfill their wish list."

"And what's expected of the Chamber members?" called Dan Reed. Tricia turned at the sound of his voice. She hadn't known he was in attendance. He must have found someone to cover for him behind the stove at his diner.

"We're asking the retail establishments in the area to put collection containers near their registers in hopes people will drop in their spare change."

"Most people pay with credit cards," Mary Fairchild pointed out. She squinted at Amelia. "Don't I know you?"

"I beg your pardon?" Amelia asked.

"Doyle. That wasn't your maiden name, right?" Mary pressed.

"No," Amelia agreed neutrally. "You might have known me as Amelia Franklin."

"Yes," Mary said, nodding. "You were a year behind me in high school."

"Was I?"

"Yes. I was Mary Wright in those days."

Amelia didn't show a hint of recognition. She merely nodded and continued speaking. "Of course, your customers can put quiet money in the collection containers, too. And we'll have literature to hand out as well."

"It's a wonderful cause," Angelica said, stepping in to voice her opinion.

Yes, it was. Except Libby's organization also had collection boxes out at many local businesses. Would having two in a shop be overkill or seem like a pressure tactic? Perhaps, Tricia decided, she might forgo the holiday collection box and just make a substantial contribution to the drive. She'd think about it.

Tricia shook herself, realizing she'd missed the end of Amelia's pitch, for the woman was heading back to her seat. Meanwhile, Angelica had donned her reading glasses and was consulting her agenda.

"Thank you, Amelia. Now, second on our slate," Angelica began, but Tricia tuned her out. She'd have to wait until the meeting officially ended before tracking Mary down and asking her what she remembered about Amelia from their high school days.

Angelica continued to drone on and on, and Tricia heard the scraping of chairs as several members ducked out of the meeting early. By the time Angelica finished, at least half a dozen people had absconded—including Mary. Well, her shop was only doors down from Tricia's. She could easily track her down. And why was she being so nosy? Was it only because Amelia hadn't seemed interested in connecting with Mary? Or was it Mary's tone, which had been slightly off when she'd asked about Amelia's past? And Tricia wondered if David might have any insight on his boss. Although, it seemed like she was currently a sore subject. Maybe she'd leave her questions to just Mary.

Finally, Angelica banged her gavel, bringing the meeting to a close with a small round of applause from the remaining members.

Tricia rose as her sister approached the table. "Let's hit the road," Angelica said. "I've got a Zoom meeting with Ginny's marketing team in half an hour."

"What are you going to say?"

"I'm not going to say a word. However, Nigela will have *plenty* to tell them."

"Good or bad?"

"Not what they'll want to hear."

"About their office space?"

Angelica nodded. "I asked Ginny not to mention my decision to them, but she indicated they had already guessed today's topic." She nodded toward the lobby. "Let's get our coats."

"Okay," Tricia said.

The sisters stopped at the coatroom, collected their coats, and tipped the attendant before they exited the building via the back door and collected Angelica's car. Once inside, Tricia continued their conversation.

"I'm surprised you're handling the marketing meeting yourself. Couldn't Antonio do it for you?"

"I don't think it would be appropriate to pin delivering the bad news on him—especially since he's Ginny's husband. I'd rather the workers turn their ire on me."

"Do you think the team will be that angry?"

She shrugged. "I'll soon find out. Come on." Once they were in the car and had pulled out of the lot, Angelica spoke again. "Did you catch Mary's tone when she asked Amelia about her past?"

"I sure did. And I intend to ask Mary about it," Tricia said.

Angelica started the car. "And after you do, be sure to tell *all!*"

"Will do," Tricia promised. "That is, unless I'm sworn to secrecy."

"Is that likely?" Angelica asked.

"Who knows?"

"Knowing you, you'll worm yourself into her confidences. You always manage to do so."

Was that a compliment or a slight? Tricia was afraid to ask.

As usual, Ginny was late to meet Tricia at Booked for Lunch. She'd always been late, but these days, she had to travel farther and had less time to spend as her commute was ten minutes longer on both ends.

"I'm sorry," Ginny apologized, and signaled for Molly, the server, to hurry to the table. "Our meeting with Nigela ran long."

"Yes, I heard she planned to talk to your team. How did it go?"

But before Ginny could answer, Molly appeared, and both women ordered the soup-and-half-sandwich combo, which on that day was beef barley soup and half a tuna sandwich.

Finally, Molly left to put their orders in, and Ginny grabbed the water glass from the setting before her, taking a big gulp. "Our meeting went great."

From her tone, it sounded more like a catastrophe.

"I'm sorry."

"No, *I'm* sorry. After having a few days to digest the idea, the team was excited. They *want* to be in Milford."

"Why are you so sad?" Tricia asked.

"I guess . . ." But then Ginny's voice trailed off.

"What's going on?" Tricia pressed.

"I don't want to speak badly when it comes to Angelica. I'm so grateful for everything she's done for me, from offering me the job as manager of the Happy Domestic, to putting her faith in my ability to jump to the head of marketing at NR Associates. . . ." And with that, Ginny ran out of steam.

"But?" Tricia asked.

Ginny sighed and looked distinctly unhappy. "I'm bummed that my team couldn't have moved into the Morrison Mansion."

"You must admit that it would be a shame to turn that beautiful, historic building into office space with chopped-up rooms and fluorescent lights."

"I guess," Ginny said, fingering her napkin before placing it on her lap.

"For what it's worth, I've repeatedly asked Angelica why she had a change of heart, but she never explained. Has she said anything to you?"

Ginny shook her head. "All I know is that once she saw the colorized pictures of the mansion's long-lost gardens, she put the whole project on hold. A couple of weeks later, she announced my team would be moving to the Milford office park."

David had given Angelica those pictures, along with a dossier on everything he could dig up on the mansion. Ginny had to know that. Would she blame David for her current work situation? He hated to see historic buildings and vintage items tossed on a rubbish heap because others saw no value in them. Tricia admired that quality in him.

Tricia decided to change tack. "Was Antonio in on the decision?"

Again, Ginny shook her head. "He was just as surprised as me. He went to bat for us, but we all knew it was a lost cause. Once Angelica makes up her mind, she doesn't budge."

Angelica *was* stubborn, but Tricia knew her sister had good instincts. She decided to probe in another direction. "Is the office park *really* all that bad?"

"Well . . ." Ginny began. "I will admit that my commute—if you could call it that—will be shorter. Half my team lives in Milford, so they're happy they won't have to go far in the winter. And there are more lunch opportunities, some within walking distance of our new offices."

"Then why are you so unhappy?" Tricia asked.

Ginny sighed. "I guess because I was left out of the loop."

It was reasonable she should feel that way. "It's just . . . I was looking forward to having an office in that old building. Angelica asked me for my wish list, and she was willing to give it to me, as she'd planned to restore at least some of the garden."

"I didn't know you were into flowers."

"Neither did I," Ginny admitted, her voice tinged with sadness. She shook her head. "But the team discussed it—without my input, I might add—and decided they'd prefer to be at the office park in Milford."

For a moment, Tricia thought Ginny might burst into tears, but then she took another gulp of water, and her facial muscles seemed to relax. "I absolutely love Angelica's plans to restore the house. In fact, I wish I could be part of the project."

"Well, why couldn't you?" Tricia asked.

Ginny frowned. "What do you mean?"

"Angelica would probably be thrilled to have a new audience to discuss the project."

"I'd love that . . . but, honestly, since Will came along, I'm almost stretched to the breaking point. I know conventional wisdom says that women can have it all, and I already have help with daycare, a babysitter, and a team that cleans my house once a week, but it still feels like it's not enough. I don't know how other moms handle the stress, and I feel guilty that I have so much help and so many other women don't."

Tricia nodded. "I know what you mean. But let me turn the equation around. You love your job, right?"

"I do," Ginny replied almost instantaneously.

"But you feel guilty because you're handing off what you feel are your wife and motherly tasks to others."

"Exactly!" Ginny agreed.

"But look at it from another perspective. You *do* have privilege. But having people come into your home to clean gives several women a job to care for *their* families. You've provided a job for your babysitter, who makes your life easier by taking care of Sofia and Will when you need to be at work. And Sofia being at daycare means she's learning to get along with her peers. She'll be a step ahead because she'll learn things like her ABCs, colors, and more before she heads to kindergarten. She does like preschool, right?"

"Oh, she loves it."

"And it's not like you and Antonio have abandoned the children to others. You have a wonderful bedtime routine, reading to them. Your weekends are pretty much devoted to family time."

Ginny nodded. "Angelica insists that everyone in the organization make family their priority. She's very generous when it comes to my team—and everyone else—when they need personal time."

"And what about your team? Can you push off some of your responsibility on any of them—or perhaps take a couple of hours or half a day once a week to spend with Angelica on the planning process?"

"I guess I could," Ginny said, sounding distinctly wishy-washy.

Tricia raised an eyebrow.

"Okay, I guess I *should*—if I *want* to take on a new project."

Tricia nodded and smiled. "You can do this. I saw how you worked with Angelica on your house. She thought she was in charge, but that home is all you—not her."

Ginny blushed. "I'm glad somebody noticed."

"She noticed it, too . . . after it was all finished," Tricia added. "But there's something you should consider. Angelica sticks out like a sore thumb on the project. As a valued member of the NR Associates team, it will appear to others that the company has a rep on board supervising her work."

Ginny looked thoughtful. "I probably would have never looked at the situation in that light."

"Think about it now," Tricia suggested.

Ginny nodded.

Just then, Molly arrived with their food, and the conversation turned to more mundane subjects. But there was a decided change in Ginny's demeanor. She seemed more at ease and truly excited at the prospect of a new project. That kind of energy was contagious. It made Tricia want to do something—like paint the shop's interior, or perhaps replace the carpet—things that weren't likely to happen anytime soon. But perhaps in the dead of winter when customers were few and far between . . . It was something to think about.

And Tricia vowed she would.

FIFTEEN

Upon returning to Haven't Got a Clue, Tricia's bright mood seemed contagious. Pixie's choice of music—from Frank Sinatra's catalog—seemed to give everyone "High Hopes." The sales weren't tremendous, but enough customers passed through the door to make the afternoon at least interesting.

"Any fun plans for the evening?" Tricia asked as her employees gathered their coats at the end of the workday.

"Laundry," Pixie lamented. "I have a stack of ironing a mile high." And all her clothes always looked freshly pressed, not a task many people still employed.

"Grace is giving a speech at the Milford Senior Center. I, of course, will accompany her," Mr. Everett said.

"What's the topic?" Tricia asked.

"Estate planning."

"Oh, dear," Pixie said.

"When one reaches our age, it's the prudent thing to do," Mr. Everett said sensibly.

"Well, hopefully, I won't need to do that for another couple of decades," Pixie said, quickly changing the subject. "What are you doing, Tricia?"

"Dinner with Angelica, and then David may drop over." She didn't want it to sound like a done deal—even if it was.

"Well, have a nice evening," Pixie said brightly, as did Mr. Everett. Tricia watched them leave, left a kitty snack for Miss Marple, grabbed her coat, and headed for Angelica's apartment.

Minutes later, the sisters sat in the living room with a tray of drinks and a plate full of crackers to accompany pumpkin hummus, which Angelica had made from scratch.

"Pretty festive for this time of year," she quipped, slathering a cracker with the orange dip.

As Tricia was motivated to help Ginny in her goal to have input to the Morrison Mansion project, perhaps this could be the time to lay that foundation.

"You haven't given me an update on the Morrison Mansion's renovations in a while," Tricia said innocently.

Angelica looked chagrined. "I'm afraid it's a bit of a sore subject with Ginny."

"So I gathered."

"As far as I'm concerned"—and here Angelica paused, looking decidedly shameless—"I'm in seventh heaven. I had fun revamping the Sheer Comfort and Brookview inns, but this renovation will be my crowning glory."

Tricia absorbed what her sister had said. "Renovation, *not* restoration?"

Angelica winced. "Well, a little of both. Sadly, too much of what once made the mansion special is gone—from lack of attention or theft. I'm trying to discern what's been lost that can either be repaired or replaced, but I want the house to be safe and comfortable for guests visiting it."

It seemed a reasonable plan.

"What work is actually going on at this time?" Tricia asked, trying out the hummus. It was good!

"Pulling out all the crap that made the rooms into office spaces." She sighed. She'd spent a considerable sum for just that purpose. "We've got to repair the plaster, sand or replace the floors where necessary, paint, and wallpaper. We're nearing the stage where I can start to think about furnishing and decorating it."

"And that's where David steps in?" Tricia asked.

Angelica's lips quirked into a smile. "Of course, but I *don't* want him to know I'm Nigela."

"Why not?"

Angelica's expression darkened. "Because . . . because I don't trust him to hold my secret. *Yet*," she amended. "When you've been together a little longer, then I'll tell him. And please, don't you spill the beans."

"I *don't* like lying to him—you know that."

"I'm not asking you to lie. I'm asking you to be discreet," Angelica said, slathering some dip onto a cracker.

"What if someone else in the village tells him? It's a pretty open secret. As Mr. Everett confided to me, people in the village who know or have guessed have kept their mouths shut because they know that Nigela has been a boon for the village. They don't want to impede any future growth or investment as it's been so beneficial to everyone."

Angelica's brow furrowed. "You mean a *lot* of the people *know* I'm Nigela?" she asked, horrified.

Tricia nodded.

"How?" Angelica implored.

Tricia shrugged. "Your relationship with Antonio, for one. They know Nigela has a family connection. Plus, our family dinners are well known."

Angelica looked distinctly unhappy. "I've tried to be discreet."

"Yeah, and *you* redecorated the Sheer Comfort Inn. *You've* been involved in the Brookview Inn. *You* revamped NR Associates real estate office. Your sticky fingers are all over NR Associates' projects."

Angelica's frown deepened. "Was I that obvious?"

"I'm afraid so," Tricia said.

Angelica sighed. "What can I do?"

Tricia shrugged. "You need to accept the possibility of coming clean about your alter ego."

Angelica shook her head vehemently. "No. Absolutely not."

"What if one of the Nashua TV channels decides to come after you?"

"Why would they?" Angelica asked, horrified.

"To stir up interest. Interest equals ratings, equals sales. Sales equal revenue."

"You don't have to tell me that," Angelica complained, and took a healthy swig of her drink.

"It might be a good idea for you and Ginny to come up with a strategy . . . just in case."

"I will . . . *when* it becomes necessary."

Again, Tricia shrugged. "Well, I think Ginny could be an incredible asset in the renovation."

"In what way?"

"Well, if nothing else, as a cover to keep your alter egos separate."

Angelica's eyes widened in delight. "That's absolutely brilliant. Ginny could be the public face of NR Associates whom I, as Angelica, coordinate with."

"Um . . . I think she'd like to be more than that."

Angelica frowned. "What do you mean?"

"Why don't you ask her?" Tricia said.

"I will. In fact, I'll text her this evening."

Tricia's expression remained bland. "Good idea." And yet, she hoped Angelica wouldn't cut David out of the renovation. If he lost his library job, working for NR Associates would keep him in Stoneham.

It was a selfish thought, but Tricia couldn't help herself.

She was tired of being alone.

Tricia left Angelica's place early, eager to see David, and hopeful Angelica and Ginny would have a meaningful conversation in her absence. But while she was in good spirits when David arrived, it was evident that he was feeling morose.

"Would you like a beer or something?" Tricia asked once he'd hung up his jacket.

David settled on one of the kitchen stools. "No thanks. They say alcohol is a depressant, and I'm already feeling up to my neck in crap. I'd just as soon skip feeling any lower."

"I'm so sorry," Tricia said. She walked up behind him and wrapped her arms around him, resting her chin on the top of his head. "Is there anything I can do to help?"

David pulled from her embrace and stood, taking hold of her hands. "Just being with you is enough." He leaned forward and planted a light kiss on her lips. "Let's go sit on the couch."

He led her to the living room, and they sat together. Soon, Miss Marple jumped onto David's lap and began to knead his thigh. He smiled and smoothed the fur on the back of the cat's neck. "Making biscuits, Miss?"

Miss Marple said, *"Yow!"*

He and Tricia laughed, which lightened the mood.

"What kind of a day did you have?" David asked as Miss Marple settled down on his lap, purring.

"Not bad. The Chamber meeting went well." And then Tricia remembered that Amelia Doyle had been there. She chose not to mention it to David. "I had lunch with Ginny. I think she might step up to help Angelica to—" But then she stopped. "To be a liaison between NR Associates and Angelica. I might find out tomorrow."

"Good for Ginny. Anything else?"

"Nothing seems to have budged on the Lauren Barker murder case," Tricia commented.

"No news is good news?" David suggested.

"Every day without an arrest means someone might get away with the crime."

David shrugged. "I don't find sleuthing so interesting now that it not only endangers my job—but the likelihood of me ever again working in my chosen field."

"Aren't you exaggerating just a bit?" Tricia asked.

David shook his head. "The average time spent as a librarian is decades long. That means job turnover isn't exactly rapid, meaning the likelihood of me finding another position as a children's librarian is as rare as finding gold nuggets in my sock drawer."

It sounded like a declaration that he'd already given up on hanging around Stoneham should the job go bust.

"I understand," Tricia said softly. She would soldier on and make her quiet inquiries or perhaps she could rope Angelica into coming along with her on her travels if the situation warranted it. If nothing else, her sister made the perfect sounding board for Tricia's theories.

"I can't help thinking about Lauren. I was wondering . . . Did the library pay her an honorarium for her library appearance?"

"Well, we *would* have."

"Was it high?"

"Yeah, a thousand bucks," he said, sounding irked. "If her estate comes after us, we'll argue that she didn't fulfill the terms of our agreement."

"Did you have it in writing?"

He nodded. "If they want to be difficult, we'll offer to pay something and see where it goes."

"Should you have reminded Lauren of the terms when she refused to do anything but sign at the event?"

"I *should* have done a lot of things that night," David remarked.

"Remind me again why Amelia didn't attend the signing. I mean, Lauren was a well-known author. This was a big event for the library."

David shrugged. "Something about having a previous engagement."

It sounded lame but reasonable.

"What made your day turn sour?" Tricia asked.

Again, David shrugged. "Just a lot of little things. But the best part is always the kids. This little guy came in all grumpy. He didn't see why his grown-up had dragged him to such a stuffy old place. And then I showed him all the wonderful things he could take home. Things like movies, board games, video games, manga, and books, books, books, and more books. So we sat down and chatted so I could figure out what he was interested in, and he had a stack of books to take out. He told me he was going straight home to read." David offered a weak smile. "That kinda thing always makes my day."

"It makes my day to hear a story like that, too," Tricia said, nestling closer to him.

"Not *just* a story—real life." He leaned his head against hers. "Thanks for asking me about my day. I feel better now."

"I'm glad. I could make you feel even better," Tricia said softly.

David sighed. "I know you could. . . . But I've got a ton of reading to get through and a paper to start. I really should be going."

"So soon? You only just got here."

"We'll have time on the weekend."

Tricia nodded, her admiration for David soaring, proud he was dedicated to his education and life goals.

"If you gotta go, you gotta go," Tricia said sadly.

"Well, maybe I could stay just a *little* longer."

Tricia faced him and smiled. "I can live with that."

SIXTEEN

October was such a fickle month weather-wise. It could be full of golden sunlight or dark and misty with a drizzle that could soak through a jacket and chill one's bones. That Friday morning, it was gray with the threat of rain, so Tricia donned her waterproof jacket and carried an umbrella—just in case.

Her walk was without incident as she contemplated what she knew about Lauren Barker's death. Gloomy thoughts on an equally gloomy day. But as she approached Haven't Got a Clue, she ran into Mary Fairchild, who was headed to her store to prepare for the retail day.

"Hey, Mary, it's good to see you," Tricia called.

Mary paused for a chat. "And you, too. What's new?"

Tricia shrugged. "I'm still bummed about Lauren Barker's death. I was at the signing she did at the library just before her death."

Mary nodded. "And your *boy*friend found her. I can see why that would be upsetting."

How Mary accentuated that word's first syllable bothered Tricia.

Several times, she'd passed someone on the street during one of her morning walks who'd snicker and cough the word *cougar* before swaggering off. It was primarily men, but a few women had also lobbed the word in Tricia's direction. She'd walked away red-faced. But then, when she spent time with David, the thought of their age difference disappeared like fog exposed to bright sunshine. They had so much to talk about—they never ran out of conversation, which she'd never encountered with any of her past paramours.

"Will you be going to Lauren's memorial service tomorrow?"

Mary sighed. "I don't know. I suppose I should. Lauren and I *were* classmates," she volunteered.

Tricia looked up sharply. "Really?"

"Oh, yeah. We were in the same loop—had most of our classes together."

"And were you friends?"

"For a while," Mary said, sounding wary. "During our freshman and sophomore years, Lauren was the class dweeb."

Tricia's mouth opened in dismay. "Was she bullied?"

"Oh, yeah. Not that I ever teased her," Mary quickly said. "I mean, I was just another member of the high school rabble and kept a low profile. I had my little clique of friends, but we were only a step above the ones who got picked on incessantly, and Lauren was definitely a member of that group."

"Why was she picked on?"

Mary shrugged. "Because of the clothes she wore, the fact that she spent every free period in the library, the books she read."

"What kind of books?"

"Baby books."

"In high school?" Tricia asked.

Mary shrugged. "The ones aimed at poor readers to get them up to speed."

"Which isn't surprising. I mean, Lauren *chose* to be an author of children's books."

"I guess," Mary said with a shrug.

"What else do you remember about Lauren?" Tricia asked.

"The summer between tenth and eleventh grades, Lauren changed. She got a new haircut, her braces came off, and she became a different person with a whole new wardrobe. She was still a reader, but she didn't talk about it. She seemed to have a lot more confidence."

"Did she gain new friends?"

"Sure . . . but after we fell out, I didn't hang with her and her new friends."

"What about teachers? Were you in Ms. Kraft's English class with Lauren?"

"Oh, yeah," Mary said sourly.

"I take it she wasn't one of your favorites."

Mary's expression hardened. "I hated the bitch."

Tricia winced at the strong words. "Why?"

Mary looked embarrassed. "Because she actually took the time to make us learn. That wasn't my priority at age fourteen. She made us read books we'd decided we'd hate . . . until we read and discussed them." Mary's gaze dipped. "I hated every single minute spent in her classroom . . . until I got older and realized what a gift she'd given me."

"An appreciation of the written word?"

Mary nodded. "I was never going to be a scholar. Hell, high school was as far as I got academically. But without realizing it, Ms. Kraft instilled in me a craving to learn. To be a better person because of the books and ideas she presented in class." Mary shook her head. "It took me years to appreciate all I learned from Ms. Kraft."

"Did you ever tell her so?"

Mary shook her head. "No," she said sadly.

"She's still around. There's still time, you know."

"You're right. But I don't think I could face her in person." Mary's cheeks darkened in a blush. "I wasn't exactly the most attentive or polite student."

"Lauren gave Ms. Kraft a nasty tongue-lashing in the hours before her death. Apparently, she never came to the same conclusion as you, that Stella Kraft was actually a good mentor."

Mary shrugged.

"If you don't want to talk directly to Ms. Kraft, perhaps you could drop her a card and tell her how you'd come to appreciate her teaching."

"I doubt she'd even remember my name."

"You'd be surprised how much that retired teacher remembers," Tricia offered. "So, will you be going to Lauren's memorial service?"

Again, Mary shrugged, looking doubtful. "I dunno. It means I'd have to be away from my shop for an hour or so on a leaf peeping Saturday." She gave Tricia a sly look. "I suppose *you'll* be there."

"Angelica and I will be representing the Chamber of Commerce." It was a better story than just being plain nosy.

"I'll have to think about it." Mary glanced at her watch. "I'd better get going. Opening time is only minutes away."

Tricia looked up the street, where there was no sign of potential customers wandering the sidewalks. "Of course, have a great day," she said.

"You, too."

Tricia nodded, and the women went their separate ways.

Tricia was running late. No sooner had she hung up her jacket when Pixie arrived at the store. She shucked her coat, looking perky in a blue-and-white long-sleeved blouse with navy piping over a navy skirt and matching pumps, appearing distinctly nautical. "The weather might be against us," Pixie predicted.

"The weatherman says the skies should clear by later today," Tricia replied.

"Let's hope so. Sunny skies bring in customers by the droves."

Mr. Everett arrived with a smile despite the gloomy atmosphere outside. "Another typical fall morning in New England," he proclaimed as the three of them got the store ready for the day. Minutes later, they sat in the reader's nook, happily sipping coffee.

"I'm sorry there're no treats this morning," Tricia apologized.

At the sound of the word "treats," a hopeful Miss Marple suddenly appeared. "Sorry, little girl," Tricia said, "but if we're out of luck, so are you."

Miss Marple leveled a disappointed look at her mistress before jumping down from the big square coffee table, her fluffy gray tail swishing as she sashayed away.

"Well, I guess she told *you*," Pixie observed, and the humans laughed. "What's on the agenda today?"

"Not much," Tricia replied. "Because of the weather, we might not be all that busy."

"Eh—unpredictable fall in New England," Pixie said, echoing Mr. Everett's previous statement.

Just then, the mail was pushed through the slot in the door by Charlie Simmons, their regular mail carrier. He gave a cheerful wave before starting down the street once more. Pixie retrieved and sorted through the stack, tossing the circulars and credit card offers before she handed the rest off to Tricia. On top of the pile was the *Stoneham Weekly News*, which Tricia was inclined to toss aside, knowing Pixie would check out the yard and estate sales set for that weekend—late as it was in the thrifting season. But Pixie looked at the front-page story and tapped the fish wrapper with her index finger. "I think you might want to read the lead story," she said, holding out the paper.

Tricia unfolded the paper and saw the headline: Local Author—Dead at the Scene.

Yes, Tricia was *definitely* interested in reading the obit Antonio had mentioned six days before at the family dinner.

> *It was to be just another author signing at the Stoneham Library, with children's author Lauren Barker, known for her Cuddly Chameleon series of books. But who could have predicted that evening would end with the esteemed author's demise?*
>
> *The evening was off to a rocky start when Ms. Barker's ninth-grade high school English teacher, Stella Kraft, of Spruce Avenue, proclaimed to be one of the author's first mentors, only to have the author dispute that assertion. The two had a lively conversation, recorded by this reporter and turned over to the Stoneham Police Department as evidence after Ms. Barker's death. Ms. Barker told the crowd of over fifty people that she had no such encouragement from her high school teachers, which led to a spirited debate between the two women.*
>
> *According to an unnamed source, Ms. Barker refused to do more than sign books available from local bookstore owner Betty Barnes, of Barney's Book Barn. Nor did Ms. Barker read from her latest release, much to the disappointment of the children and parents who'd assembled to hear just that.*
>
> *Reports have surfaced that Ms. Barker spoke to an unnamed male during her time at the library. Who is this mystery man? Was he Barker's friend or foe? That, dear readers, is the question.*

Tricia frowned. Yeah, who was that guy? Had Chief McDonald been on the lookout for him? Would he show up for Lauren's memorial service the next day? Those were questions Tricia had no answer for. She folded the paper without looking at the rest of its contents, handing it back to Pixie.

"I think I'll start work in the office," she said.

"Sounds like a plan," Pixie agreed.

"We'll hold the fort," Mr. Everett said, and got up from his seat, heading for the back of the store, with Tricia following. He turned right to retrieve his lamb's wool duster, and she turned left for the stairs and the office below.

After firing up the computer, Tricia Googled Lauren Barker's death and found a link to the TikTok video Patti Perkins had uploaded of the altercation between Lauren and her former high school English teacher. Lauren sounded shrill and unreasonable, and the look on Stella Kraft's face was one of absolute hurt and confusion. And, as on that night just a week before, Tricia felt sorry for the older woman, who'd remembered the events of the past in a distinctly different light.

And yet . . . Lauren was dead. On gut instinct, Tricia believed Stella Kraft had nothing to do with Lauren's death, but what would the big news outlets make of the humiliating video the *Stoneham Weekly News* had shared with them?

Tricia also had several significant disputes with the story. Identifying Lauren as a local author was definitely off the mark. The woman had left the area over thirty years before. She identified a town in Connecticut as her home base. And there was apparently no love lost between Lauren and the children and parents who'd come to see the author in person, hoping for a connection that Lauren wasn't willing— or capable—of supplying.

Then, there was Mary's news of Lauren being picked on by other students. If events were different, and Lauren had been the bully, someone from her past might have had a motive for murder. It seemed extreme, but anything was possible when one could be shot and killed for simply pressing a doorbell or pulling into a driveway to turn a car around.

Tricia put the computer to sleep and headed up the stairs to the shop, where she found Pixie ringing up a sale with Mr. Everett bagging the purchase. Just another day in Booktown. Still, Tricia felt antsy, and she couldn't say why. Maybe it was her own kind of spidey sense warning her that something was about to break when it came to Lauren Barker.

She'd just have to wait and see.

When Pixie and Mr. Everett returned from their midday break, Tricia donned her jacket and jaywalked across the street to Booked for Lunch, which was teeming with people. In fact, Angelica had given up their usual booth that sat four to accommodate more customers and waited for her sister at one of the tables for two in the front of the café.

Tricia shrugged out of her jacket, setting it on the back of the chair opposite her sister. "Tight squeeze," she said.

"On days like this, we really should just have a sandwich at my place to accommodate more of the café's customers."

"Shall we do that tomorrow?"

Angelica nodded.

Tricia missed the comfortable—roomy—booth in back and felt a little exposed sitting where everyone who walked by could stare at them eating. Also, the table wasn't as private—not that she was planning on sharing any secrets, but she had planned on bringing Angelica up to date on what she'd learned about Lauren that morning. Angelica got the conversational ball rolling before she could even bring up the subject.

"I got a call from Marina over at the Sheer Comfort Inn a little while ago."

"Did anyone ever pick up Lauren's belongings?" Tricia asked.

"Yes. She said Chief McDonald did so after you asked about it. But that's not the interesting thing."

"Do tell."

Angelica leaned forward and lowered her voice. "It looks like Lauren might have been branching out as an author."

Tricia donned a wicked smile. "Don't tell me; she was working up a proposal for a tell-all book on Becca Chandler titled *Working for a Tennis Shrew?*"

Angelica did not look amused. "No. Marina only glanced at the first few pages, but it looks like a true-crime manuscript."

Tricia's eyes widened. "Actual pages?"

Angelica nodded.

"Where was it found?"

"Under the bed."

"Had anyone else been in the room since Lauren?"

"Of course. It's leaf peeping season. Lauren had reserved the room for Thursday and Friday nights. We lost Saturday—our busiest night of the week—because of the police investigation and had to put a couple up at a motel on the highway, but it's booked solid for the rest of the month. Marina was vacuuming this morning and nearly sucked up the pages."

"Is Lauren's name listed on the title page?"

Angelica shook her head. "No title page, but it was in the header along with the page numbers."

"What's the subject?" Tricia asked.

"An unsolved murder on Cape Cod that happened some twenty years ago."

Tricia looked thoughtful. She remembered the list of books from

Lauren's e-reader and had even taken a photo of the true-crime titles but hadn't thought to look them up. She'd try to remember to do so upon returning to Haven't Got a Clue.

"I wonder if Lauren already had a contract for that book," Tricia mused.

"It might be something that Chief McDonald could ask her agent or publisher," Angelica suggested.

"I suppose Marina's already turned the manuscript over to the police," Tricia lamented.

Angelica pursed her lips and glanced down at her perfectly polished nails. "Um . . . not quite yet."

Tricia's brow rose in interest. "Oh?"

"I thought maybe *you* might want to make a copy of the pages before they're turned over to the police."

Would she ever!

"How thick a manuscript is it?"

"About a hundred pages."

Something that large would take too long to replicate on the little printer/copier in Tricia's basement office. "I'd have to take it to the big office supply store outside of Milford to efficiently do the deed."

Angelica nodded.

Tricia didn't feel hopeful. "What would Marina say to the chief?"

"That she found it. Unless he asks, she doesn't have to tell him *when* it was found."

"He's sure to ask if anyone else knows about it."

"And she can tell him she told me."

"So . . . would you take custody of it?"

"Of course. I'm co-owner of the inn. I'll report it, and then Marina won't have to lie."

"But *you* would?" Tricia pressed.

Angelica shook her head. "I *don't* lie. If asked, I'll tell him I showed it to you, which would be the truth. He doesn't have to know you have a copy."

All of which sounded a little sneaky. Heck, *really* sneaky! But Tricia *so* wanted to read those pages.

"When would you pick it up?"

"This afternoon."

"And when would you turn it in?"

"Later this afternoon."

Over fish tacos and nachos they worked out the logistics of the handoff and Tricia's trek to the office supply store. Angelica didn't want to appear on the office supply store's video surveillance—and neither did Tricia—but there was no way she could ask Pixie or Mr. Everett to do her dirty work, either. It would have to be Tricia who committed the crime . . . er, act.

The sisters decided that Angelica would meet Tricia at Kaley Park in Milford and hand off the manuscript, then she'd wait for Tricia to return before making her way to the Stoneham police station.

Tricia's gaze wandered out the window to the sidewalk outside, watching as tourists filed past. Her gaze fell on the face of a man who headed north up the street, and it took a moment for her to realize she'd seen those features before. In an instant, Tricia shot out of her chair and headed for the café's door, but a couple waiting to be seated blocked her way. By the time she got past them and left the building, the man had disappeared. Tricia stepped to the sidewalk's edge to peer up the street but could see no sign of the bomber jacket worn by the man she sought. A wave of frustration passed through her as she reentered the café.

"What was that all about?" Angelica asked once a flustered Tricia flopped back into her chair.

"I just saw the mystery man Lauren was talking to the night she died."

"Are you sure?" Angelica asked.

Sudden doubt filled her. "Pretty sure," Tricia said.

"Why do you think he's hanging around the village?"

"Beats me."

Molly, the server, arrived to clear the table and, upon finishing, gave Angelica a nod in the direction of the door, where a man and woman waited to be seated.

"We'd better go," Angelica said, gathering her things.

"But I didn't get to tell you what else I learned this morning," Tricia protested.

"You can tell me during happy hour."

"Oh, all right," Tricia said, grabbed her jacket, and donned it. The sky had cleared, but there was still a brisk wind.

Angelica led the way out and Tricia followed.

The sisters crossed the road together, risking double jaywalking tickets, but there wasn't a cop in sight.

"Meet me at the park in half an hour. Don't be late," Angelica warned.

Tricia met her sister's gaze. "I won't."

SEVENTEEN

Tricia entered Haven't Got a Clue, where the after-lunch lull was in full force, and Pixie and Mr. Everett were seated in the reader's nook, and judging by their placid expressions, each was engrossed in a satisfying read. Neither seemed surprised when Tricia said she had to run an errand.

"I should be back in an hour or so," she promised as she headed out the door.

"We'll be here," Pixie called to Tricia's retreating back.

Angelica's car was missing from the municipal parking lot. She must have gone directly from Booked for Lunch to the Sheer Comfort Inn to pick up the manuscript. Sure enough, Angelica was already at the park when Tricia arrived. Another car was parked at the far end of the lot near one of the baseball fields. Across the lawn, Tricia saw a woman walking a dog around the perimeter.

"I'll try to hurry," Tricia told her sister as Angelica handed over the manuscript.

"Take your time," Angelica assured her. "I brought my laptop. I can get some work done while you're gone."

Tricia nodded and turned, a shiver of excitement coursing through her as she walked back to her car, clasping Lauren's manuscript, held together by a single large binder clip. After gingerly placing it on the passenger seat, Tricia drove carefully to the big office supply store.

Tricia did feel like a sneak as she exited her vehicle. Of course, the hat and sunglasses she'd donned only helped to reinforce the sense of guilt she felt. But she didn't feel bad enough to abort the mission, either.

After waiting five minutes for the large-capacity copier to free up, the clerk told her how to use it and left her to her copying. Upon finishing the job, Tricia paid for the pages and was given a paper bag to hold it and the originals. She returned to her car, noticing her hands shook a little before she started the engine and headed back to the park.

Angelica was focused on her laptop's screen and started when Tricia knocked on her window.

"My goodness! You scared me."

"Sorry." Tricia handed over the manuscript.

"Did everything go all right?" Angelica asked.

Tricia nodded. "I'd better get back to my store."

"Are you just going to walk in with the manuscript under your arm?"

"The bag it came in has the store's name on it." Tricia thought about it. "I'll stop at the grocery store and pick up a few things. Then I can squirrel it away in my tote bag, and no one will know the difference. See you at happy hour at your place, or do you want to come to mine?"

"I don't like to leave Sarge alone when I've already been gone for a while. In fact, I should probably go home. I'll just finish up what I'm doing and see you at closing."

"I'll be there," Tricia said, and returned to her car.

At the store, she picked up a twelve-pack of beer, eggs, bacon, and some vegetables. That ought to hold her for a week's worth of interesting breakfasts she could make for David. Things he liked. She wanted to please him. Wanted whatever time they had together to be pleasant.

Was she being silly or just practical?

She didn't want to know.

Upon returning to Haven't Got a Clue, Tricia carried her groceries (and the manuscript) to her apartment. After putting the food away, she was tempted to start reading the pages, but she knew if she did she probably wouldn't put it down until she finished it—and it was getting near to closing time.

Pixie and Mr. Everett were getting ready to leave as Tricia rounded the bottom of the stairs that led to her apartment.

"See you on Sunday after the sales," Pixie called as she headed for the door.

"And I shall see you tomorrow, Ms. Miles," Mr. Everett chimed in.

"Have a good evening," Tricia called as she collected her jacket and headed out the door after them. June was locking up the Cookery and let Tricia inside before she, too, left for the day. "Have a good one," Tricia wished.

"You, too!"

After locking the door, Tricia made a beeline for the stairs to Angelica's apartment and was greeted by Sarge. Was he eager to see her or more interested in the dog biscuits she gave him? Tricia hung up her jacket and started for the kitchen. She tossed the dog his treat to quiet him, looked at her sister, and demanded, "Well?"

Angelica stirred the mixture in the crystal pitcher. "Well, what?"

"What happened when you visited the police department?"

Angelica shrugged. "The chief wasn't in. I left the manuscript with Polly, and he called me about twenty minutes later."

"And?" Tricia asked eagerly.

"I told him how Marina found it and that she gave it to me to turn over to him."

"And that was it?" Tricia asked.

Angelica nodded. "Pretty much."

After all the intrigue, Angelica's tale seemed anticlimactic.

"Let's sit in the living room and enjoy our drinks and snacks," Angelica said. That night, it was a slice of brie on a round butter cracker, with a dab of pepper jam on top.

The sisters settled themselves and Angelica poured the drinks.

"So, what did you want to tell me about your adventures earlier in the day?" Angelica asked.

Tricia recounted her conversation with Mary Fairchild, reading the *Stoneham Weekly News*'s front-page story on Lauren's death, and her online search for more background information on Lauren.

"I guess I should read Patti's story," Angelica said, not sounding at all enthused, "and probably before the service tomorrow morning."

Tricia had almost forgotten about that.

"I suppose you'll be going with David," Angelica said with just a hint of a pout in her tone.

"Why don't the three of us go together?" Tricia asked.

Angelica shrugged. "I suppose."

"And then after that, aren't you and David going antiques shopping?"

Angelica perked up at the word *shopping*. "Oh, yes. He said he saw a gorgeous set of antique porcelain china he thought I might want to look at for the Morrison Mansion. At least twenty place settings."

"Isn't that an awful lot of dishes?"

"Breakage, my dear. One must consider a worst-case scenario," Angelica said with a distinctly superior tone.

Tricia polished off her second queen olive. "I wonder who'll show up at the service. I doubt many of the Chamber members will bother coming. Why would they? Did anyone but Mary and Becca even know Lauren?"

"I doubt it," Angelia said.

"Most of the booksellers aren't local, but perhaps some of her old classmates might show up out of curiosity," Tricia suggested.

"Not likely," Angelica remarked. "I suppose Amelia Doyle will be there to represent the library."

"I don't know, but I'll ask David when I speak to him later." Tricia was so psyched to read Lauren's manuscript that she was willing to forgo a night of romance. David wasn't a fan of true crime, finding it too grisly for his taste. Which reminded Tricia . . . she still hadn't investigated the titles she'd seen on Lauren's e-reader. Tricia made a mental note to check that out.

"What else is new?" Angelica asked.

Tricia's heart sank. "Nothing much. It seems like no one is really interested in finding Lauren's killer."

"I'm sure that's not true."

"I was surprised at how little news her death generated. I didn't find anything more than casual notices of her death online. Was I wrong in thinking the Cuddly Chameleon books were more popular?"

"Kids like Sofia adored them. But let's face it, how seriously was Lauren taken as an author?"

Picture books were popular with the toddler set, and Lauren had sold a boatload of them, but she was trying to branch out as a true-crime author. She must have thought there was more money in the genre . . . or was she just bored writing children's books? Tricia had spoken to authors who'd written what they called the *book of their heart* only to be rejected by fans unwilling to try a favorite author writing in a different genre. The same fans were also the ones who claimed the author's work had gotten stale. They were damned if they tried something different and damned if they wrote the same-old, same-old book. Some readers just couldn't be pleased. And now Lauren would never get to be published in a different genre. It made Tricia sad. And yet she hadn't yet read Lauren's unfinished manuscript. Could she have been taken seriously as a true-crime writer? The world would never know.

Tricia sighed. "What's for supper?" she asked, feeling mildly depressed. She wanted some kind of comfort food, although she didn't have a clue what it should be.

"Chicken pot pies. Tommy's trying them out for our winter menu. He thinks he can do at least twenty a day—fresh, not mass-produced and frozen. I'll be interested to know what you think about them."

"Any chance of mashed potatoes as a side?"

Angelica grinned. "You got it. And how about a hot roll with butter, too?"

Tricia felt just a little bit better. She'd had issues with food in the past, but she'd recently embraced the calming effect of comfort food.

"I'll put the pies in the oven, and they should be ready by the time we finish our second drink," Angelica said.

"I'm all for that," Tricia agreed.

She watched her sister head for the kitchen to get their dinner started. And, once again, she thought about the manuscript that awaited her in the reading nook of her bedroom suite. Could those pages be the key to Lauren's death?

Tricia was eager to find out.

EIGHTEEN

Tricia stayed up far too late reading Lauren Barker's manuscript. As she read each page, unease crept through her. Her former lover Marshall Cambridge had owned a store devoted to true-crime books, but Lauren's manuscript wasn't like the tomes Marshall sold. It was nothing Tricia could put her finger on, so she put down the manuscript and powered up her laptop. Google truly *was* her best friend. She entered the name of the victim mentioned in Lauren's manuscript and got no hits. She added keywords like the name of the town where the murder was to have taken place and still got nothing. She Googled unsolved murders in Connecticut, where Lauren had said the murder had taken place, and again came up with nothing that matched.

The subject of her tale stemmed from the killer's sense of being wronged, something the narrator of the story seemed to think was an inconsequential slight but that the perpetrator of the crime viewed as akin to high treason.

As Tricia kept reading, a single thought kept circling through her brain . . . the possibility of an unreliable narrator. Lauren had painted the victim in an unflattering light. Was the author in sympathy with the perpetrator?

As she set the last page aside, Tricia wasn't sure how she felt about what she'd read. Unsettled. The manuscript hadn't read like a true-crime tome, nor did it follow the rules of mystery fiction. Was that because the genre was strange to the author? It sounded like an acceptable answer. And then Tricia asked herself a question, knowing the answer. Had it been a published book, would she have finished reading it? The answer was no. The narrative hadn't been enough to hook her. If Lauren hadn't been murdered, Tricia probably would have given up on it long before she'd reached the one-hundred-page mark.

So what did that say about Lauren Barker?

That she should probably have stuck to writing children's books, and yet, that wasn't a fair assessment. Tricia had probably read a first draft of a genre new to the author, so she probably should cut Lauren some slack. Lauren would have undoubtedly worked on the manuscript for months, maybe years before it saw print—if it ever did. And because Lauren's success had been with a print publisher, Tricia's gut feeling told her Lauren wouldn't be satisfied transitioning to another genre without the backing of a traditional publisher.

Sometimes independent authors struck gold, but it was a hard slog, and just because anyone could self-publish a book didn't mean it was good. Subscription services made thousands—maybe millions—of titles available, but that didn't mean they were worthy of regard, either.

As she prepared for bed, Tricia thought about all the elements of the manuscript that seemed wrong, leaving her frustrated and grumpy. When she awoke the following day, she decided she needed an attitude adjustment before attending the gathering in Lauren's honor. Despite more gray skies, she managed it thanks to her morning walk. Tricia almost always felt rejuvenated by exercise. Afterward, she fixed herself a one-egg omelet and a piece of toast with jam before showering and dressing for what she knew would be a somber occasion.

Fifteen minutes before the start of the service, Tricia met Angelica and David at the municipal parking lot.

"How was that new book you were telling me about?" Angelica asked coyly.

"Not as good as I'd hoped."

"Well, then. You'll have to tell me about it later. We'd better get going. The service should be starting soon."

Angelica unlocked the car, and the three of them got inside, with David riding shotgun.

Contrary to what Tricia might have expected, the Stoneham High School gymnasium was packed when they arrived for what had been advertised as Lauren's celebration of life. However, most of the faces in the crowd were unfamiliar. Those she did recognize were Stella Kraft, Dan Reed, Mary Fairchild, and, of course, Amelia Doyle, representing the library where Lauren had spent the last hours of her life.

A table sat at the back of the cavernous room, piled high with commercially baked sugar cookies slathered with pink frosting and colorful sprinkles. A coffee urn and sweating pitchers of ice water stood nearby, along with the thermal paper cups for the hot drinks and plastic cups for the cold. And, inevitably, adjacent to that table was another stacked high with copies of Lauren's books, along with an apron-clad teenager standing behind a cash register, ready to sell them. Instead of a coffin or urn, a smiling, life-sized photo cutout of Lauren holding a copy of one of her books stood near a lectern.

"Did I not warn you the whole thing would be gauche?" Angelica whispered.

"You did," Tricia muttered.

David shifted near Tricia's elbow. For the unhappy occasion, he'd donned what *Seinfeld* fans knew as a "puffy" white shirt with ruffles on the sleeves and cascading from the neck over a black brocade waistcoat. His shoulder-length hair was again captured in a ponytail, and he looked like the hero in an eighteenth-century French novel. "Ladies, may I get you some refreshments?"

Angelica turned a sour eye on the cookies on offer. "No, thank you."

Tricia shook her head. "None for me, either, but thanks."

David shrugged.

"What do you make of the crowd? We hardly recognize anyone here," Tricia said.

David nodded. "Apparently, they seem to be mostly school and public librarians from all over New England."

"And what do they have to say?" Angelica inquired.

"That the Cuddly Chameleon books enticed a lot of kids to want to read. I'd say that's one hell of a legacy. Hopefully, those books will keep ushering in new readers in the years to come, too."

"They've sure captured Sofia's heart, and I don't doubt baby Will will enjoy them when he's a little older."

"About Sofia—" David began, but Tricia grabbed his arm, squeezing it, signaling that now was not the time to make such inquiries. He did not look pleased but gave her a nod in understanding.

"Should we mingle or try to find some seats?" Tricia asked.

"Mingle with whom?" Angelica asked.

The question was moot as Betty took her place before the podium and spoke into the microphone. "Testing. One. Two. Three."

Tricia, Angelica, and David walked up the aisle that divided the rows of folding chairs, reminding Tricia of wedding guest factions. Bride's family and friends on one side; groom's on the other. But she suspected few in this audience knew more than one or more people in attendance. Still, Betty Barnes may have dug up a few people to share remembrances of Lauren Barker.

They took seats in the second row, with David on Tricia's left and Angelica on her right.

Once those attending found seats, Betty cleared her throat and looked over the crowd. "I think I speak for all of you who've gathered here today when I say that we all mourn the loss of Lauren Barker's work for the generations of children to come. But her stories live on—and autographed copies of such are available for purchase at the back of the room," she added, and a portion of the audience members turned, craning their necks to take in the table with piles of books that bore Lauren's signature.

"Today, we'll hear from a number of friends that Lauren left behind," Betty continued, "but first and foremost, I'd like to welcome to the podium one of the tennis world's greatest players, and a newcomer to our humble village: Becca Dickson-Chandler." And with that, Betty clapped her hands, lifting her head to acknowledge a newcomer at the back of the room.

Everyone turned as Becca emerged from the gymnasium's double doors and walked down the aisle between the chairs toward the podium. The mood of the crowd seemed to change from somber to excitement as Becca, clad in a black linen suit, crisp white blouse, and three-inch heels, made her way down the aisle, their applause thunderous. For a moment, Tricia expected Becca to start blowing kisses to the throng while her acolytes tossed rose petals to soften her footsteps.

"Gimme a break," Angelica muttered, rolling her eyes.

Upon reaching the head of the room, Becca acknowledged Betty, who'd moved aside while the former tennis star took over the lectern and waited for the commotion to die down. After adjusting the microphone, Becca gazed over those assembled, gripping the podium.

"Ladies and gentlemen," she began in earnest, "let me tell you about my *dearest* friend Lauren Barker."

Tricia scowled. That wasn't how Becca had described the woman to her.

"Lauren and I met near the beginning of my esteemed career that spanned almost two decades and brought me fame as the winner of trophies from Wimbledon to the French and Australian Opens. And during several of those years, Lauren was there for me, serving as my go-to girl and an integral part of Team Becca. She got me where I needed to go, enabling me to win the most prestigious awards the tennis world had to offer. Lauren was a small but vital cog in the glory of my illustrious career." She paused dramatically to allow applause to follow.

"Oh, brother," Angelica grumbled. "I thought we were here to celebrate Lauren's life—not Becca's."

"Shhh!" Tricia admonished her sister.

"I'm with Angelica," David muttered, which garnered him an ingratiating smile from Tricia's sibling.

"It was while working for me," Becca said, "that Lauren developed her much-loved character, the Cuddly Chameleon."

"On company time? And she was okay with that?" David whispered.

"Not so much," Tricia responded, remembering Becca's assessment days before.

"So," Becca continued, "I like to think that *I* might, in my own small way, have been a *big* part of Lauren's literary success."

"Good grief," Angelica grated, but the rest of the audience had given Becca their rapt attention, apparently grateful to her for honoring the deceased author.

Becca yammered on for another five minutes, mostly tooting her own horn, but had the good grace to sense her audience was getting restless. "But I'm not the only one whose life Lauren touched." She turned to Betty, who clambered to the podium again, snatching the microphone from its stand.

"Thank you, Ms. Dickson-Chandler, for sharing your memories with us here on this most solemn occasion."

Becca made a grab for the mic, but Betty pivoted and encouraged those assembled to give the ex-champ a round of applause. Then Betty dispatched Becca to an empty chair at the end of the first row, just a few seats away from Tricia. Becca made eye contact with Tricia but quickly took her chair.

Betty returned the microphone to its stand and leaned into it. "Our next speaker is Mary Fairchild, a darling school friend who traveled the same public school path here in Stoneham as dear Lauren—every step of the way." She lifted a hand as a gesture of welcome, and Mary stood. Judging from her rather terrified expression, Mary hadn't expected to be called upon.

With dragging steps, Mary approached the lectern. Betty stepped back, and Mary's startled gaze took in the audience. "Uh . . ." she began. "I . . . I guess I knew Lauren Barker since we both started kindergarten in Mrs. Morrow's class." She paused. Someone coughed. A cell phone's ringtone broke the silence before being abruptly silenced. Mary looked out over the crowd like a deer caught in an SUV's headlights.

"I, uh, can't say Lauren and I were ever as close as she and Ms. Dickson-Chandler, but my best friend, Lori-Lynn, and I could always depend on Lauren to loan us a buck or two when we wanted to buy a couple of hot chocolates or a doughnut from the high school Future Business Leaders of America club." She gave a nervous laugh. "We used to call her Lauren the Loner. We always paid her back," Mary assured the audience. "That way, we always had a banker friend in Lauren, who only charged us ten percent interest."

Those assembled, primarily women, looked at Mary with cold gazes. Her remembrance had not endeared her to them. Sensing this, Betty rushed back to the podium.

"Thank you, Ms. Fairchild, owner of the village's craft store, By Hook or By Book. If you're into yarn, Mary's got you covered," Betty gushed, but Mary only looked embarrassed by the endorsement. She ducked her head and practically ran back to her seat.

Betty plastered on a plastic grin and continued. "Our next speaker is Dan Reed, owner of the Bookshelf Diner, Stoneham's most *cozy* eatery."

"That's just crap," Angelica grated. "Booked for Lunch and even the Dog-Eared Page are cozier than Dan's dump."

"Shush!" Tricia ordered.

"If your tummy needs a refill, check out the Bookshelf Diner, only two blocks south from where I stand right now," Betty encouraged. Had she sold commercial time to the people she recruited, or imposed upon them to speak on Lauren's behalf?

Dan rose from his seat, just a little unsteady, Tricia noted, and made his way to the podium. Betty stood back, beaming.

Dan leaned onto the podium. "Welcome, welcome, welcome," Dan slurred. Good grief, was the man drunk?

"I'm here today to tell you that the Cuddly Chameleon—Lauren Barker's series of kids' books"—he shot her cutout a look of contempt—"were written to blatantly brainwash our kids—not just here in Stoneham, but around the entire world." And with that statement, Dan gestured to take in the whole room, nearly losing his grip on the lectern.

Betty looked appalled but didn't move forward to stop him from elaborating.

"Do we want our children thinking about such subversive rhetoric? Subversive, I tell you! Nothing and no one can change their colors. Not even a slimy little lizard."

David raised a hand. "Uh, excuse me, sir. But chameleons can do *exactly* that. When frightened, their skin *does* change color so they can blend in with their environment to be safe from predators. It's a scientific fact."

Dan narrowed his gaze. "And you're a slimy little creep. You're another one poisoning our children. And just look at the way you're dressed. You shouldn't be allowed to be near impressionable kids!"

But then Betty stepped forward and yanked the microphone from its stand. If she hadn't known about Dan's unfortunate view of the world before this, she did now.

"Thank you for speaking with us today, Mr. Reed."

"I haven't finished what I've got to say!" Dan complained, but no one in the audience seemed to care to listen.

"Thank you," Betty said again, and gave Dan a little shove, indicating his time in the limelight was over. Dan retaliated by reaching out both hands, planting them on Betty's shoulders, and pushing so hard the poor woman crashed to the floor, landing squarely on her bottom.

The crowd erupted in a collective gasp as Dan turned back to the lectern and Lauren's picture, giving it a good kick to send it flying before grabbing the microphone again. "Our children have been perverted by the kind of crap people like Lauren Barker spewed—" he began, and the crowd began to rumble in protest. Those assembled were Lauren Barker fans.

"That bitch—and people like her—are the reason our country is in the kind of trouble we're in today!"

But before Dan could elaborate, Police Chief Ian McDonald charged toward the podium, grabbed the microphone with one hand,

and captured Dan's arm with the other. The man yelped as though in pain, but McDonald didn't let go. "I'm sorry, folks," McDonald said, the Irish lilt in his voice coming on strong—and charming.

By then, Betty had been helped to her feet by several women from the front row of seats and was dusting herself off. Dragging a protesting Dan with him, McDonald conferred with Betty, and as Tricia sat so near, she could hear the whole exchange.

"Are you all right, ma'am? If you'd like to press assault charges, just let me know."

"I . . . I don't know," Betty said, still shaken.

"Take some time to think about it and get back to me."

"Thank you, Chief. I will," Betty said.

"Mr. Reed and I have a previously scheduled meeting to attend." McDonald glanced at the crowd before continuing. "We'll be going now. Please carry on with Ms. Barker's memorial," he said sweetly.

McDonald then dragged a protesting Dan out of the gymnasium while the eyes of all those in attendance stared after them.

It took Betty another minute or so to regain her composure. By then, the entire audience had her back.

"Our next speaker," Betty began, her voice just a little shaky, "is someone well known to our community, who was Lauren's very first employer." Betty looked over the audience. "Mr. William Everett, will you come up and tell us what you knew about Lauren Barker?"

Tricia's head whipped around so fast she should have suffered whiplash. When they'd entered the gym, she hadn't seen a sign of Mr. Everett, but there he was, accompanied by Grace, rising from his seat and heading toward the front of the assemblage.

The gym was deadly quiet. Most of the mourners had no clue who the next speaker was. And Tricia wondered why Mr. Everett hadn't mentioned that he'd known Lauren Barker.

Though he was someone Tricia had always thought of as a shy and unassuming person, Mr. Everett stood ramrod straight in front of the microphone, and when he spoke, his voice was vibrant and strong.

"As Ms. Barnes explained, my name is William Everett, and in the past, I owned Everett's Grocery on Stoneham's main thoroughfare. I personally interviewed each and every employee who worked in my store, and Lauren Barker, then known as Lauren Cox, was hired as a part-time cashier. Lauren's work was exemplary. She always showed up on time, never called in sick, and could be depended upon to do any task asked of her. She was, what one would say in those days, a good girl. She treated our customers with respect; she often regaled her fellow employees with songs she made up. Her beautiful soprano accompanied many tunes played on the store's speakers. I often wondered if she might find a career as a vocalist. But that she found her niche as a writer filled my heart with joy, as I, myself, am a bibliophile. I know from my own grandchildren"—and at this, Angelica positively beamed—"that her stories touched the hearts of many a young girl and boy. And I mourn that her voice has now been silenced."

Tricia had to swallow to not cry at her dear friend's loving tribute to someone he probably hadn't had contact with for twenty or thirty years. She raised her hand to give him a wave and Mr. Everett caught sight of her, giving her a small, warm smile before he left the lectern.

"Thank you, William," Betty said as she watched his retreating back.

Eileen Harvick waved a hand to get Betty's attention. So, at least one other Chamber member had attended the occasion.

"Yes?"

"Will Ms. Barker be buried here in Stoneham?"

Betty blushed. "I haven't been told."

"And who would tell her?" Angelica muttered.

"Angelica!" Tricia hissed.

"If I learn of another ceremony in Lauren's honor," Betty continued, "I'll be sure to share it with all the Chamber members and, of course, the *Stoneham Weekly News*."

Patti Perkins would probably already know if there was news on that front. Tricia looked around, surprised that Patti—and the other two women who kept the weekly fish wrapper in business—didn't appear to be in attendance. Tricia thought she might give the office a call on Monday.

"Would anyone like to share a memory of Lauren?" Betty asked.

As most of the audience hadn't personally known the deceased author, it wasn't surprising that no one volunteered to speak. Betty looked expectantly at the assemblage for an uncomfortably long time before she wrapped up the proceedings.

"Thank you all for coming. Before you leave today, I hope you'll drop by the refreshments table and help yourselves. And, of course, if you'd like a remembrance of Lauren, there's a large assortment of autographed copies of her work that can be purchased by cash, check, or credit cards."

Tricia's gaze wandered but it seemed those around her found Betty's invitation to be just as crass as she did.

Silence.

For a long minute.

Then a chair scraped across the gymnasium's lacquered floor, and someone stood as though giving the rest of the crowd permission to leave.

Tricia, Angelica, and David waited until those behind them had cleared the aisle. No one seemed to be partaking in the cookies or the invitation to buy books as they shuffled out of the room. Tricia looked back to see Betty still standing at the podium with a look of fury coloring her cheeks.

* * *

Once outside, Tricia saw Stella Kraft heading for her car. She wore a large floppy hat, and despite the overcast day, sunglasses. "Stella!"

The older woman turned, saw it was Tricia who called her, and gave a halfhearted wave.

"I'll be with you in a moment," Tricia told Angelica and David, and hurried over to speak with Stella. "I was surprised to see you here."

Stella frowned. "No more than me." She shook her head. "After the way Lauren treated me at the book signing . . ." She let the sentence hang. "But she *was* my student. I wasn't sure anyone local would show up—and from the looks of it, not many did."

Tricia nodded. "What did you think of the remembrances?"

Stella eyed Tricia, probably wondering if she should be honest or keep her opinions to herself. "Pie in the sky," she said before her gaze narrowed. "You didn't answer my last few text messages."

"I'm sorry to say I have nothing to report."

Stella glared at Tricia skeptically. She nodded to Angelica and David. "You need to go. Your store will be opening soon."

It was a pretty blunt dismissal, but Tricia nodded. "We'll talk soon."

Stella said nothing and turned for her car.

Tricia joined David and Angelica once again.

They drove back to Haven't Got a Clue, in what seemed to Tricia like strained silence, where they let her out. "Have fun shopping," she told them.

David gave a weak smile.

"See you for dinner at my place," Angelica said.

Did that mean she planned on having lunch with David? Tricia hoped she wasn't about to grill the poor guy.

Angelica nodded, glanced in her side mirror, and pulled the car away from the curb. Tricia could see David's reflection in the side-view mirror. He didn't look happy. Then the car sped up and out of view.

Tricia turned to see that the lights were on inside her shop. Mr. Everett had arrived before her. He had the beverage station up and running and had donned his apron, ready for the retail day.

"Thanks for getting everything ready."

Mr. Everett rewarded her with a wan smile. "Just part of my job."

"I'll just hang up my coat and then join you at the reader's nook."

By the time she returned, Mr. Everett was seated in the nook with a steaming mug of coffee before him, and one in front of Tricia's seat. After so many years, he knew how she took her brew.

"Thank you," Tricia said, picking up her cup. "I was sure surprised to see you at Lauren Barker's remembrance service. That was an eloquent eulogy you gave her," Tricia commented.

Instead of accepting the compliment, Mr. Everett just looked sad. "I like to think I remember only the best of the people I've been acquainted with during my life's journey," he said.

Tricia could tell by her friend's expression that he hadn't told the whole truth when it came to his recollections of Lauren Barker. The man kept most of his opinions to himself, so Tricia had little hope he'd confide in her when it came to Lauren's shortcomings. Still, she felt she needed to ask.

"Was there something about Lauren's character you felt you couldn't share?" she asked gently, not expecting an answer.

Mr. Everett mulled the question over for a long moment before answering. "Lauren was not what some would call a team player. She did her job, but she didn't get along with a number of the other employees."

"In what way?" Tricia asked.

Mr. Everett shook his head but didn't look Tricia in the eyes. "There were always tensions and animosities among the teens in the store. Petty rivalries. Boys and girls going steady and then breaking up. On occasion, it led to a lot of drama."

"Was there anyone in particular Lauren didn't get along with?"

Mr. Everett shrugged. "The little tragedies of those days are now lost to me."

That was too bad. But that Mr. Everett remembered such strained relations was enough for Tricia to hold as fact. But who could verify those trifling jealousies?

Mary Fairchild, for one, but who else?

NINETEEN

Along with yet more gray skies, Lauren Barker's remembrance service had cast a pall over the day. Tricia didn't hear from Angelica or David, and as the hours crept closer to the end of the workday, Tricia found herself feeling antsy. She texted David to confirm their getting together later that evening at her place, but received only a terse reply that said, *See you there.*

So, with trepidation, Tricia climbed the steps to Angelica's apartment after the close of business. Both Sarge and Angelica were in high spirits, which seemed like a good sign. Angelica stirred the martinis while Tricia carried the tray of glasses, garnishes, and a plate of cheddar cheese wrapped with prosciutto and skewered with toothpicks to the living room's coffee table.

"You're in a good mood," Tricia said as Angelica took time to pour the cocktails. "Did you and David have a good time shopping?" Tricia asked, trying to sound like it hadn't been on her mind since Angelica had driven away that morning.

"Did we!" Angelica handed her sister a glass. "I bought that set of china David spoke of. It's beautiful, and because it doesn't have gold rims, it can go in the dishwasher. Have you seen the pattern?"

"No."

Angelica whipped out her phone, scrolled through her gallery of pictures, and handed it to Tricia. "Yes, that's a pretty design."

"Twenty place settings," Angelica gushed, as though she'd just lost twenty pounds and wanted to crow about it.

"What else did you get?"

"Well, it's not so much what I got as what I learned. I had no idea David was so knowledgeable when it came to nineteenth-century architecture and furnishings. We talked about rugs, art, and even the appropriate potted plants for the time period. How does one so *young* accumulate that level of expertise?"

Tricia didn't take offense at the term *young*—this time. "By being exposed to such things. His grandmother—"

"Oh, yes, he spoke very highly of her. Such a nice young man."

Tricia let out a mental sigh of relief. That said, she didn't want to push her luck and decided she'd better change the subject.

"Between wondering how you two got along—"

"Famously," Angelica interjected.

"—and Lauren's remembrance service, I had a lot to think about during the day."

"Sales weren't great, were they?" Angelica said, her mood seeming to deflate.

"No. We need a few sunny days to get the tourists back."

Angelica nodded and sipped her martini. "Speaking of Lauren's service, Dan Reed sure made a fool of himself this morning."

"That he did," Tricia agreed.

"I'm not sure if I should be angry with him or feel sorry."

"He's got my pity—not because he's a nice guy—but because he's *not*," Tricia asserted.

Angelica nodded, and her expression changed to quizzical as she toyed with the blue frill pick in her glass. Had she chosen the color to go with her silk blouse? "Uh, what have you heard about the Bookshelf Diner?" Angelica asked, her voice just a little bit higher.

Tricia frowned. "Not a thing. And why would I? I rarely darken its doors."

"Yes, and apparently, you're not the only one," Angelica said coyly.

The Bookshelf Diner had originally been called Dan's Place before Bob Kelly, who'd bought up most of Stoneham's Main Street when the village more resembled a ghost town almost two decades before. Those already in business adapted to the Booktown theme.

When Bob had gone to prison for murder, with a twenty-five-years-to-life sentence, most of the properties he'd owned had gone up for sale—some of them for auction to the highest bidders, who'd low-balled their offers. Dan Reed had been such a recipient, acquiring the building that housed his diner for a song. Oddly enough, if he were to declare bankruptcy, he might suffer the same fate as Bob when it came to liquidating his assets.

"Go on," Tricia encouraged.

"Antonio forwarded me an anonymous e-mail begging NR Associates to please buy the diner before Dan Reed runs it into the ground."

"Did they say what was wrong?"

Angelica nodded. "After his wife went to jail, Dan decided to take over as the short-order cook, and not only can't he stand the heat in the kitchen, he can't cook, either. Burned pancakes and burgers, tasteless salads, moldy bread, sour milk. It seems he just doesn't have the chops for the job."

Chops—as in pork or lamb? Tricia mused. She said, "And?"

"Apparently, the locals have abandoned the place, which explains why business at Booked for Lunch and the Dog-Eared Page have been up more than twenty percent this past quarter."

"Are you thinking of buying the business?" Tricia asked.

"Not a chance," Angelica quipped, reaching for a piece of the cheese. "But I wouldn't be opposed to buying the building and moving my café to the larger space."

"When does the lease for Booked for Lunch run out?"

Angelica chewed and swallowed before answering. "Unfortunately, it was just renewed for another two years. But there's nothing stopping me from subletting the space should I move my café to a new location."

"Sounds like you've got everything figured out," Tricia said, and took a sip of her martini.

Angelica frowned. "You don't sound pleased."

Tricia shrugged. "I'm not a fan of Dan Reed . . . but I guess I do feel a little sorry for him."

"Whatever for? He's an obnoxious man who mistreated his wife, drove her to crime, and has harangued his customers with his outlandish conspiracy theories!"

"You're right," Tricia remarked.

The sisters sipped their martinis in silence for a long minute or so.

"Well?" Angelica finally demanded.

"Well, what? *Is* there a chance Dan will sell the building?"

"I might have to wait until he's filed for bankruptcy."

"Isn't that taking advantage of someone when he's down and out?"

Angelica shrugged. "What do you suggest?"

"Well, you could throw the man a lifeline."

"In what way?"

"Offer him a fair market price for the building—and offer to sublet the space Booked for Lunch now occupies should he want to continue in business. I don't think he has any other marketable skills."

"That's a fine idea in theory, but Dan hates me for opening my café and competing against him."

"Couldn't NR Associates buy the space and lease it to you?"

"Probably, but if it did, I'd never be able to spend a shift waiting tables, baking desserts, or manning the kitchen ever again."

"What do you mean?"

"Right now, Booked for Lunch is a two-to-three-person operation. I estimate I'd need ten to twelve people to man two to three shifts seven days a week at a bigger location. It would be a much larger operation."

"Is hands-on experience all that important to you?"

"I don't do it every day, but I do occasionally enjoy it." Which meant once or twice a week—more during peak summer hours or during the holidays.

"You're a control freak," Tricia accused her sister.

Instead of taking offense, Angelica nodded. "Sometimes. But are you any different?"

"Of course."

Angelica scoffed. "Then how come Pixie is your *assistant* manager? The woman may only have a GED but is smart as a whip. She knows your stock—hell, she finds most of it these days. She's great with customers and is as loyal as the day is long. So why haven't you given her a bigger role in the store?"

Everything Angelica said was true. Still . . .

"Because *I'm* the manager. It's *my* store." And then a thought occurred to Tricia. Her gaze narrowed. "Are you thinking of poaching her?"

"I would never do that," Angelica protested.

"The heck you wouldn't! You poached Ginny to manage the Happy Domestic."

"And didn't she not only excel, but prove she had more to offer?"

It was true. Ginny hadn't gone to college, either, but she was as business savvy as anyone with a degree in marketing. She'd taken it upon herself to learn what she needed to succeed.

"What kind of position would you offer Pixie?"

"Perhaps head of the house at a revamped Booked for Lunch." Angelica looked thoughtful. "If the business is going to be open from dawn 'til dusk or after, I'd definitely have to change the name."

"You've obviously thought about this in great detail," Tricia accused.

"Just as a possibility," Angelica remarked.

Tricia let out a weary sigh. "What would you offer Pixie?"

Angelica offered a similar sigh. "It would be a lot more responsibility than she has now. Of course, that would warrant a substantial raise, along with guidance to learn the ropes. I would not want her to fail."

The thought of not interacting with Pixie every day made Tricia feel a terrible ache of sadness. Still, what Angelica had to offer—and the faith she had that Pixie could—no, *would*—succeed was an opportunity Tricia wouldn't try to interfere with. Then again, Angelica had previously offered Pixie a full-time position at Booked for Beauty, Angelica's day spa, and Pixie had turned it down. Would she do the same for this kind of break?

"Okay," Tricia said reluctantly. "*If* she'd accept the opportunity, I wouldn't stand in her way."

"It would be her decision, but you can't let her loyalty to you stop her from learning and growing."

Tricia stared into her nearly empty glass. "I suppose if it came to it, I *could* fire her. And I don't think you'll get her to break her thrifting addiction."

"Why would I want to when it benefits the Cookery and the Happy Domestic?"

"Not to mention Haven't Got a Clue and several other businesses along Main Street." Tricia heaved another heavy sigh, feeling like she was about to lose a good friend. "When would you approach her with an offer?"

"Not anytime soon. Not until I could acquire the building. It's *not* a given."

Then why had she brought up the whole subject?

"If nothing else, you could have Antonio put out some feelers," Tricia offered.

"That's a good idea. Thanks."

"Not at all."

They sipped their drinks, took pieces of the cheese, and looked at each other.

Sometimes, Tricia wished her sister wasn't such a phenomenal business success.

"Hey, you were going to tell me about Lauren's true-crime manuscript," Angelica reminded Tricia.

"What a bust. Not at all worth the intrigue for obtaining it." She explained the lack of factual information that would clue someone in on the murder or where it had happened.

"So, it doesn't sound like the crime garnered national attention?"

"*If* the crime was even real."

"How can true crime not be real?"

"When it's fiction."

Angelica looked puzzled. "Tell me more."

"First, it's not especially well written. To the contrary. I couldn't find any corroborating information on the presented facts. Lauren may have wanted to keep key elements of the story hidden, like the victim's real name and the crime's location. But other people mentioned were given generic identification such as Witness 1, 2, 3 or Officers A, B, or C. Not at all helpful."

"I see."

Tricia toyed with the frill pick in her glass. "And why would Lauren want to jump from writing children's books to true crime, anyway? It's so far from her successful genre."

"Unless she had it published under a pseudonym," Angelica pointed out. "Then again, is it good enough to be traditionally published?"

Tricia shrugged. "It would have taken a lot of work, but maybe Lauren was up for it. Who knows."

"So, it's a dead end?"

Tricia looked thoughtful. "Possibly. I wonder if any of Lauren's friends or colleagues knew she was working on the book. Surely, her agent had to be aware of it."

"Maybe. But, like you said, hopping genres is difficult. One usually doesn't take one's readers along with them."

"Perhaps she was thinking of turning the manuscript into a podcast. Plenty of celebrities have podcasts that have nothing to do with their professional careers."

"I guess it's a possibility," Angelica said, although she didn't sound convinced.

"I guess it really doesn't matter. Lauren won't have the opportunity to finish the book. I wonder if there's another Cuddly Chameleon book in the pipeline."

"Surely the publisher would have announced it when news of her death broke—if only to gin up interest."

"You're probably right."

Angelica looked at the clock on the wall. "I'd better pop our supper into the oven, or we'll be eating at midnight."

Tricia watched as her sister headed for the kitchen, feeling just a little depressed. Still, after she left Angelica's place, she'd be meeting up with David, and the thought immediately lifted her spirits.

Just a couple more hours.

She could wait.

TWENTY

"She wants to poach Pixie from Haven't Got a Clue?" David asked, sipping his beer.

Tricia nodded sadly. "But only if she can wrangle leasing the building should Dan Reed run his diner into the ground."

"He's sure done that," David said. "The last time I was in there, I ordered a BLT and one side of each of the slices of bread was burned to a crisp. The server had him make another one, but I couldn't get that burned taste out of my mouth." He shuddered at the thought.

Tricia had set out a bowl of pretzel twists, picked one up, and dipped it into honey mustard. She wasn't hungry, realized it, and set the pretzel down on the napkin before her on the kitchen island.

"I don't think you have to worry," David consoled her. "Pixie loves you and Mr. Everett. She's always singing your praises. And she loves talking vintage mysteries to your customers. My guess is she'd turn down that kind of promotion. But . . ." He paused, sipped his beer, and took one of the pretzels, chomping on it. "You could offer her more money as kind of a pre-incentive to stay."

Bribery was such an unpleasant suggestion.

"We'll see," Tricia said, and ate the pretzel she'd previously abandoned. "At least you and Angelica had a good time shopping. Well, she apparently did. How did it go for you?"

"Great. Your sister talks a lot but she also knows when to listen."

"I neglected to ask her if she would accompany you and Pixie on your sales tomorrow."

David shook his head. "Not her thing. She's looking for high-end furnishings and accessories. Pixie and I look for affordable items."

Tricia nodded. She dipped another pretzel into the mustard. "What did you think of Lauren Barker's service this morning?"

David's expression soured. "Depressing. Becca Chandler's tirade seemed pretty self-centered. Dan Reed was just a jerk."

"And Mr. Everett?" Tricia asked.

"Perfunctory."

That was a pretty odd description. Then again, had everyone caught that though Mr. Everett had spoken well of Lauren, there hadn't been any kind of emotional connection? Of course, it wasn't a secret that Mr. Everett kept his feelings to himself, so perhaps because Tricia, and maybe even David, knew him better than most, they paid more attention to what the older gentleman *hadn't* said.

David polished off the last of his beer, and Tricia noticed that the bowl of pretzels had mysteriously emptied—as had the pot of mustard.

"What do you want to do this evening?" Tricia asked.

David smiled. "We could just . . ." He looked toward the stairs that led to her bedroom suite.

"There is that."

"But before that . . . what do you say we listen to some music and . . . *read.*"

"You want to read?" she asked, surprised.

"Well, I have this test coming up . . . and you *always* have something you want to read. It's not exactly romantic—"

"Oh, I don't know about that . . ."

"—but it would be enjoyable."

Tricia smiled. "That might be the sexiest thing a man has ever said to me."

"I doubt it," David said.

"Maybe, but I like the way you think."

"I like everything about ou," David said.

Tricia batted her eyelashes, her mouth quirking into the barest hint of a grin. "You're just saying that because it's true."

He nodded. "Now, what have you got in the way of music?"

Tricia thought about the CDs Pixie had brought in that sat near the stereo system in her store.

"How about a little Sinatra?"

"I thought you'd never ask."

After breakfast the next morning, David headed home to get ready for his thrifting outing with Pixie. Tricia walked him to the municipal parking lot, kissed him good-bye, and watched as he drove north on Main Street, heading for his apartment in Milford. On that morning, she decided to start off in the same direction.

When Tricia approached Barney's Book Barn, she saw Betty Barnes gazing out the window, as though she'd been waiting for her to pass. Betty disappeared from view only to suddenly burst from the shop's door. "Tricia! Do you have a moment?"

Tricia paused on the sidewalk, dreading the conversation to come. Still, she squared her shoulders and put on a manufactured smile. "Sure. What's up?"

"Uh . . . I was just wondering, does the Chamber of Commerce ever provide low-interest loans to their members?"

Tricia took a step back. "Uh, no. It's not one of our services."

"Oh, darn," Betty said grimly.

It was an awkward moment. Tricia was dying to ask why Betty needed a loan—guessing the answer but being too polite to actually inquire.

"I find myself in a bit of a financial bind," Betty volunteered. "You know, now that the tourist season is waning. This gray, gloomy weather hasn't helped, either."

"Things will pick up after Thanksgiving," Tricia reminded her. "May I suggest you speak with Billie Hanson, the manager at the Bank of Stoneham? I'm sure she could help you out."

Betty chewed her bottom lip, looking anxious. "Maybe."

Another uncomfortable silence ensued.

Tricia cleared her throat. "It was a lovely gathering you hosted for Lauren yesterday."

"Yeah," Betty muttered, "lovely. Unfortunately, I expected book sales to cover the cost of the event. Do you know not one person bought *any* of Lauren's books? They came to honor her, and yet no one had the courtesy to—"

"Pay up?" Tricia suggested.

"No!" Betty cried, taking umbrage. She glared at Tricia for long seconds, but then her gaze shifted. "She was the best-known author I ever hosted at a signing, but apparently I made a grave mistake when it came to Lauren Barker's popularity."

"Betty, the *library* hosted Lauren. You just supplied the books." And if Betty hadn't alienated Lauren by having her sign so *many* books, Lauren likely would have read for the children in the audience, entertaining them with the antics of her Cuddly Chameleon creation—exactly what she'd been asked to do.

"I'm the *only* children's bookstore in Stoneham. Lauren *had* to come to me to acquire the books," Betty asserted. Not so. David had asked Betty to supply the books, but any bookstore owner could have ordered them from their distributors. It was a courtesy that he'd contacted her. Lauren probably had no clue who Betty was nor had heard of her store before arriving the day of the signing.

"Why did you order so many books?" Tricia asked.

"As I said, I miscalculated the woman's popularity," Betty uttered bitterly.

"And now you need to unload them quickly?"

"I refuse to lose money on the deal," Betty said through gritted teeth.

Tricia felt she had to reply to that statement. "Well, I'm sure if you're patient, the books will eventually sell."

"I'm running out of time *and* patience."

So was Tricia. It was time to cut this conversation short. "You'll let me know if the Chamber can be of any further help, won't you?"

"Why would I when you've been absolutely useless so far," Betty said, pivoted, and stalked back into her store.

Tricia continued on her way, with plenty to think about during the next half hour or so.

Out of curiosity, upon returning to her store, Tricia checked eBay for autographed copies of Lauren Barker's books. Sure enough, Betty Barnes had relisted the different editions of the Cuddly Chameleon series with starting bids of five hundred dollars each. Whether she would get that kind of money for an autographed book was doubtful. Betty had only to bide her time to sell the rest of her hoard. Then again, the longer Lauren was dead, perhaps the more valuable her books would become. That was a pretty big *perhaps*. Tricia sat back and contemplated the other suspects. The mystery man was at the top of her list. Now, who could he possibly be? A lover? A relative?

Then, on a whim, Tricia decided to look up the name of the person who'd illustrated all but the first Cuddly Chameleon book, which had been sold to a small press—and who apparently still owned the rights, for it hadn't been republished by Lauren's much more prominent, New York–based publishing house.

Tricia Googled the name B. R. Woodward and was rewarded with a URL for a website. Upon clicking it, she saw examples of the artist's work; chief among them was the cover of the latest Cuddly Chameleon book. Upon clicking the bio link, Tricia was rewarded with a picture of a dark-haired, lean man with classic good looks. She'd seen an older version of the man just an hour or so before Lauren had been found dead in the Stoneham Library's parking lot and on the street two days before.

Now . . . how was she going to track him down?

TWENTY-ONE

Tricia spent the rest of the hour on the hunt for Brian Woodward. Not that he was difficult to find—at least online. In no time at all she read every bio she could find, plus reviews of his decades of work as an award-winning illustrator. She knew where he lived, had his contact information from his website, and considered leaving him a message. But what could she say? The police would like to talk to you? That was another problem Tricia wrestled with. Should she tell Chief McDonald she'd discovered the identity of Lauren's mystery man? And then what? If she did, she'd probably never get to speak to the man, which she was sure most people would think was appropriate.

Finally, Tricia decided to put the whole Woodward dilemma on the back burner and instead turn on the oven. She had just enough time to bake a batch of brownies, which she knew to be David's favorite dessert. He liked them with chocolate frosting, which would also delight Sofia when they were presented as dessert at that evening's family dinner at the Barbero-Wilson abode. David had already told her he'd be in attendance. Since the previous day's shopping trip with Angelica, he seemed to have lost most of his anxiety about spending time with her.

Tricia saved a couple of the brownies, dusting them with confectioners' sugar, as a treat for herself and Mr. Everett. She had the coffee ready when he arrived for work just before noon.

"Good morning, Ms. Miles." He glanced at the clock. "It still *is* morning, at least for the next seven minutes."

"Good morning to you, too."

In minutes, Mr. Everett had donned his apron and joined Tricia in the reader's nook. "You baked?" he asked.

"I did. And there's more where this came from—but just for the family," she said, indicating the brownies that sat on napkins decorated with cheerful pumpkins.

Mr. Everett smiled. "I shall look forward to this *and* dessert tonight."

"David will be joining us again."

"How nice. He's a fine young man."

Tricia tried not to wince every time someone described David in that manner.

The two enjoyed their coffee, brownies, and chatted until the first customer of the day arrived some ten minutes later. Mr. Everett sprang into action while Tricia tidied the large coffee table and washed their mugs. Mr. Everett made the sale, and the shop was quiet once more. Tricia put on another of Pixie's CDs for background music, while Mr. Everett retrieved his lamb's wool duster.

As there were no customers, Tricia decided to do a little research into the titles that had been listed on Lauren Barker's e-reader. Retrieving her laptop, she set it up on the shop's display case that doubled as a cash desk.

As she suspected, the books were all true-crime titles. Had Lauren used them as inspiration, or was her book to be another take on a murder that had already been dissected by other authors?

A couple of Granite State tour buses arrived in the village, spilling a hundred or so visitors onto the street and eager to visit the stores and eateries on Main Street. Tricia felt sorry for those who chose the Bookshelf Diner, as they were sure to be disappointed with Dan manning the grill.

It was well after four when the activity waned and Tricia examined the gaps on the shelves in her store. It had been a profitable day, but she hoped Pixie had scored big on her thrifting forays.

It was nearly five when Pixie and David arrived at Haven't Got a Clue, both of them looking extremely proud of themselves.

"So, what did you get?" Tricia asked as Pixie and David both set boxes on the glass display case.

"Remember that sale I went to on Thursday and bought the best of the lot?" Pixie asked.

Tricia nodded.

"I got five cartons of the rest for a great price. They were motivated to get rid of the books. Plus, we found more at the other sales we went to. Seven cartons in all."

"That's great. And how did you do?" Tricia asked David.

"I found some wonderful vintage storybooks at the same sale. They sold them for a song, but they're worth so much more to me."

"I can't wait to see them."

"We already dropped them off at my place, along with everything else I got, but I took some pictures I can show you and, of course, you can see them in person the next time you come to my place." He grinned. "I may have to do a dramatic reading."

Tricia laughed. "I'll look forward to that. "Did you find anything for Angelica?"

"A ginormous and gorgeous Persian rug in fantastic condition," Pixie said. "It wouldn't fit in my car, so Angelica will have to figure out how to get it to the mansion."

"I'm sure with her connections she'll have it delivered in no time. Can I help you bring in anything?"

"We can handle the rest," Pixie assured her.

Once inside, and with all hands helping, the books went down the dumbwaiter to the basement for inventory. It pleased Tricia that the gaps in the shelves would be filled within a day or so.

Pixie drove off with a wave, and as it was time to close shop, Tricia, David, and Mr. Everett walked to the municipal parking lot where they picked up Tricia's car and headed for Antonio and Ginny's home. Angelica and Grace had already arrived.

It seemed that everyone was in high spirits and Sofia was giggling up a storm as she chased Sarge around the kitchen and family room. The wine was flowing and Angelica's cheeks were pink with pleasure as she made her way around the family room, offering sausage rolls to everyone. Meanwhile, David showed pictures of the new-to-Angelica rug around. Ginny was particularly interested in hearing all about it.

Antonio held a bottle of wine, ready to top up glasses. "Oh, Tricia, did you hear that they caught the man who"—Antonio paused, catching sight of Sofia, who was within hearing distance, and mouthed the word *killed*—"Lauren Barker?"

Tricia nearly choked on her wine. "When did that happen?"

"Apparently late this morning."

Tricia set her glass down on the coffee table before her, her hands shaking. "Was it her illustrator?"

Antonio blinked. "Sorry?"

"B. R. Woodward, the mystery man she was talking to at the library just before—" Her gaze slid to Sofia and back to Antonio. "Before."

"I do not think so. It's said the man is an unhoused person."

Tricia frowned. "Really?"

Antonio nodded.

"But what would his motive be?"

Antonio shrugged. "I'm sure we will learn more in the coming days."

It all sounded rather fishy to Tricia. It wasn't unheard of that people with no means of support, and nowhere to go, often confessed to crimes—and the more spectacular the better. Jail wasn't a particularly nice place to be, but when your options are nil, a person could at least depend on a roof over their head, a shower, clean clothes, and three meals a day.

"I'm always glad to hear when a person who commits crimes is taken off the streets," Grace said.

"As am I," Mr. Everett agreed, but he fixed his gaze on Tricia, his expression indicating that he wasn't quite willing to believe they'd caught the right person.

Angelica had a strict rule that cell phones were verboten during their family dinnertime. Once, she'd even confiscated Antonio's phone when he went to check his text messages. But Tricia was eager to leave the family room and escape to the powder room to get an update from one of the Nashua TV channels. Her phone was in her purse, which was in the kitchen.

Luckily, an opportunity opened when Angelica suddenly announced, "Oh, dear. We've run out of appetizers. I'll just get the next batch out of the oven and—"

"I'll get them," Tricia volunteered, leaping to her feet, grabbing the empty platter, and racing to the kitchen. She picked up a pot holder from the counter, removed the rolls from the oven and turned it off, then returned to the family room, offering the tasty morsels around.

"These are delicious," Grace said, helping herself to another.

"I seem to make them a lot," Angelica said, "but you all seem to enjoy them so much. I hope you don't get bored of them."

Ginny laughed, taking another. "Not a chance."

Once she'd made a circuit around the room, Tricia set the platter on the coffee table. "As long as I'm on my feet, I think I'll visit the restroom."

Nobody seemed to notice her slip away as the conversation again turned to the rug David had purchased on Angelica's behalf. Grabbing her phone, Tricia hurried to the powder room just off the kitchen. In seconds, she read the news story chronicling the arrest of one John Mason, a seventy-seven-year-old man who'd confessed to the crime to the Nashua police. A photo showed a grizzled old man in handcuffs looking like a good gust of wind could knock him over.

Tricia frowned. That he'd confessed to the cops in a city at least a twenty-minute car ride from Stoneham was telling in itself. How did a man with presumably no assets—like a car or cash—get from Stoneham to Nashua? Hitchhike? In these days, not likely. Why did he wait over a week to confess to the crime? Would a person that age have the strength to strangle to death a woman more than twenty years younger than himself?

Everything about the confession seemed ridiculous. It would take a day or two for the cops to pinpoint the older man's whereabouts on the night in question, but eventually they would, either through video or the testimony of his fellow unhoused acquaintances.

Tricia checked two other sources, which mirrored the original, before she heard a knock on the door.

"Tricia, are you all right?" Angelica asked, sounding concerned.

"Yes. Coming right out," Tricia said, flushed the toilet for effect, and washed her hands before exiting the room. Angelica saw the phone in her hand and was not pleased, but said nothing.

It was time to serve the dinner. Tricia lent a helping hand, as did Ginny, and within minutes the whole makeshift family was sitting at the table passing dishes that had been prepared by the catering staff at the Brookview Inn.

Dinner conversation was lively and laughs abounded, but Tricia found her thoughts kept circling back to the man who currently sat in the county jail. A man who had probably never even heard of Lauren Barker until a day or so ago and had pounced upon the opportunity to improve his lot in life.

"You seemed preoccupied all evening," David said as he drove Tricia's car back to his apartment in Milford. "What's going on?"

"I'm sorry I wasn't good company. When Antonio told us about Lauren's supposed killer, I just couldn't wrap my head around it." She spent the next few minutes explaining why.

"Yeah. It sounds like you could be right. But I'm sure the Nashua cops will figure that out in a couple of days."

"And it doesn't bring them one step closer to finding out who actually *did* kill Lauren."

"May I remind you that it's *not* your problem?" David asked.

"You can do so, but that doesn't mean my mind won't stop thinking about said problem."

"Tricia, my love, sometimes you think too hard."

"That's easy for you to say," she muttered as David pulled into the driveway of his apartment.

He yanked the electronic key from the ignition and handed it over to her. "Well, what do you want to do?"

Tricia pouted. "Eat a pint of ice cream, and that's not something my former self would have ever admitted, let alone done."

"We can hit the grocery store if you want, because I've only got frozen veggies in my freezer, but I don't think you mean it."

Tricia frowned. "No, I guess I don't."

David reached up a hand to stroke the left side of her jaw. "Oh, lady, why are you so hard on yourself?"

Tricia shrugged. "Beats me. This whole fake confession has got me discombobulated."

"Well, you don't look it. But it's just as well, I really need to—"

"Study," Tricia completed for him. He nodded. "By the way, thanks for coming to our family dinner tonight. Do you think you might want to do it on a regular basis?" she asked hopefully.

"Tonight was fun. A lot less tension than I felt other times." David shrugged. "I wouldn't mind coming back, especially if the food continues to be this great. It's a good thing I'm not a sports fan, though. Pixie told me she's currently a Sunday football widow."

"Yes, but she makes the most of her time while Fred watches the games."

David nodded. "She bought a couple of damaged leather purses and is going to merge the two to make one spectacular bag."

"I'll have to keep my eye out for it."

Another silent interlude stretched between them. Finally, David reached out a hand to take Tricia's. "We really should say good night."

"We should," she agreed.

But then they sat there in silence, just holding hands for a long time before David leaned over and kissed her. "Good night, my love."

"Come to my place tomorrow evening and I'll have a scrumptious dessert for you."

"Only me?"

"Well . . . us."

David frowned. "I don't know. I've got a project deadline coming up for one of my classes. But we'll at least talk." He kissed her again and then they both got out of the car, with Tricia crossing to the driver's side. She got in and rolled down the window. "Until tomorrow."

David leaned down and kissed her one last time.

Not bad. Not bad at all.

TWENTY-TWO

David waved as Tricia pulled out of the driveway and started for home. But after parking her car in the municipal lot, she decided to divert to the Dog-Eared Page. Tricia knew Ian McDonald often spent evenings sitting in the pub, nursing a beer and watching or playing darts. Its Celtic charm reminded him of home.

The crowd wasn't exactly boisterous on that chilly October evening. Still, lively music issued from the pub's sound system, and Tricia saw Ian sitting alone at a table reading a book. She walked up to him and cleared her throat. "Is this seat taken?"

McDonald looked up. "Tricia, what brings you out and about on this fine evening?" Before she could answer, he plowed on. "Where's your boyfriend?"

At least he didn't emphasize the word *boy*. But Tricia considered answering with a lie because the truth would only validate McDonald's—and everyone else's—opinion that she was robbing the cradle.

Still . . . "He's studying. He'll get his graduate degree in library science in the spring." She indicated the empty seat across from him. "Well?"

"Where are my manners," McDonald said, rose from his chair, and pulled one out for Tricia. "What would you like to drink?"

"Nothing for me, thanks." She glanced at the book on the table. "Hey, are you a Grisham fan?"

McDonald's mouth quirked in a smile. "Sometimes fiction is a good way to learn the ways of a country new to one."

"Well, he does write about the law," Tricia agreed. But she wasn't interested in talking about fiction just then. "I wanted to ask what you think about John Mason's arrest."

McDonald reclaimed his seat and scowled. "Probably the same as you. It's a waste of taxpayer's money to process him into and then out of the penal system. This country should do more for those with nowhere to go and no one to look out for them."

Tricia thought of Hank Curtis, a navy veteran living rough in a tent on the outskirts of the village just the year before. Angelica had helped the man get back on his feet by giving him a job managing the Brookview Inn, at which, thanks to his military training, he'd excelled. Tricia didn't mention it, though. There were other things on her mind.

"What do you think will happen to Mason?" she asked.

McDonald shrugged. "They'll fail to find a corroborating witness who can place him in Stoneham on that night or find someone in Nashua who can place him there. My guess is he'll be released either tomorrow or the next day. Meanwhile, my team is still chasing up some real leads."

Tricia bit her tongue so as not to refute him. "Has the medical examiner come up with a cause of death?"

"A pretty cut-and-dried case of manual strangulation," Ian replied, as Tricia had suspected. "I'm curious: Who do *you* suspect is responsible for Ms. Barker's death?"

Tricia's gaze dipped to the wood tabletop. "I don't have a guess. But . . ." She hesitated. "I'm pretty sure I've identified the man Lauren spoke to at the library not long before she was found dead."

McDonald's eyes widened. "Go on."

"I saw him again yesterday, walking north on Main Street. I'm pretty sure it was Brian Woodward, the artist who illustrated Lauren's Cuddly Chameleon books."

"Why didn't you mention this before now?" McDonald demanded.

"I should have," Tricia admitted, "Except . . ."

"What?" McDonald asked.

"It might be my word against his."

"Maybe not. We should have the contents of Ms. Barker's phone and text messages in the next day or so."

"It's taken more than a week to get it?"

"Sometimes it takes even longer." He retrieved a small notebook and a pen from his jacket pocket. "And who was the artist?"

Tricia repeated what she'd already told him and how she'd tracked down the information on Woodward. "Why do you think Woodward would hang around the village?"

McDonald shrugged. "If he's innocent, he might be doing the same as you—poking around to see what he can dig up on Lauren's death. If he's the perpetrator . . . sometimes they just like to return to the scene of the crime."

"Other people in the village must have seen him. You might want to show Alexa Kozlov his picture. I saw him in the early afternoon. I suppose he could have had lunch right here in this pub."

McDonald pulled out his phone and searched online for a picture of the artist. When he found what he was looking for, he passed the phone to Tricia. "Is this the man?"

Tricia studied the face. "Definitely."

McDonald nodded. "I'll ask the crew before I leave tonight and try to catch the day staff tomorrow."

Tricia nodded.

"Anything else?" McDonald asked.

"I guess not," Tricia said, but didn't immediately leave her seat. "What's happening with Dan Reed?"

"I'm not at liberty to say just now. But stay tuned."

McDonald's words had intrigued her, but Tricia wanted to know what McDonald had found out during his inquiries yet knew better than to inquire further, especially in a public place.

"I'd better get going," she said at last.

"Would you like me to walk you home?" McDonald said.

Tricia shook her head. She only had to cross the street and walk another twenty or so feet along the well-lit sidewalk. Tricia vacated her seat. "Perhaps we'll talk again soon."

"Perhaps," McDonald said, and stood.

Tricia nodded and turned to leave. The door opened as she approached the exit, and Becca Dickson-Chandler charged in. She stopped abruptly upon encountering Tricia. "Oh. I'm surprised to see you here."

"Why?"

"Oh, it's just . . . I didn't think someone who was *with* someone would come to a bar alone." She said it as though Tricia might be trolling for a one-night stand.

"I came to speak with Chief McDonald." Tricia looked over her shoulder where McDonald was looking at the women's encounter with what seemed like interest.

"About Lauren's murder, no doubt," Becca said with more than a hint of disdain.

"Yes."

Becca nodded.

"You'll solve this yet," Becca chirped. "Don't you *always*?"

Tricia felt heat rise up her neck to color her cheeks. "Gotta go," she said with false bravado. "Have a good evening."

"I sure hope I do," Becca said, and again charged forward.

Tricia left the bar but didn't immediately cross the street. Instead, she walked past Booked for Lunch before she pivoted and backtracked. Looking through the Dog-Eared Page's front window, Tricia saw that Becca had settled in the chair she'd only a minute or so vacated and was gazing into Ian McDonald's green eyes.

Tricia turned and, looking both ways, crossed the street. Why was she bothered that Becca had come to see McDonald? It wasn't her business . . . but for some reason, it bothered her, and she didn't want to probe too deeply to discover why.

With nothing much to occupy her time, Tricia worked on the article about the Harvicks' bees for the next Chamber newsletter. She wrote a rather stream-of-consciousness story, printed it out, and retreated to the reading nook in her master suite to edit it. Once it was trimmed to a little over seven hundred words, she closed her laptop and got ready for bed.

The next morning, she reread the article, tweaked it, and printed out a clean copy, folded it, and placed it in an envelope to drop off at the Bee's Knees that morning for correction and approval by Larry Harvick. But first, she took her morning walk. Once again, she turned down Maple Avenue and again encountered Lois Kerr, the former Stoneham Library director, raking leaves. "Good morning," Tricia called as she approached.

"Good morning, Tricia," Lois said, paused in her efforts, and leaned against her bamboo rake. "What's new?"

"Not much," Tricia admitted. "Although . . ."

"Out with it, girl," Lois barked. It seemed like a commandment.

"I was just wondering about why you hired David Price."

Lois scrutinized Tricia's face. "He's your beau, isn't he?"

"Well, yes. We are together," Tricia sheepishly admitted.

"Good for you! Enjoy your life with anyone who makes you happy because, believe you me, those opportunities don't come around all that often. Even if it doesn't last, you can at least say you had one helluva good time."

Tricia got the distinct impression that Lois had had an opportunity at love and had missed it. She didn't want to ask why.

"To answer your question," Lois continued, "I thought he was wiser than his years, and I put him in a situation with a couple of children to see how he'd react. He connected with a little girl, made her giggle, and found some books that she seemed thrilled about. And then I had him react with a teen who wasn't all that keen on the written word. He found a way to connect with that young man, as well. That's what I wanted—someone who could inspire children to read. Too often, schools assign kids to read books that don't interest them—especially older ones. If you don't catch a child when they're young, they may never become a lifelong reader, limiting their entire existence. I wanted someone who could connect with kids of all ages, and that's why I picked David, even though he hadn't quite finished his education."

And Tricia was so grateful for the trust Lois had put in David. Still, she didn't think she could verbalize her gratitude. It would only sound self-serving.

"And what about Amelia Doyle?"

Lois nodded. "The board searched for almost a year, interviewing more than a dozen candidates for the job."

"And?"

"Amelia had a good résumé." Lois said the words with a level tone, one devoid of acceptance.

"Did you feel she wasn't right for the job?"

"Her credentials were absolutely perfect."

"But?" Tricia asked.

Lois shook her head. "After I retired, I ran into Stella Kraft."

"Oh, yes. I know her."

"We'd been acquaintances for years," Lois elaborated. "I would coordinate what her class was reading in case her students couldn't afford to buy the books she assigned in class."

"And?" Tricia asked.

Lois frowned. "Well, as part of her application, Amelia included a glowing recommendation from Stella."

"And?" Tricia pressed.

Lois scowled. "Stella told me she'd written no such recommendation. Not that she wouldn't have done so, because she remembered Amelia as an acceptable pupil, but that she hadn't been asked to do so."

"Did you report that to the library board?" Tricia asked, aghast.

Lois shook her head. "I quickly found out that once I was no longer a part of the library system, my opinion was no longer valued," she said bitterly.

"I'm so sorry."

"Thanks to people like Dan Reed and his ilk, who are actively advocating for book bans and more from the library system, there are far too many people who believe as he does and want to keep young and old people from exploring facts that might not align with their cynical view of the world."

"It's so sad," Tricia lamented. She dealt with mystery fiction, but the genre could and was used to expand critical thinking on the part of the reader. That some might encourage the dumbing down of children and adults was a frightening scenario. Inspired by her beloved grandmother, Tricia had always had a thirst for knowledge and found it in books, magazines, and musical entertainers. She felt those various sources of expression made her a more well-rounded person. That some wanted to curtail that experience was sad, and a source of smoldering anger.

Lois looked around her yard littered with leaves. Tricia asked why she was again raking when so many of them were still on the trees.

"Exercise. Besides, I've got nothing better to do." Lois sounded sad.

"Have you thought about doing some volunteer work? I know the Stoneham Food Shelf is always looking for helpers."

"I've thought about it. I might look into it after the holidays," Lois said, but Tricia could tell her heart wasn't into it.

"How about throwing in your hand for a spot on the library board?"

Lois shook her head. "As I mentioned, my voice isn't one they want to hear. They're looking for input from a younger generation."

How sad to reject all the knowledge Lois possessed. Someone should point that out to them. It probably shouldn't come from Tricia, as people tended to think of her as a meddling busybody. But if she put a bug in Antonio's ear, perhaps the *Stoneham Weekly News* could run an opinion piece on that subject.

Tricia nodded. "Well, I won't keep you from your work any longer. It was nice speaking with you again."

Lois laughed and looked at the tree canopies above. "I'll probably see you again soon if you walk this way."

Tricia grinned. "Then I'll plan on it." She waved good-bye and continued on her walk, her thoughts returning to what Lois had told her. Why would Amelia fudge a job recommendation? Was it because she needed to reestablish some local connection and figured no one would check?

Tricia continued on her way, again passing the Morrison Mansion, wondering when the large Persian rug would be delivered. She'd seen the picture of it on David's phone, but the small screen couldn't do it justice when it came to size.

Upon reaching Main Street, Tricia headed straight for the Bee's Knees. It wasn't yet open, so she slipped the envelope with her story through the mail slot and continued on to Haven't Got a Clue.

The October days were waning. The lack of sunshine, which had been so rare that season, seemed to have leached the joy from the village. But—rain or shine—the tourists who'd booked travel months before kept showing up.

TWENTY-THREE

Thanks to the influx of leaf peepers, seating at Booked for Lunch was again limited, so Tricia met Angelica at her apartment for their midday meal. The intoxicating aroma of homemade soup filled the apartment. "What have you got for us?" Tricia asked.

"Some chicken vegetable soup and toasted cheese sandwiches. Tommy at the café made the soup; I'm making the sandwiches. Would you prefer Swiss, provolone, or American cheese on yours?"

"Swiss, please."

"Same here."

Tricia poured herself a cup of coffee and sat at the kitchen island. "Anything new?"

"Darling Tricia, it would take me hours to update you on what's happening in NR Associates Land. Suffice it to say that Antonio has everything under control so that I can concentrate on the Morrison Mansion renovation."

"And the update is?"

"I had the big rug delivered to a place where it will be cleaned and should have it back in a week. I can't wait to see how it will look in the front parlor."

"Surely the room isn't ready," Tricia protested.

"You're right. I'll just roll it out to admire it and then put it in storage until the room is completed." Angelica buttered two slices of bread before placing them in a hot skillet. "What's going on in your world?"

Tricia mentioned the story about the Harvicks' bees and her conversation with Lois Kerr that morning.

Angelica shook her head. "I never know why people lie on their résumés and such. They're sure to be found out."

"As Lois said, no one on the library board seemed concerned."

"No, but it says something about Amelia's character that she would pull a deplorable stunt like that."

Tricia thought so, too, but didn't comment. "Oh, I also spoke to Ian McDonald at the Dog-Eared Page last night."

"I thought you were taking David straight home after dinner."

"I did. Afterward, I went to the pub on my own."

Angelica raised an eyebrow. "Was that wise?"

Tricia frowned. "What do you mean?"

"I mean, if you're dating one man, should you be meeting another, and in a public place for the wagging tongues?"

"I was there to talk shop," Tricia declared.

"You and Ian don't work together," Angelica countered.

Tricia couldn't refute that statement and watched as Angelica placed cheese on the toasting bread, capping it with more buttered slices. "I told Ian what I know about Lauren's illustrator."

Angelica busied herself by checking the color of the bread in the skillet. "Uh-huh."

"Oddly enough, as I was leaving, Becca Chandler sashayed into the pub."

"Is that so strange?"

"Apparently, she was there to meet Ian."

Angelica turned to study her sister. "Are you jealous?"

"No!" Tricia protested. "I'm with David and we're perfectly happy."

Angelica looked skeptical. "Sure," she said, drawing out the word and flipping the sandwiches.

Tricia felt heat creep up her neck and settle onto her cheeks, a surge of irritation coursing through her that she should have such a reaction. "Anyway, I just thought it was a little weird."

"That an attractive man should be drawn to an attractive woman? Why?"

"Not at all," Tricia protested, but then she had no factual rebuttal, either.

"Oh, I almost forgot!" Angelica exclaimed. "Dan Reed was arrested last night."

"What? For Lauren's killing?" Tricia asked, shocked.

"No, but it turns out he was one of the people who was harassing her."

"Wait a minute. Where did you hear this?"

"Our own Patti Perkins from the *Stoneham Weekly News* got wind of it and told Antonio, who told me. It turns out Patti's quite the little crackerjack reporter. And to think Russ Smith thought her only worth was as a typist."

"Yes, yes, Patti's terrific. Now, what did she say?"

"That Chief McDonald arrested him yesterday afternoon for cyberstalking Lauren for the past month."

Irritation made Tricia frown. The chief hadn't shared that information with her the previous evening. "What did Dan do? Send Lauren threatening e-mails?"

"Yes, and some of them were pretty obscene."

"Did Patti get to see any of them?"

"No, but her informant did."

"Who's that?" Tricia asked.

"Patti's not about to out someone who gives her confidential information, not if she wants to keep getting hot tips."

"What about the threats?" Tricia asked.

"Lauren was told if she came to Stoneham to spread word of her filthy books she would never leave the village alive."

Tricia frowned. "Because a chameleon naturally changes color?"

Angelica nodded.

"But that's what chameleons do."

Angelica nodded.

"How many times did he e-mail her?" Tricia asked.

"Four hundred and thirty-seven times over a period of three weeks."

Tricia blinked. "When did the man have time to grill a burger at the diner?"

Angelica shrugged and plopped the sandwiches on plates before slicing them into triangles. "Maybe he stayed up late."

"They were able to trace Dan's IP address?"

"Apparently."

"Why did it take so long to find this out?" Tricia asked.

"Well, maybe the fact that Lauren was a woman had something to do with it," Angelica said sourly.

Tricia's brow furrowed. "You don't think law enforcement protects genders equally?"

Angelica glared at her sister, nearly dropping the plate in front of her. "Restraining orders," she said flatly. "How strenuously are they enforced? And sometimes women can't even get them if some judge, usually a *man*, decides the threat isn't real if the abuser isn't a family or household member."

"That's ridiculous," Tricia said.

"That's the law."

"And you know this because?"

"Let's just say I lived to tell the tale. Not all women do. But that's not a story I wish to tell because I do have some good news about Dan," Angelica said, and returned to the stove to ladle the soup into bowls.

Tricia was more interested in hearing about her sister's tale of harassment but felt she couldn't pursue it right there and then. "What about Dan?"

"He contacted Antonio about selling his building to NR Associates."

"Wow," Tricia said, dread seeping into her soul. "Was this before or after his arrest?"

"After. Maybe it finally sank in that he could be in real trouble for what he's done."

"Why wouldn't he go through a real estate agent?"

"Apparently he wants a quick sale and figured NR Associates had the deepest pockets."

"So, you're getting what you want," Tricia stated.

Angelica brought the bowls to the island and took her seat. "That depends on what the appraisal brings up. If Dan has been so lackadaisical with the food he serves, he may have treated his property in the same manner."

"It certainly seems like standards fell once his wife was out of the picture," Tricia agreed, picking up her spoon. "Do you have a timeline for moving in?"

Angelica shook her head. "The place will have to be gutted, and Tommy will probably want a whole new kitchen."

"So, you intend to keep Booked for Lunch open until you can move into the bigger space?"

"I might even keep it open afterward. I haven't made up my mind."

"Have you spoken to Pixie yet?" Tricia asked, dreading the answer.

Angelica shook her head. "No. There's no need for that until or unless I decide to open the new restaurant space."

"You realize that if you acquire an additional place, you'll have a complete lock on food services for the entire village." Not only would Angelica own the new restaurant, but she already owned the Dog-Eared Page, the Brookview Inn, and the Eat Lunch food truck.

Angelica looked thoughtful. "I hadn't looked at it that way." She smiled and struck a pose. "Angelica Miles, restaurant mogul." Then she laughed.

Tricia didn't find the idea funny. "What if Dan finds out you and Nigela are the same person?"

Angelica immediately sobered. "Is that likely?"

Tricia shrugged. "So many people already know that it's a distinct possibility."

Angelica didn't look concerned. "I assume he's going to want a quick sale. If he won't sell to me, he might have trouble selling at all before he's in bankruptcy court."

"Dan's stubborn. He might go down and refuse to sell to you on principle."

"And I would still get it because if it goes into foreclosure, the bank will sell it to the highest bidder."

It seemed to Tricia that her sister sounded more than a little smug. "Don't you feel even a little bit bad about not giving someone else the opportunity to open an eatery?"

Angelica looked at her sister with a blank stare. "No. Other locations in and around the village could be converted. If Becca were smart, she'd open a high-end restaurant on the lot she owns down the road, and it should play on her brand. It could be a destination spot."

"I doubt she wants to be in the hospitality business," Tricia remarked.

"She could build it and lease it."

"Could the village support another restaurant?" Tricia asked.

"I think so," Angelica said. "Maybe I'll suggest it to her the next time I see her."

"You do that," Tricia said, hoping she'd kept the sarcasm out of her voice. "But you also said Dan was *one* of the people stalking Lauren. Do they know who—or how many others—were harassing her?"

"Apparently, the investigation is ongoing."

For all Dan's foibles—and stupidity—Tricia wasn't convinced he was a murderer.

But then, who did kill Lauren Barker?

Tricia returned to Haven't Got a Clue feeling unsettled after her conversation with her sister—especially when learning about Dan Reed and his despicable harassment of Lauren Barker. But there were also other things on her mind, like her encounter earlier in the day with Lois Kerr. Tricia knew that Grace Harris-Everett was a member of the Stoneham Library board and wondered what she would have to say about Lois to the library's other members. On impulse, she picked up the phone and dialed the Everett Foundation, speaking with its secretary, Linda Fugitt.

"Hi, Linda, it's Tricia Miles. I wonder if Grace would have time this afternoon to talk to me. I'd only need ten or fifteen minutes."

"Let me check her calendar."

Tricia waited impatiently for what seemed like eons but could have been only fifteen or twenty seconds before Linda came back on the line. "She's got time this afternoon. Would four o'clock suit you?"

"Perfect. I'll see her then."

"Great. I'll let her know you're coming."

"Thanks." Since the appointment was forty-five minutes away,

Tricia decided to busy herself in the store's office with a keen eye on the clock.

At 3:59, she crossed Main Street and arrived at the foundation office at precisely four o'clock, and Linda quickly ushered her into Grace's office.

"Tricia, you don't have to make an appointment to see me," Grace protested. She looked regal sitting behind her desk, with her perfectly coiffed hair, and wearing a gray silk blouse and pearls.

"I know how busy you are with all the requests for help that come into the foundation. I didn't want to interrupt you."

"It's no interruption. Now, what can I do for you, dear?"

Tricia took a seat in front of Grace's desk. "I spoke to Lois Kerr this morning, and she seemed to think that despite all her years of experience with the library, there would be no place for her on their governing board."

Grace folded her hands, and her gaze dipped to focus on the top of her desk. She didn't speak for long seconds; when she did, her words and tone were measured.

"Lois was extremely good at her job as library director, which is why she held it for decades. Let's just say she had clashes with the current board. Several members rejoiced when she announced her retirement."

"Was she that difficult to work with?" Tricia asked.

"I suppose it depends on your definition of 'difficult.' I would describe Lois as passionate about her work and what was good for the library. She assembled a superb staff, including young David."

Once again, Tricia fought not to wince at that descriptor.

"From what I understand, David has a remarkable rapport with both the children *and* their parents who use the library."

"But you said Amelia might want to get rid of him."

"I still hope she'll drop that idea. In just the short time David has been the children's librarian, the library has seen an uptick in children's books being checked out, and we've had good feedback from not only parents but from several elementary school teachers that their students who use the public library are already showing increased interest in reading. David has the knack to find out what they'd enjoy and encourages them to explore different things to read. He knows what's on the shelves and who they'll appeal to."

A thread of pride and affection coursed through her and caused Tricia to smile, but then she sobered, needing to get the conversation about Lois back on track.

"In what way did Lois clash with the board?"

Again, Grace seemed to want to tread softly when speaking about the situation. "Let's just say some board members"—she paused and mouthed the word *men*—"thought she was strong-willed. It was hoped Amelia Doyle would be more attentive to the board's whims."

"But wasn't it Lois who suggested Amelia for the job?"

"Yes."

"And how is she doing so far?"

"Adequately. She hasn't had the position long enough for an evaluation, although she seems to be trying to make it her own in as short a time as possible."

"You mean like deciding to fire David?"

"Amelia doesn't have that ability, but as his direct supervisor, she *does* have input should she complain to the board."

Tricia nodded, not feeling at all reassured.

"Did Lois mention that she'd like to become a board member?" Grace asked.

Tricia shook her head. "She more or less said she wouldn't be considered."

Grace nodded. "That's too bad. I have always enjoyed working with her. She's got spunk."

The descriptor made Tricia smile. "Yes, she does." Again, the smile was short-lived. "As Chamber co-president, it's my responsibility to work with Amelia on promoting the January library book sale."

"You don't sound like you're looking forward to it."

"I'm not. I feel conflicted because of my relationship with David."

Again, Grace nodded. "Couldn't Angelica handle that?"

"Honestly, with everything she's juggling, I don't see her having the time to take on another project."

"She *is* a busy woman," Grace agreed. "I'm so glad she makes time for our little family. We can't express how happy visiting with Ginny and the children makes us. Sundays are our favorite day of the week."

"Mine, too," Tricia said, again experiencing a flush of warmth and affection for everyone in their little family circle.

The phone rang in the outer office, and seconds later, the intercom buzzed. "Grace, it's Libby Hirt from the Food Shelf. Do you want to take the call?"

Tricia immediately stood. "Go ahead and take it. I need to get back to my store," she whispered.

"Uh, yes," Grace told Linda. "Please tell her to hang on a moment."

Tricia backed toward the door. "I'll see you Sunday." And she blew a kiss before exiting.

Grace nodded and smiled before answering the call. "Yes, Libby, thank you for returning my call," Tricia heard Grace say as she closed the office door.

Tricia waited for traffic to pass before she crossed the street and returned to Haven't Got a Clue, where she got a status update from Pixie. With less than an hour to go before closing and only a few customers in sight, Tricia again excused herself to ostensibly work in the office, but instead she logged on to her computer to Google the latest news on Lauren Barker's murder.

The first item that came up was an update on John Mason, the man who'd turned himself in, confessing to her murder. Unsurprisingly, he'd been released from the county jail earlier in the day for lack of evidence. She wondered if the poor old man had a place to sleep and hoped the Nashua PD hadn't just turned him loose to fend for himself. There didn't seem to be any other information. Checking her e-mail, Tricia was surprised to see a reply from her query on Brian Woodward's website, which had arrived half an hour before. She tapped the link and eagerly read the reply.

I'd be interested to learn what you think you know about Lauren Barker. Reply to this e-mail. You may or may not hear from me again.

Well, that was something. Tricia would have preferred a face-to-face Zoom meeting or even a phone conversation with the illustrator, but she'd take what she could get.

She typed: As her collaborator, I assume you know what was going on in Lauren's life. The harassment on more than one front and that she looked up an old friend for advice on security measures. You spoke to her just before her death. . . . I saw you not only on the evening of Lauren's death but also three days after walking along Stoneham's main drag. I'm sure the Stoneham police chief would like to know about that, too, if he hasn't already contacted you by now. I realize you have no obligation to tell me what you know about Lauren's situation, but . . .

But what? Tricia hadn't known Lauren personally. Had never spoken to her. How could she explain her interest to a man who may or may not have murdered the woman? Wasn't that just asking for trouble? Of course, Woodward could be completely innocent. Just a business associate, a friend . . . or was he Lauren's lover? Was Tricia setting herself up as a target by contacting the man?

Woodward indicated that he may or may not reply. Tricia studied the keyboard for long seconds, figured what the heck, and hit the enter key, sending her message to the illustrator. She didn't picture him sitting in front of his computer, eager for her reply, and she had things to do.

Tricia emerged just five minutes before closing to find that the shop was in tip-top shape, the carpet vacuumed, the beverage station cleaned and ready for the next day, and her staff eyeing the clock.

"Time to close," she called cheerfully. Mr. Everett took off his apron, collected Pixie's, and headed for the back of the store to hang them before bringing back their coats.

"Have a nice evening, Ms. Miles," Mr. Everett called.

"See ya!" Pixie said cheerfully, and the two of them practically waltzed out the door. Tricia doled out a snack for her cat before grabbing her jacket and heading for Angelica's apartment. She wasn't all that hungry for food, but she was hungry for solace. Too many things she'd learned that day had been . . . *upsetting* was too strong a word. Perhaps *discomforting*. For now, she craved a quiet setting, a chilled martini, and the company of her sister, who was her best sounding board. . . .

When she could get a word in edgewise.

TWENTY-FOUR

Angelica was in high spirits, bubbling over with news about where she wanted to put the new-to-her rug. Ginny had used her lunch hour to track down a vintage dining room suite that might be suitable for the mansion. And with no one to man the grill, the Bookshelf Diner hadn't opened that day.

Angelica seemed bored with Tricia's news about Lois and the library board. And though she had no other plans for the evening, Tricia was motivated to leave her sister's early. But when she got home, she felt restless, so she decided to change into her nightgown and robe.

Tricia was about to settle into her bedroom's reading nook when her phone pinged. It was a text from David.

How's my lovely lady?

Instead of texting a reply, Tricia scrolled through to David's number on her contacts list and poked her phone's call icon. He answered right away.

"Hey, what's up?"

Should she tell him about her e-mail from Brian Woodward? *Not yet*, she decided.

"I'm all alone," she said, feeling sorry for herself.

"I'm sure Miss Marple would have something to say about that. I've been thinking I might get a Beta fish so I have someone to talk to when I can't be with you."

"Fish have even less to say than cats," Tricia pointed out.

"That's true. I've only got another six weeks of classes, and then I have a whole month without them. We can spend a lot of quality time together then."

"Promise?"

"I do."

That is, if he didn't lose his job and pack to return to his parents' home. She didn't voice that concern. There was no use burdening him with her fears. Instead, she asked him about his day, and he answered with another heartwarming encounter he'd had with one of the library's younger patrons. He loved that job and had such a good rapport with the kids. It would be such a shame if it had to end.

"How about you?" David asked. "Did you do any sleuthing?"

"Only a little."

"Tell me all about it."

She gave him the short version of all she'd learned that day and waited for him to comment.

"You know, it seemed odd that Lauren just left the library without saying a word to anyone or even trying to collect her honorarium.

What happened to her between when she left the library and when we found her?"

"Yes, the missing half hour. Lauren had to run into her killer in the parking lot. Why would she let the person in her car? When I'm in a dark lot, the first thing I do when I get in the car is lock the doors."

"It was a rental car, right? Maybe she didn't immediately know where the lock button was."

"Maybe," Tricia agreed. "As I recall, I heard one of the officers say the car was in park, and the keys were in the ignition. I suppose the killer could have been waiting, and when Lauren entered the driver's side, he jumped right in."

"Who says it had to be a man?" David asked.

"Well, a lot of men kill women."

"And women kill men quite often, too."

Tricia couldn't argue that point. "I bet the killer was wearing latex or other gloves, or we probably would have heard if any DNA was collected from the car or under Lauren's fingernails."

"Yuck!" David said. "Chief McDonald hasn't discussed that with you, has he?"

"He didn't discuss much of anything with me," Tricia remarked.

"When would he have the opportunity to do so?"

Oops. Tricia hadn't mentioned her conversation with the chief the evening before. She did so, and David didn't seem to react to the news, which was a small source of relief. She mentioned Becca joining the chief, as well.

"Maybe they'll get together. I can tell you how lonely it is when you arrive at a place like Stoneham, not knowing anyone, and he was here months before me. Becca, too, right?"

"Yes. But . . . I don't know; Becca can be a bit caustic. I don't think she's right for Ian."

"How many people have told you I'm not right for *you*?" David asked.

"Nobody," Tricia said emphatically.

"But?" David prodded.

Tricia said nothing.

"I know what they've been saying. I've heard it—been teased about it. I'm sorry we aren't closer in age, but I'm not sorry to be with you. I just wish I could get through my last two semesters quicker."

"One thing I can say from experience is that time goes much faster than you think," Tricia lamented.

"Not when you're studying for a test."

"Will you have to study tomorrow?"

"I'll let you know. Right now, I need to get back to work. It'll all be worth it in the end."

"Yes. Well, when you finally stop burning the midnight oil, sleep well, my love."

"You, too. Talk to you tomorrow."

"Good night."

Tricia ended the call and set her phone down. Almost immediately, the shop's landline rang. She didn't answer it after the shop closed, and after the third ring the call went to voice mail.

"Ms. Miles . . . this is Brian Woodward."

Tricia nearly tripped in her haste to grab the phone.

"Hello? Mr. Woodward. This is Tricia Miles."

"I found your store's number online. I hope you don't mind me calling instead of using e-mail. I find it tedious when I can wrap up a conversation in a few minutes."

"Thank you for giving me the time."

"I Googled you," Woodward said. "I see that you own a bookstore and have been associated with several murders in the Stoneham area."

Tricia laughed. "I didn't commit them."

"But your name *is* linked to them," Woodward said flatly.

Tricia sobered. "Yes. In the past, I *have* helped the police with their inquiries. Like Lauren, I have an interest in true crime."

"I see. Maybe you ought to start a podcast," he said flippantly, but there was an edge to his tone.

"I only listen to them. However, I managed to get a copy of Lauren's true-crime manuscript," she said, hoping he wouldn't ask how. "I wasn't able to verify anything about it."

"That's because it's fiction. Lauren had this idea of writing a novel like a true-crime account. It was going to be a breakthrough for her . . . if it was ever published."

"Have you read it?"

"A couple of chapters. I'm not into murder mysteries."

How sad, Tricia thought.

"That said, it *was* based on an incident from Lauren's past."

"You mean the murder was committed for petty reasons?"

"Yes."

"Did Lauren have a contract for this book?" Tricia asked.

"She was writing it on spec," Woodward replied.

"I see," Tricia remarked.

"So, what do you think you know about Lauren?" Woodward asked.

"Lauren seemed frazzled and anxious on the night of her death."

"For several reasons. She was scheduled for hand surgery the week after her death, and was dreading it."

"Did she tell Betty Barnes about it?"

"You mean the woman who supplied the books for the signing?"

"Yes."

"Oh, yeah—but the bitch insisted. Somehow, she cowed Lauren into doing it."

Betty *could* be forceful.

"What else?" Woodward asked.

"I know Lauren feared for her safety and spoke with her former boss Becca Chandler about security concerns."

"Lauren thought hard about accepting the invitation to speak in her adopted hometown."

"And why was that?" Tricia asked.

"Because she feared facing someone from her past. Lauren told me she'd been bullied as a teen, and lately, she'd been getting bombarded with hateful messages and threats. She learned to guard her back but felt she had to accept personal appearance requests to keep the Cuddly Chameleon series in front of the public."

That seemed logical.

"But it was somehow different lately?" Tricia asked.

"Yes."

Tricia considered her next query and decided she ought to try to draw out Woodward before getting to harder questions. "How was Lauren as a collaborator?"

"To be honest, it wasn't a factor. We never met—or even talked—until I'd illustrated five of her books."

"Is that unusual?" Tricia asked, somewhat surprised.

"Not at all. I've illustrated scores of books and have only spoken to or met less than a handful of the authors I'm associated with. The publishers tell me what they want, and I deliver."

"But you *did* meet Lauren before the night of her death."

"Yes. We made a few appearances at conferences. We got along quite well."

"Were you romantically involved?" Tricia asked, hoping the man would answer honestly. Surprisingly, he laughed.

"Lauren was ten years older than me."

Tricia's cheeks suddenly burned with embarrassment. She was

twenty years older than David, who valued her for her life experience and knowledge and didn't judge her by their age difference. Just how shallow was Brian Woodward?

"So, you weren't even friends?"

"I wouldn't say that. Once the series was a success, we exchanged e-mails and, as I said, promoted the series together at bigger book events. And we became friendly acquaintances. I'll miss her," he said sadly.

Tricia waited a few seconds before continuing. "What will happen to Lauren's character?" Tricia knew that other writers would often take over a series as successful as the Cuddly Chameleon, and the books would continue to be published long after the original author's death. It happened with the likes of Tom Clancy and other big-name authors who'd passed away.

"I have a contract for three more books. I'm waiting to hear from my agent."

"The night of Lauren's death," Tricia began. "Why did you meet her at the library?"

"As I'm sure you know, I don't live all that far from Stoneham."

Yes, just twenty or so miles across the state line.

"Lauren asked me to come to the signing as moral support. I wasn't up for a personal appearance and didn't want to be put on display, so I told her I'd be there in the audience and we could talk afterward."

Tricia considered the artist's description . . . *on display*. Yeah, that accurately described some author (and apparently artist) meet and greets. Not every author felt comfortable in the limelight. Tricia had hosted authors whose books entertained the masses, but who were uncomfortable when it came to face-to-face promotion. Writing was a solitary occupation, after all.

"As I mentioned, I saw you and Lauren speaking near the library's checkout counter."

"I thought her appearance was a disaster but didn't tell her so. She was pretty upset about how it had gone. She said she was thinking about returning to her B and B room, grabbing her stuff, and heading home. I encouraged her to do so."

"But she didn't have the opportunity to do it."

"No." He uttered the word with such sadness and finality. "I could kick myself for not hanging around to make sure she was safe. I'll carry that with me for the rest of my life."

"I'm sorry for the loss of your collaborator," Tricia said.

"Yeah, so am I. For all her eccentricities, I'll miss Lauren," he said again.

"Has the Stoneham chief of police contacted you yet?"

"Yes. He said someone—presumably you—had identified me."

"I did."

"We spoke for ten minutes or so. He updated me on the arrest of the man who'd harassed Lauren. And I'm to return to Stoneham to make a statement."

There didn't seem to be much more to say or ask.

"I appreciate your speaking with me," Tricia said.

"It didn't help, though, did it?"

"I wouldn't say that," Tricia said, but inwardly conceded that he was right.

"I don't suppose we need to speak again," Woodward said.

"No," Tricia agreed.

"Then I guess I'll just watch the news for updates on Lauren's case—if there are any—and hope for closure."

"I hope you'll find that soon," Tricia said sincerely.

"Thanks. Well, good-bye."

"Good-bye."

Tricia put down the receiver. She'd hoped speaking with Woodward would give her a greater understanding of who Lauren was. Instead, she felt less informed.

Miss Marple wound around Tricia's feet. Cats had a way of grounding a person. Tricia petted her kitty before heading back down to the kitchen to give Miss Marple her nightly treat. With nothing better to do, Tricia retreated to her bed with another Hercule Poirot tome, but it wasn't enough to keep the day's frustrations at bay. She finally gave up and turned off the light.

TWENTY-FIVE

 Perhaps it was her conversation with Brian Woodward that gave Tricia an unsettled night with dreams of Lauren's dead body slumped over the steering wheel of her car. That morphed into depictions of Tricia running away from an unknown, faceless assailant. She'd wake up, take what seemed like eons to fall back to sleep, and fall into the same pattern.

Upon waking, Tricia needed something to distract her . . . something that might take one of the worrying bricks off her shoulder. First, she texted Pixie and asked her to come to work half an hour early. Of course, Pixie was agreeable. Then Tricia decided to once again bake. She found it soothing to measure ingredients and savor the aroma that filled her kitchen and lifted her spirits, if only a little bit.

The coffee was brewing, and the fresh batch of cookies sat on one of the pretty floral plates David had thrifted and gifted to Tricia when Pixie arrived at Haven't Got a Clue. Tricia poured coffee and moved the cookie plate to the reader's nook. Except for the kelly green apron, Pixie was dressed in all black, from her shirtwaist dress to her stockings and her pumps. She looked positively grim as she took her seat.

"Good grief, you look serious," Tricia commented.

"You hardly ever call me in early to talk," Pixie said gravely. "What's up?"

Tricia bit her lip. "I probably shouldn't say anything, but it's not betraying a confidence, so . . ."

"What?" Pixie asked, anxiously.

Tricia let out a heavy sigh. "Angelica may be buying the Bookshelf Diner."

Pixie looked puzzled. "I didn't know it was for sale."

"It's not a done deal. But if she *does* buy it, she was thinking of asking you to be her front of the house."

Pixie blinked. Then she sat back in her seat and laughed loud and long.

"What's so funny?" Tricia asked, confused.

"*Me* taking care of a restaurant? Angelica must be pretty desperate to think of me for the job."

"No, she's not. She thinks you'd be perfect. You're good with customers; you're good with handling money. She thinks you'd be great hiring staff and everything else that goes with managing it for her."

Pixie reached for a cookie. "I'm flattered she thinks so. But what about my job here?"

"You know I wouldn't stand in your way," Tricia said, desperate to sound noncommittal.

"Oh, yeah. I know that, but it's not something I'd be interested in."

Tricia felt like heaving a sigh of relief, but she kept her composure. She waited as Pixie took a bite of her cookie and washed it down with a sip of coffee.

"We went through all this when Angelica offered me a full-time job at Booked for Beauty. I haven't changed my mind. I love my job here at Haven't Got a Clue. I love you and Mr. E and Miss Marple. Why would I want to risk all that to take on more work? And believe me, I know how much work it takes to be successful at managing a restaurant. I was a waitress for way too many years. It's not an industry I want to be around at this point in my life."

"It would probably involve a substantial raise in pay," Tricia remarked.

"For the first time in my life, money isn't the most important thing to me. I've got Fred, our cute little house, and the best job in the world. I'm happy where I am."

Tricia swallowed, relief draining away the angst she'd been shouldering. "I'm glad you feel that way. What will you tell Angelica if the deal goes through?"

"The same thing I just told you. And I won't let her know that you mentioned it to me," Pixie added.

Relief coursed through her, and Tricia offered her friend and employee a grateful smile. "I'm so glad you feel that way. Haven't Got a Clue wouldn't be the same without you."

Just then, the bell over the door tinkled, and Mr. Everett stepped over the threshold. "Good morning, ladies. Isn't it a fine day?"

Tricia had so much on her mind that morning that not only hadn't she checked the weather, she'd forgotten to take her daily walk. If things were slow, perhaps she'd work one in after lunch.

In the meantime, Mr. Everett donned his apron, poured himself a cup of coffee, and joined them in the reader's nook.

Unless a bus descended upon the village, sales before noon were often few and far between. So Tricia decided that once the Haven't Got a Clue morning coffee klatch had ended, she would catch up on an errand, leaving Pixie in charge.

Tricia hadn't heard from Larry Harvick about the article she'd written for the Chamber newsletter. Since she and Angelica were both getting low on honey, she decided to visit the Bee's Knees and hope Larry was on-site, although she was sure his wife, Eileen, had probably read the article as well.

The Bee's Knees was the smallest retail space on Main Street, and the scent of honey inside it was intoxicating. However, if the shop had more than three or four customers, it could feel positively claustrophobic, but on that morning, Tricia was their only customer.

"Tricia, great to see you," Eileen Harvick greeted her. "What brings you here?"

"Besides needing honey and a few candles, I was wondering if you and Larry have had a chance to read my article for the Chamber newsletter."

"We did, and it's wonderful. You even got the Latin name for our bees correct. We wouldn't change a thing, thanks."

Tricia's gaze took in the tiny retail space. "Is Larry around? I was wondering when he will remove the bees from the Stoneham Public Library."

"Sorry, he's working on the property today. We haven't yet decided when the bees are being moved. Why?"

"Well, I know he wouldn't need my help, but I would love to see the whole retrieval operation. I'm fascinated with everything to do with beekeeping."

"I'm glad to hear that, but to be truthful, I'm not keen on anyone being around when we move our hives. I guess I'm just paranoid that there could be a problem," Eileen said gravely.

"You mean beestings?"

"*I'm* not afraid of the bees, and, of course, neither is Larry. But . . ." Her sentence trailed off. Amelia Doyle was afraid, so the bees had to go.

"I understand," Tricia said, feeling more than a little disappointed.

"You said something about honey and candles," Eileen prompted eagerly.

Tricia bought a large jar of honey for Angelica and a medium-sized jar for herself, happy the containers were glass and not plastic, so that when the honey began to crystallize, she could pop it in the microwave to refresh it. She also purchased a box of eight tapers, intending to split it with her sister. She paid for her purchases and headed for the exit. "We'll be e-mailing the newsletter on the first of November, so please look for it then."

"I will. And I'll cross my fingers that it'll inspire fellow Chamber members to visit our store."

"That often happens," Tricia said. "See you again soon."

Tricia returned to Haven't Got a Clue, removing the items she intended to keep to take to her apartment and placing the decorative bag with the Bee's Knees logo and the things she'd purchased for Angelica behind the display case that doubled as a cash desk. She'd ask David when the bees were to be removed, as she wanted to at least observe the operation. Surely, the Harvicks would have to schedule a time—either before the library opened or closed—to do the deed.

Thankfully, another Granite State tour bus arrived at about eleven thirty, disgorging some fifty or sixty potential customers, and a number of them visited Haven't Got a Clue, giving the store a handsome sales day. But it wasn't only books that sold. Other items, such as store-logo mugs, bookmarks, and even a couple of T-shirts, which had been Pixie's suggested promo item, sold, too. Angelica was right: Pixie was almost as PR-savvy as Ginny!

When it was her turn to leave for lunch with Angelica, Tricia grabbed the string-handled paper bag Eileen had packed the honey and candles in, and started off for Angelica's home for her midday meal.

Sarge must have conked out, for he didn't bark as Tricia mounted the steps to Angelica's apartment.

"Howdy Doody," Tricia called as she entered her sister's home.

"Buffalo Bob," Angelica answered the call. It wasn't something the women knew about from their childhoods, but something their grandma Miles used to say and they'd adopted, not knowing until adulthood that it related to an old TV show their parents had seen in childhood.

"What have you got there?" Angelica asked as Tricia set the bag onto the kitchen island. Taking out each item, she placed them on the counter and folded the bag for reuse.

"I visited the Bee's Knees this morning."

"How much do I owe you?" Angelica asked.

"Nothing. Think of it as an early Christmas present."

Angelica laughed. "I was hoping for a little more, but I'll take what I can get."

"I got you the larger jar of honey because you seem to use more of it than I do."

"I like it in my tea."

"I like it on hot biscuits," Tricia countered.

"And fried chicken," Angelica responded.

"Really?" Tricia asked.

Angelica actually winked. "Try it sometime."

Tricia decided she would. "The Harvicks loved my article."

"That's nice. So what else is new?"

"I figured out who Lauren met at the library the night of her death."

Finally, Tricia caught her sister's attention.

"A serial killer?" Angelica asked anxiously.

"No, the guy who drew the Cuddly Chameleon."

Angelica frowned. "Well, that's hardly exciting."

"I agree, and I don't think he had anything to do with Lauren's death."

"So, who are the viable suspects?"

Tricia thought about it. "I would think the police might suspect Betty Barnes because she had Lauren sign a mountain of books. If Betty thought she could make a proverbial killing on the books when the author suddenly died, it would make a compelling reason for murder."

"But?" Angelica asked.

"But Lauren was no Chris Van Allsburg, Maurice Sendak, or Dr. Seuss."

"So, your next best guess?" Angelica asked.

"I think the police might suspect Stella Kraft. The confrontation between Lauren and her was pretty brutal."

Angelica looked unconvinced. "But Stella is an old lady. I hardly think she would have the physical strength, let alone the passion, to kill a former student, no matter how obnoxious Lauren was."

"Maybe."

"So, who's left?"

"Dan Reed?" Tricia offered.

Angelica nodded. "He's just crazy enough to lose it and do something as extreme as murder. But . . ."

"But what?"

"Have you got another suspect?"

"I wish I could say I did. The thing is, Lauren was getting multiple threats. Just because there are people here in Stoneham who were angered by her appearance at the library doesn't mean she didn't alienate just as many people across the country. People like Dan, who looked for hidden, horrific meanings in something as innocent as a children's book."

Angelica looked thoughtful. "I didn't think Lauren's books were exemplary, but they weren't subversive, either. They were just stories that entertained little kids."

"I agree," Tricia said. She bit her lip, thinking. "But if I were into comics, my spidey sense would tell me that her killer either came here to murder Lauren or has been here all along."

"Gut instinct?" Angelica asked, skeptical.

Tricia nodded.

Angelica puttered around in the kitchen.

"What are we having for lunch?"

"Your favorite: a tuna salad plate."

"Oh, lovely," Tricia deadpanned. Since birth, she'd eaten probably a thousand pounds of tuna and far too much of it canned and without mayonnaise.

"It's on a bed of romaine lettuce with all the celery and onion crunchies you adore."

Adore? No, but that made it tolerable.

"Is there soup to go with it?"

"Yes, I made a pretty big pot of leek-and-potato soup. What we don't have today, I'll freeze in single portions. You can have some to take home, if you want."

"I'll definitely want," Tricia said. "I just wish I'd brought an empty pickle jar to put it in."

Angelica ignored the comment. And while she doled out their soup and salads, Tricia reflected on their conversation. It seemed that no one on her suspect list had a strong enough reason to murder the children's book author. Then again, there was no telling what it would take for a warped mind to kill, especially these days. People were murdered for the most frivolous of reasons. The world seemed to be spiraling out of control and there was nothing Tricia—or anyone she knew and trusted—could do to stop it.

At last, Angelica set bowls of soup and the salad plates on the kitchen island and took her seat. "Bon appétit," she said.

As Tricia poked at her soup and salad, she kept thinking about the suspects associated with Lauren Barker's murder and felt that she'd missed something—something pretty big, with no clue how to suss the motive or suspect out.

As she dipped her spoon into the soup or her fork into her salad, Tricia contemplated what she knew about the crime and the terrible gap of missing information. She knew that, on average, only 51 percent of murder cases ever brought the killer to justice. Would Chief McDonald—or the county or state police—be able to suss out who was responsible for Lauren Barker's death?

Sadly, it was anyone's guess.

TWENTY-SIX

As Tricia stepped out of the Cookery, she saw Mary Fairchild advancing toward her shop with a white bakery bag—probably her lunch freshly made from the Patisserie. "Mary," Tricia called. "I've been trying to catch up with you for days."

"You should have stopped by my shop. I've been so busy decorating it for the fall—which I should have started weeks ago. But my best friend fell last week and broke her leg. Let me tell you, I'm in total sympathy with her after what happened to me on the *Celtic Lady*. I've been advising her and her husband to figure out what would best help her navigate her home in the weeks to come."

"I'm sorry to hear about your friend," Tricia began, "but I was wondering about something that happened at Lauren Barker's memorial service, and I wanted to ask you about it."

Mary frowned in confusion. "I don't remember anything out of the ordinary—I mean, apart from Dan Reed being a jerk, but then he always is."

"Something in your tone when you spoke about Lauren sounded off."

Mary's eyes widened, and she took a step backward. "I don't know what you mean."

"It wasn't what you said . . . it was what you *didn't* say about her," Tricia said.

Mary's lips pursed, and she swallowed, her gaze dipping. Then she looked around the quiet street. Across the road, a woman walked a pit bull mix Tricia had seen on many of her morning walks. The dog wagged his tail as the two continued on their jaunty circuit. Meanwhile, Mary seemed to squirm.

"I would rather not have this conversation on the street. In fact, I would rather not have this conversation at all," Mary asserted.

"Why?" Tricia asked, knowing Mary was under no obligation to elaborate, but she hoped the years of friendship the women shared would cause her to reconsider.

Mary looked profoundly embarrassed and heaved a heavy sigh. "I need to get to my shop. Come with me, and I'll make us a cup of coffee."

"And?" Tricia asked.

"And I'll confess one of my deepest regrets."

A solemn Tricia nodded, and the women proceeded to Mary's craft and book shop, By Hook or By Book. Once inside, Mary ushered Tricia onto a stool that sat before a table of sewing pattern books. Mary's shop specialized in the needle arts but was most heavy on yarn for knitting and crocheting. But Mary did offer bolts of fabric for customers who were into dressmaking or quilting, along with a section full of what Tricia had come to know as fat quarters of a yard of fabric samples.

Mary hung up her jacket and puttered around in her back room for a few minutes, calling out to ask Tricia how she liked her coffee.

Finally, she emerged with two mugs bearing the shop's logo—probably marketing samples, as Mary didn't offer them for sale.

"I'm sorry I don't have any cookies or anything. I know you offer them to your customers, but my margins are pretty slim. I just can't afford it."

Tricia offered her customers cookies, tea, coffee, and cocoa. She often made the cookies, mainly because she enjoyed her newfound love of baking.

The women sipped their coffee for a minute or so before Tricia asked the question that had been on her mind for days.

"So, what about Lauren Barker seems to haunt you?"

Mary looked guilty. "It wasn't only what Lauren did . . . but what I did, as well."

"And that was?" Tricia asked, her voice rising.

Mary took a deep breath. "After emerging like a butterfly from a cocoon, Lauren had a tendency to be a . . . a mean girl. A bully."

Tricia's brow furrowed. "But you said that Lauren was bullied by other students during her high school days."

Mary nodded. "But that's not the worst of it. For a time, I was a mean girl, too."

It must have taken a lot for Mary to confess that, for she looked absolutely mortified.

Because of what Woodward had told her, Tricia wasn't sure how to react to those admissions, so she said nothing.

"There was one girl in particular that Lauren liked to bully. She had shabby clothes. She packed a lunch of a peanut butter sandwich and nothing else every single day of high school."

Tricia's eyes widened at the words *peanut butter.*

"This girl," Mary continued, "didn't participate in any after-school activities because she had to take care of her brother and sisters after school." Mary gulped her coffee and swallowed it. But then, she swallowed again, and Tricia was sure it was due to guilt as Mary's cheeks darkened.

"I'm sorry to say that I joined in on Lauren's taunts—as did a bunch of other girls. Kids can be such mean little buggers," she added bitterly.

"What happened?"

Mary's gaze remained fixed on the floor. "One day, the bullied girl came up to me in the hall between classes and said that what I was doing was not nice. That's the phrase she used, 'not nice,' and in my heart, I knew she was right."

"What did you say to her?"

Mary forced a laugh. "That I was sorry, and I wouldn't do it again."

"And did you?"

Mary shook her head. "And after that, Lauren and I kind of . . . fell out because I wouldn't berate that poor girl. That's when Lauren started in on me. After that, *I* didn't have many friends." Mary swallowed a few times. "I told my mom about it, and she told me I'd done the right thing, but the thing is . . . I lost most of my friends because I decided *not* to be one of those mean girls. It hurt. It really hurt. But after a while, I realized that I didn't want to be friends with girls who would pick on someone just because they didn't have the right clothes or dated the wrong guys, or couldn't afford to buy a hot lunch. Heck, most of us didn't date *anyone*. I wasn't the only one who didn't get asked to the prom," she remarked.

Tricia thought she knew the answer to the question she was about to ask, but she did so anyway. "And who was it that Lauren bullied and you confronted?"

Mary looked Tricia straight in the eyes. "Amelia Doyle."

Tricia nodded. "I take it you and Amelia never became friends."

Mary shook her head. "After the day she confronted me, we never spoke again until the Chamber meeting last Thursday."

Tricia nodded, and the women sipped their coffee for a long minute.

Again, Mary's gaze sank to the floor, and a tear cascaded down her left cheek.

"Have you considered telling Chief McDonald about those incidents?" Tricia asked.

Mary looked up sharply. "Why would I?"

Tricia hated to make the accusation, but it had to be said. "Because a long-held grudge could be a motive for murder."

Mary shook her head. "I don't think so. . . ." But Tricia picked up on the shadow of doubt in Mary's tone. That said, she didn't offer to go to the chief of police. She didn't need Mary's approval for that because Mary hadn't cautioned her that anything they spoke of was in confidence, and she wanted to keep it that way.

Tricia drained her cup and stood. "Well, I'd best be getting back to my store." She glanced at her watch. "I need to open in another fifteen minutes."

Mary gave a mirthless laugh. "At least you have employees to help you. I've never made enough to have that luxury." It was true. Tricia knew Mary ate her lunch between customers and often had to put up a CLOSED sign when she needed a bathroom break or had to do a quick restock of product.

"Thanks for speaking with me. I do hope you'll reconsider sharing your story with Chief McDonald."

Mary's expression soured. "I have no doubt he'll come to see me once you have a chance to chat with him."

"A woman—Lauren—was murdered," Tricia reminded her.

"And you have no proof that Amelia Doyle was responsible," Mary said.

What she wasn't saying was that if Amelia Doyle was willing to kill Lauren Barker, a second death wouldn't be as hard—and perhaps Mary Fairchild didn't want to be her next victim.

"We'll talk again soon," Tricia said.

"Fine," Mary said succinctly, distinctly unhappy.

Tricia wasn't sure, but as she closed the door behind her, she thought she heard Mary utter a single word. "Snitch."

Great. First, she was known as a jinx or a black widow. Lately, she'd been called a cougar and now a snitch.

Although it was a cliché, Tricia began to believe that truly no good deed—or piece of good advice given and ignored—went unpunished. She didn't want to be known as a snitch, but she also wanted Lauren's killer to be identified and punished.

Was that really such a bad thing?

The rest of the afternoon dragged, with Tricia feeling lower than a mine shaft. Both Pixie and Mr. Everett noticed her blue mood, and when a few jokes and lighthearted banter didn't affect her, they backed off, respecting her need for a little alone time.

It was after four thirty, and Tricia stood behind the cash desk, studying a publisher's catalog and contemplating a new order, when the bell over the shop's door tinkled, and Stoneham Police Chief Ian McDonald darkened her door. As her mood was so black, *darkened* seemed the proper adjective.

"Hello, Ian. What brings you to Haven't Got a Clue?"

"A little while ago, I got a call from Ms. Fairchild of By Hook or By Book," McDonald said.

"Oh?" Tricia asked, feigning innocence, as Pixie and Mr. Everett skulked away to the back of the shop to give them some privacy.

"Yes, although she asked to speak to me personally, she seemed quite reluctant to talk about Lauren Barker's past and only did so because, if not, she was convinced you would, which could bring her trouble."

Tricia tried not to sound at all interested. "And what do you think of what she told you?"

McDonald shrugged. "It doesn't seem likely that someone held a grudge for thirty years and then spontaneously decided to murder her former tormentor."

Maybe so, but David had described Amelia as petty and vindictive. Surely that kind of personality could find it within herself to lash out in a fit of pique—and damn the consequences.

"What do you think?" McDonald asked.

Tricia hesitated before answering. "Perhaps you should ask some of Amelia's employees what they think of her."

McDonald raised an eyebrow. "Mr. Price?" There was something about his tone. . . . Annoyed? Sneering?

"Among others," Tricia answered.

"Anything else?"

Tricia shrugged. "I thought Mary's experience was information you should have and that it would be up to you to determine if it was something you and your team wanted to pursue—particularly because she apparently ate peanut butter sandwiches for years on end. She could have sent the sandwiches to Lauren."

McDonald nodded.

"And did Mary accuse me of being a snitch?" Tricia asked blandly.

"Uh, yes, I do believe that word was mentioned."

Tricia nodded, her heart sinking, feeling that she'd lost Mary as a friend. They'd had their ups and downs, but perhaps Mary would now decide to steer clear of her Main Street neighbor. Well, it wouldn't be the first time Tricia lost a friend because she valued her integrity over someone else's blatant disregard for the law or what was morally right. Still, she guessed she'd known the friendship might be over when she'd heard Mary utter "snitch" under her breath. No doubt Becca felt the same. Still, Tricia felt the need to be true to her sense of duty and fairness . . . even if it meant alienating people she'd viewed as friends or acquaintances.

Still, it isolated her from people and it also eroded her faith in humankind. When had it become acceptable to flout the social contract—that people acted in their own best interests instead of considering their fellow travelers on life's journey?

"I'm sorry," McDonald said.

"For what?"

"Just . . . just sorry," McDonald said.

Tricia nodded. "So am I." She forced herself to sound more cheerful. "So, how *is* the investigation going?"

"It's going," he replied blandly.

She wasn't likely to get any more information from him. But then, he probably thought it a breach of his duty to do so . . . more's the pity.

"I appreciate you coming to speak to me," Tricia said, not that he'd revealed much. "Will you pursue Amelia Doyle as a suspect?"

"We'll do some investigation before we speak to her."

Did that mean he'd start with David? Would that put him in jeopardy? Suddenly, Tricia wished she'd never spoken to Mary. Should she warn David?

All at once, the sense of depression she'd been experiencing since talking to Mary escalated to near panic. David had texted her earlier that he was free for the evening, and that was the carrot that coaxed her to get through the day until they could be together.

"When will you speak to library personnel?" Tricia asked, her tone level.

"Not until at least tomorrow. I need to think about how to couch my questions so my target isn't so obvious."

Tricia nodded.

"I will speak to more than Mr. Price," McDonald added. "I'd appreciate it if you wouldn't speak of this to him."

"Yes, of course," Tricia said, keeping her tone neutral. Then, for some unfathomable reason, Tricia blurted, "How are you and Becca Chandler getting along?"

A crooked smile crossed McDonald's face. "We shared a drink and talked the other night. She's led a much more interesting life than me."

"I wouldn't say that," Tricia countered. "A cruise ship's security director must have many fascinating tales to tell. Have you ever thought about writing a book?"

McDonald shook his head sadly. "Unfortunately, I had to sign a nondisclosure agreement upon leaving my post with the Celtic Cruise Line. But . . . I haven't discounted the idea of writing fiction."

Tricia's eyes widened. "For the mystery or thriller genre?"

McDonald shrugged. "It's something else I need to contemplate. But for now, I'm focusing on my job as Stoneham's police chief. So far, it's been far more interesting than I could've ever imagined."

Was that because some considered the village to be the murder capital of New Hampshire?

It wasn't a question Tricia was willing to ask.

TWENTY-SEVEN

That evening, Tricia was not good company. She listened to Angelica go on and on about the renovations at the Morrison Mansion and how she was choosing wallpapers for the six guest bedrooms, but Tricia hardly listened. Of course, Angelica picked up on her lack of participation in the conversation.

"Are you okay?"

Tricia poked at the food on her plate. "I'm just in a funk."

"What happened?"

"Nothing, really," Tricia lied. "I just feel flat."

Angelica squinted at her sister. "Are you fixating on Lauren Barker's murder?"

"A little."

"And maybe your relationship with David?" Angelica probed.

Tricia nodded. "More than a little."

Angelica shook her head. She'd warned Tricia not to fall too heavily for the guy, but thankfully, she didn't (yet again) voice that opinion. Instead, she changed the subject.

When David arrived at Tricia's place, he immediately picked up on her melancholy. He clasped her hand and drew her to sit on the couch.

"Something's been bothering you for days. I wish you felt comfortable enough to tell me about it," David said, sounding just a little hurt.

"It's just . . ." Tricia wasn't sure how to approach the conversation and instead blurted, "I don't know how I'll get along after you're gone."

David looked puzzled. "Gone where?"

"If you lose your job at the library."

"I'm not going anywhere," he said, sounding confused.

"But if your job disappears?"

"I'd be staying here to be near you."

"But?"

"Did you think I'd leave you just because of a job?" he asked, sounding offended.

"Well . . . yes."

David studied Tricia's face, frowning. "If you'd only mentioned it to me, I could have allayed your fears."

Tricia looked into the distance. "That's not an option I've had in the past."

"What?" David asked, sounding puzzled. "Are you saying you couldn't be honest with the other men in your life?"

Tricia thought about it. In some way or another, every man she'd ever been with had betrayed her. It was enough to make one want to forget about love. Would David one day betray her, too? Her still-wounded heart ached, but if she was honest, she remained a hopeful optimist . . . and the gap in their ages was a pretty formidable obstacle.

She looked away, thinking of the muttered taunts of "cougar" that had lately been bandied her way on far too many occasions. Worse, some thought David was exploiting their relationship for gain. So far, no one had said it aloud, but she was pretty sure some had come to that conclusion.

"Let's just say they weren't always honest with me."

David shook his head sadly. "Oh, Tricia . . . why would you think I'd leave you?"

"Because . . . you've worked so hard to get your degree. Because you love working with children—something I can never give you. Because . . ."

"I'm young, and commitment means nothing?" he asked, his voice flat.

"I don't know . . ." she waffled.

"Just so you know, commitment means a lot to me," David asserted. "*If* I lost my library job, there are other things I could do right here in Stoneham, or at least in southern New Hampshire or northern Massachusetts."

"Like what?" Tricia asked, not believing such a thing could be possible.

"Like being a corporate librarian."

Fat chance of that happening, Tricia thought. Those kinds of positions were almost as rare as children's librarian jobs.

"And who says I *have* to be a librarian?" David asked.

"I thought that was your lifelong dream," Tricia said, suddenly confused.

"Not really," David remarked. "I mean, I *do* love it, but I could be happy doing something else."

"Like what?" Tricia asked, still doubtful.

"Like being a consultant."

"In what field?"

"Vintage furnishings. Or I might open an antiques shop. Although, my first coup would be stealing Pixie from you and having her come work for me. The woman has an uncanny eye for salable vintage merchandise."

"Why does it seem like everyone on the planet wants to poach her from me?" Tricia cried.

"You mean Angelica and Nigela Ricita?"

Tricia nodded. "Pixie's knowledge of vintage clothes, books, furniture, china, and glassware is a hot commodity."

"Angelica *and* Nigela?" David asked pointedly.

Tricia remembered her promise to her sister not to divulge the truth about her dual personalities. "Yes," she said simply.

"It's time to come clean," David said.

"In what way?"

"That Angelica and Nigela are one and the same."

"Who says?" Tricia bluffed.

"Half the village."

As Tricia suspected.

David continued. "Angelica—as Nigela—has already offered me a position to work with her company as a consultant."

"To do what?"

"Work with the landscape architect and help outfit the Morrison Mansion with appropriate furnishings and decorative items."

"Is that something you'd like to do?"

"If I lost the library gig? Yeah, in a heartbeat, and I'd be tempted to sell my soul just to do it on a volunteer basis during the off-hours from my day job. Not many people get paid to explore their hobbies for fun and profit."

Tricia tried to digest what he was saying. "Then . . . you aren't thinking of leaving Stoneham?"

"That would mean leaving you, and that's not something I'm prepared to do." He looked at her tenderly. "I love you."

It was the first time he'd said those words, bringing tears to her eyes.

"And I love you, too," she admitted.

David reached out a hand, and that was all it took for her to fall into his embrace. Tricia held on for a long, long time. When they pulled apart, they kissed, and then Tricia settled her head against David's chest and sighed. "You've lifted a huge weight from my shoulders."

"How long have you been carrying that?"

Tricia had to swallow before she could answer. "Since the night Lauren Barker died."

"I'm sorry about that. We should have had this conversation when the trouble started between me and Amelia Doyle. I mean, she's had it in for me since the day she came on board as library director. But I'm not the only one in her sights. She instantly disliked anyone and anything that Lois Kerr hired or approved of. Why are some people so damned petty and vindictive?"

"I wish I knew," Tricia remarked.

"Well, that's not how we operate," David said, wrapping his arm tighter around her shoulder. "Besides. Mrs. Everett told me that Amelia can't just fire me. It would be up to the board to get rid of me. She's let me know she's on my side and thinks others on the board would be, too. Now, if any of my co-workers quit because of Amelia . . . that's a different story. That is, unless there's a mass exodus, and then the board would have to ask themselves why."

"So, you're not thinking about quitting?"

David shook his head. "Although . . . the offer to work full-time on the Morrison Mansion project is awfully tempting."

"As you said, even a part-time job on the restoration could be pretty exciting."

"I wanted to get your opinion before I accepted it. It means that some of my free time that I could spend with you would be spent elsewhere."

"My darling David. I work a seven-day week. I already feel like all the time we have together is stolen. But you have weekends off. I would encourage you to spend that time doing something you love and that fulfills you."

"Thank you."

Tricia heaved a sigh. "Angelica wants me to work with Amelia on the January library book sale."

"Better you than me," David said under his breath.

"One of the things I want to ask her is when the bees were going to be removed from the library's roof. Eileen Harvick didn't want to reveal that information, as though it should be kept top secret. She's worried about a lawsuit should someone get stung."

"Won't happen," David declared, shaking his head.

"What do you mean?"

"The library board made sure insurance would cover any mishaps. I was told they were thrilled to be a part of so-called urban beekeeping. Stoneham Village is hardly an urban area. Lois Kerr thought it might be a great learning experience for kids. She had the Harvicks talk to a couple of groups of kids. They all got little sample pots of honey, too. Apparently, they were gobsmacked."

"Have you heard when the bees will be removed?"

"Tomorrow, late afternoon between five and six, when there's a lull in library patrons."

"Are you going to hang around to watch their removal?"

David shrugged. "I don't know that there'll be all that much to see. I imagine Mr. Harvick will be covered in his beekeeping suit and lower the hives to someone below. I heard his son helped him put them up there in the spring on a pulley system. But no matter what, the bees have to be gone before the end of library hours tomorrow, and as it gets darker earlier than later, the supper hour is when it has to happen."

"Hmmm. I wonder if I might be able to delay happy hour with Angelica so I can watch the operation. I mean, I'm fascinated with the whole idea of beekeeping."

"How about if the little buggers crawl all over you—or sting you?"

"I wouldn't be keen on that," Tricia admitted. "But I love honey, and I recently bought some beeswax candles. I should have lit them tonight. They give off an amazing scent."

"How about lighting them the next time I come over?"

"I will. I should also look up some recipes that call for honey. I like the idea of using it instead of granulated sugar. Maybe I could make some honey-based cookies for Pixie, Mr. Everett, and my customers."

David laughed. "If you do, save a few for me, will you?"

"I will. I'll bake you anything you like. I love to try new recipes. I'm nowhere near being the best cook in the village, but I'm getting pretty good at baking," she bragged.

"If you want to experiment, I'll be your willing taste tester."

The idea of baking for David pleased her, and she would keep him in mind the next time she baked cookies or prepared a dessert for the Sunday family dinners.

David yawned. "I'm beat. With all this studying, I've been burning the candle at both ends. I'll get a tiny break around Thanksgiving, but I think my parents will expect me to come home. It'll just be the three of us, as my brother and his wife are going to her parents' house for dinner, unless you want to come," he said hopefully.

"Would they be open to coming here? I'm sure Angelica, or Nigela, could find them a room at either the Sheer Comfort Inn or the Brookview Inn—*and* with the friends-and-family discount."

"I'll e-mail my mom and ask. It would be great if they could come. They already love the village. Seeing it all decorated for Christmas would be nice."

"I'm sure there'd be no problem with Angelica or Ginny, as we'll probably have the meal at Ginny's house, and you know there's plenty of room to add two more to the mix."

"Yeah, I'll ask," David said. He sounded pleased.

Tricia snuggled closer to him. She liked his parents. They seemed to like her. She *wanted* them to continue to like her.

David yawned again. "I'm sorry. It's been a long couple of days. I'm bushed."

"Want to go to bed?" Tricia asked with just a hint of a tease in her voice.

"I wouldn't say no," David said.

Tricia stood and held out her hand. "Then let's go."

Tricia pulled David to his feet and then turned off all the lights before they started toward the stairs to her bedroom suite, with Miss Marple scampering ahead of her, and David trailing only a step behind her.

After that, she put all thoughts of business, murder, beekeeping, and Chamber business out of her mind. Now it was time to concentrate on connecting with another human being who seemed to understand her, and whom she understood.

And it was about time.

The next morning, Tricia started the day by making breakfast while David showered. By the time he reached the kitchen, Tricia had again assembled her version of a fast-food breakfast sandwich. Down it went with a cup of coffee and not a complaint.

Afterward, they walked to the municipal parking lot, where they once again parted company with a kiss and went their separate ways. David took off in his Jeep and Tricia started off on her walk.

The weather on that day was mild, with temperatures rising to the high sixties and the morning clouds were supposed to burn off before the noon hour—perfect leaf peeping weather. The addition of another tour bus was sure to make the day a perfect success.

As she walked, Tricia made a mental list of what she needed to accomplish. She decided she'd procrastinated enough about calling Amelia Doyle to discuss the upcoming library sale and decided she'd do that as soon as she returned to her shop. Pixie had mentioned it was past time to haul out the Halloween decorations. It wasn't Tricia's favorite holiday, as her mother hadn't let her eat the Halloween candy she'd trick-or-treated, telling her it would make her fat. And despite operating a mystery bookstore, Tricia wasn't fond of decorating with faux skulls and skeletons. As they pleased Pixie, Tricia would have to endure the macabre décor for a couple of weeks. It was much more fun to decide how to mix up their other holiday decorations.

As Tricia was about to unlock the door to Haven't Got a Clue, she once again saw Mary Fairchild exit the Patisserie with a white baker's bag—no doubt containing her breakfast.

"Tricia—I'm so glad I ran into you," Mary said, grinning.

"Oh?" Tricia said warily. After their last encounter, she wasn't sure if Mary should be considered a friend or foe.

"I did as you suggested and sent a thank-you card to Ms. Kraft."

A flush of relief spread through her. "I'm so glad," Tricia said.

"Not only that, but Ms. Kraft—Stella—invited me to her home for tea. I actually closed my shop for a few hours to visit her."

"And?" Tricia asked, and by Mary's joyful expression, anticipated a positive response.

"We had a wonderful conversation." Suddenly, Mary's eyes brimmed with tears. "She'd kept a copy of an essay I'd written about my grandma, who taught me how to crochet, knit, and sew." Mary dipped a hand into her slacks pocket to withdraw a tissue that she used to dab her eyes. "I don't even remember writing that homework assignment, but when I read it again it brought back all those sweet memories of my wonderful grandma, and I cried like a baby."

A lump rose in Tricia's throat. She was a sucker for such feel-good stories.

"Ms. Kraft—Stella—gave me that copy of the essay. I had no idea she'd made it, but she explained that she tried to save her students' best work to remember them by."

"That's so sweet."

"I'm going to frame that essay and hang it in my store so I can see it every day and remember Grandma and how much she taught me about the domestic arts and—more importantly—life."

"Did you learn anything else about your former teacher?"

Mary laughed. "Yeah. She makes the best molasses cookies I've ever tasted and gave me the recipe. And you know what else? We're going to stay in touch."

"I'm so glad to hear you say that. Stella was so demoralized the last time I spoke to her."

"I spoke to a couple of acquaintances from school who came to the same realization about our former teacher. We're going to organize a reading group, and we've asked Ms. Kraft to not only join us, but suggest what we should read. The girls agreed to meet on Sunday mornings so I wouldn't have to close the shop to attend."

"That's fantastic."

"And it's all because of you," Mary said gratefully.

"Oh, no," Tricia protested, but Mary wouldn't accept her denial.

"Nope. You made it happen. Maybe someday you'll join us."

"That would be nice."

Mary giggled. "We're going to rotate bringing treats to the

meetings. I thought I might try a couple of the recipes from one of Angelica's cookbooks."

"I'm sure she'd be thrilled to hear that."

Mary glanced at her watch. "Oops! Gotta go. I heard another bus full of tourists could pull in today. I need to be ready."

"I hope you have a great sales day."

"You, too," Mary said, and waved at Tricia before she started off in the direction of her shop.

TWENTY-EIGHT

Once she returned to her store, Tricia looked up the library's main number and made the call she'd been avoiding. She was told Amelia was in a meeting. After explaining the nature of her call, Tricia was assured that Amelia would contact her at her earliest convenience.

Hmm.

Tricia returned to her apartment, showered, and dressed in her standard uniform of dark slacks, flats, and a peach sweater set to compliment the season, and headed down to her store to set up the beverage station for the day. Pixie was the first to arrive that day, and she, too, had gone for an outfit with an orange tinge, along with black hose and shoes. Pixie looked striking no matter what she wore. Mr. Everett wasn't far behind, and the three of them started their day as usual with a coffee klatch in the reader's nook. Their chat was interrupted soon after the store's official opening when Tricia's phone rang. Sure enough, it was the library's main number.

"Hello?"

"Ms. Miles, it's Amelia Doyle. How may I help you?"

Tricia explained about the Chamber's support of the upcoming library sale.

"I wasn't aware of that. I have so many new duties. When would you like to meet to discuss the project?"

"My schedule is pretty flexible. When would it be convenient for you?"

"I don't have much on tap on Friday. That is, of course, unless you'd like to meet late this afternoon. Could you come to the library about four thirty?"

"Yes. I don't think our first discussion will take more than half an hour."

"Great. I'll see you then."

"Good-bye." And the connection was broken. Tricia set down her phone and stared at it.

"Is anything wrong, Ms. Miles?" Mr. Everett asked.

Tricia sighed. "I don't know. I don't feel comfortable speaking with Ms. Doyle."

Mr. Everett nodded. He knew all about the conflict with David and Amelia, thanks to his wife being on the library board.

Pixie, as ever, spoke her mind. "Why, what's going on?"

Tricia explained how Amelia blamed David for the unsuccessful book signing at the library almost two weeks before.

"Well, that doesn't seem fair. Like David orchestrated the fiasco? Things happen. She can't blame David because the event didn't go as planned."

"I just hope that in time things will mellow out."

"Hear, hear," Mr. Everett said, and raised his coffee cup in solidarity.

Tricia's ringtone sounded again. She glanced at the phone's screen, seeing that it was Ginny.

"What's up?" Tricia answered.

"Hey, Tricia, I'm sorry, but I have to cancel our lunch today. Will's got a fever, and I didn't want to send him to daycare. I'm going to be working at home to take care of him. I hope you don't mind."

"Mind? Of course I don't. You take care of that little bambino so he'll be in the pink for our dinner on Sunday. And take care of yourself, too."

"You are an angel," Ginny said.

"No, little Will is."

"Thanks for understanding. I'll see you on Sunday," Ginny promised.

"Looking forward to it," Tricia answered, and they ended the call.

"Oh, dear," Mr. Everett said, sounding upset. "Do you think the baby will be all right?"

Pixie waved a hand in the air. "I'll bet he's just cutting a new tooth. Kids are resilient. He'll be fine by the weekend. Mark my words." So said the former EMT.

"I'd better text Angelica to see if she's free for lunch," Tricia said.

"You do that," Pixie said, and got up, taking her cup with her.

Just then the shop's door opened with their first customer of the day.

Mr. Everett rose from his seat, and while Pixie greeted the patron, he headed to the back of the store to wash his cup and returned with his lamb's wool duster. Meanwhile, Tricia texted her sister, who was free for lunch but again suggested they meet at Angelica's apartment. She knew as soon as their online chat ended that Angelica would be calling Ginny to be apprised on little Will on an hourly basis for the rest of the day.

See you at one o'clock or thereabouts, Tricia texted back.

Suddenly, a big Granite State tour bus roared up the street.

"Get ready for the onslaught," Pixie called happily. "I predict it's going to be a great day."

"From your lips to God's ears," Tricia said, and the three of them laughed.

After the bus disgorged its occupants, there was usually a ten-to-twenty-minute lag as the tourists made their way south along Main Street. So Tricia, Pixie, and Mr. Everett prepared the shop for what they hoped would be a great sales morning.

Pixie chose upbeat music to greet the customers, and Tricia's employees were in high spirits as the first of the day's customers entered the shop. Still, her meeting with Amelia hung heavy on her mind. She consoled herself with the knowledge that she'd have a pleasant lunch and dinner with her sister, and then, as icing on the cake, could reconnect with David. And there was also the anticipation of possibly seeing Larry Harvick remove the bees from the library's rooftop. Yes, it was going to be a great day.

Pixie and Mr. Everett arrived a few minutes late from their lunch hour because they had to wait for a table at Booked for Lunch—and finally settled for a couple of seats at the counter. Tricia wasn't concerned about their tardiness because that meant that Angelica's retro café was doing great business. They decided that if the weather was fine the next day, they might bring their lunches and eat on a bench in the village's square.

When it was Tricia's turn for lunch, she hurried next door to the Cookery, climbed the steps to Angelica's apartment, and rapped on the door.

"Come in," Angelica called above Sarge's joyful barking.

Once inside, Tricia tossed the dog a couple of biscuits and settled on one of the stools at Angelica's kitchen island. Angelica stirred a steaming pot with a wooden spoon.

"What's on tap for lunch?" Tricia asked.

"Beef barley soup with buttered, seeded rye bread."

"Sounds great to me," Tricia said.

"What do you want to drink?"

"Water's fine."

Angelica turned to the fridge, grabbed a glass pitcher, turned to one of the kitchen cabinets, and plucked a tall glass, filling it with the chilled water and presenting it to her sister.

"So, what's going on?" Angelica asked.

Tricia sighed. "I'm supposed to meet with Amelia Doyle this afternoon to talk about the January book sale."

"About time you set that up," Angelica said, getting out bowls and plates for their lunch.

"I wonder if it'll be an awkward conversation."

"Why should it be awkward?"

Tricia told her sister about her conversation with Mary days before—and her uttered oath of *snitch*.

"Yes, that certainly could be awkward," Angelica said as she ladled soup into bowls, setting one in front of each of their usual places, and a plate with several pieces of bread.

Tricia tasted the soup. Mmm . . . good! She buttered a slice of bread. "Anyway, I'll try to keep the conversation on topic."

"And what if Amelia wants to talk about possibly being accused of murder?"

Tricia shrugged. She took another spoonful of soup. "Of course, it wasn't me who reported Amelia's past interactions with Lauren Barker. It was Mary."

"But it was only at your insistence. I'm sure if there's any flack, Mary will want it known that she only reported it under duress."

"Maybe." Tricia ate more of the soup, but her enjoyment had soured, thanks to Angelica's words.

"Do you honestly believe Amelia Doyle is capable of murder?"

"I didn't think Grant Baker was, and look what happened," Tricia countered.

Angelica nodded solemnly. She'd had several counseling sessions after discovering the former police chief's body.

"And," Tricia added, "Ms. Doyle isn't exactly loved at the library."

"So David says," Angelica said.

"Yes. But she's not only been hard on him but other library workers, as well. He seems to think she can't outright fire him because the disaster of Lauren's signing and then death on the property weren't his fault. Grace seems to have his back."

"Good for Grace. But speaking of David, I texted him this morning to see if he wants a tour of the Morrison Mansion this evening."

"Oh?"

"Yes, the rug was delivered, and I want to unroll it and see how it'll look in the front parlor. More importantly, to see if it'll fit."

"What if it doesn't?"

"I'm sure it'll go somewhere else. There are six bedrooms on the second floor."

"How did you get the rug back from the cleaner so soon?" Tricia asked.

"Money talks," Angelica answered simply. "Anyway, I thought the three of us could go together and then have dinner at the Brookview Inn. What do you think?"

Tricia nodded. "I'd like to see what you've done in the past few weeks and how you envision David and Ginny helping out. It's too bad Ginny can't be there with us."

"She's going to start working with me on Friday afternoons beginning next week. If you can spare an hour or so, you could come by and sit in on our gabfest."

"That would be fun. Thanks for the invite."

"Wonderful. If I speak to her before Sunday, I'll let her know. Otherwise, we can mention it at our family dinner."

The sisters polished off the soup and bread, and Tricia rinsed the dishes, handing them to Angelica to place in the dishwasher.

Tricia glanced at the clock. "I'd better get back to the shop. Next week, I'll host at least a few of our meals. You've done far more than your share of late."

"Well, I *do* love to cook, and I'm not doing nearly enough of it now that we have our family dinners at Antonio's house. And since I work from home, it's not a big deal for me to whip up something for us for lunch or supper. Soon, leaf peeping season will be over, and we can go back to our usual routines."

Tricia nodded. "When and where do you want to meet to go to the mansion?"

"Why don't you and David meet me there after your meeting with Amelia? Then you two young people can go back to your place and have another riotous evening of reading separate books."

"Stranger things have happened," Tricia remarked. "I'm off," she said, and headed for the door. "See you later, alligator."

"In a while, crocodile."

Tricia smiled all the way down the stairs and through the Cookery. It wasn't until she opened the door to Haven't Got a Clue that her thoughts again turned to her upcoming meeting with Amelia, and her mood immediately soured. At least she had something to look forward to. If she could just get through the rest of the afternoon, she could spend a pleasant couple of hours with David and Angelica while they made plans for the future.

And that, she decided, was that.

TWENTY-NINE

 Tricia arrived at the library at precisely 4:25 that afternoon, her stomach tied in knots. *If nothing else, just act
professional,* she told herself.

Part of the lot had been cordoned off, and as she pulled into a
parking slot, Tricia noticed Larry Harvick's pickup truck parked near
the south side of the building behind the yellow caution tape. The
bees were going back to their home. Tricia saw no sign of the beekeeper, figuring he must be on the roof, getting the bees ready for
their ten-minute drive down the road to the Harvicks' property, and
wondered if they'd be relocated in the spring. She'd ask the next time
she saw either Larry or his wife.

Tricia grabbed her purse and a leather-bound notebook and exited
her car, walking around the building to climb the stairs at the front
entrance.

At the reception desk, she asked for directions to the conference
room Amelia had mentioned during their morning conversation and

found that she was the first to arrive. She turned on the lights and took a chair facing the door at the long table that easily sat twelve people—most likely for staff meetings.

Minutes ticked by.

No Amelia.

Surely the person at the reception desk had notified Amelia that Tricia had arrived. Or was this a tactic Amelia used to make people—including her employees—anxious?

Tricia scrolled through her phone but wasn't entertained. She noted the time—eleven minutes since she'd arrived. If Amelia didn't show in four more minutes, she'd go looking for David and hang out with him until it was time for him to clock out. She could conduct whatever business she needed with Amelia by e-mail or phone.

Just as Tricia was about to get up, a somber Amelia arrived, closing the conference room door behind her. She looked downright grim dressed in a black blazer, white blouse, and dark slacks. "I'm sorry I'm late," she said gravely, taking a seat opposite Tricia. "I was detained by a visit from Chief of Police McDonald."

Tricia inwardly cringed. She said nothing.

"Some *people* around here think I might have killed Lauren Barker. What do you know about that?" she demanded.

Tricia had run this scenario through her mind countless times during the afternoon. She hadn't expected Amelia to jump into that topic without preamble.

"Well?" Amelia demanded.

Tricia could fudge, or she could come right out and ask.

"Well, what?" Tricia asked.

"Did you put it into the chief's head that I might be responsible for Lauren's death?"

Uh . . . not directly.

Tricia composed herself before replying. "I'm a mystery bookseller.

I've literally read thousands of tales of murder and mayhem. I suppose countless people could have had a motive for killing Lauren."

"For example?" Amelia asked, stone-faced.

"Dan Reed. He kicked up a fuss at Lauren's signing and her memorial service. He's since been arrested for harassing her online."

"And?"

"Lauren purposefully humiliated her former high school English teacher at the signing. Their unpleasant discussion was captured on video and distributed to the press and went viral, causing Stella Kraft tremendous embarrassment."

"Anyone else?"

"You," Tricia said nonchalantly. "She *did* bully you in high school, right?"

"That was decades ago. Do you think I'm petty enough to hold a grudge for all these years?"

"I don't know. Are you?"

Amelia's eyes widened, her mouth turning into a straight line. "How dare you accuse me!" Amelia's voice rose higher with each word.

"It wasn't an accusation; it was a question."

Amelia's gaze dipped to the tabletop, and she chewed her bottom lip for long seconds. Finally, she nodded. Her head tilted up, and she looked Tricia straight in the eyes.

"Yes, I killed that sorry bitch. But that's the thing. I couldn't wrangle an apology from her."

Tricia blinked, shocked that Amelia would confess her horrendous deed so casually.

"Why?"

"Isn't it obvious? That *woman* made my life a living hell for three long years."

"She wasn't a woman when it happened. She was a misguided girl."

"Who hadn't changed in the interval. I confronted her in the parking lot, and she taunted me. She bragged about her movie contract and merchandising deals. She had a high school diploma and is a multimillionaire while I'm still struggling to pay my student loans from a quarter of a century ago!"

And Lauren had to die for that?

Tricia wasn't sure what she should do next. As she'd wondered during her conversation with Mary Fairchild, would a person who'd killed once find it easier to do it again? That seemed to be the trend.

Tricia swallowed. "What are you going to do now?"

"I'm going to kill you," Amelia said matter-of-factly.

Oh, yeah. It would definitely be easier the second time around.

"Why?"

"Because you know."

Tricia feigned a calm she didn't feel and nodded. "And they already suspect you of the *possibility* of murdering Lauren. Everyone's given the presumption of innocence until proven guilty beyond a reasonable doubt."

"Since I've already told you I killed her, you'll undoubtedly be the first to give evidence against me."

Tricia *had* testified several times at murder trials. It was never a pleasant experience.

"So, what happens next?"

"As I said, I'm going to kill you. It's the ultimate punishment for betrayal."

"That just means you'll spend even more time in jail," Tricia countered.

"I don't intend to spend a single moment in jail. I had an inkling of that when I choked the life out of Lauren. And let me tell you, it was sweet revenge. But I don't intend to be punished for it. My life is already over. I may as well join you in death."

That wasn't what Tricia wanted to hear. "Surely you don't intend to kill me *here*."

Amelia nodded. "Of course not. I wouldn't want to scare any children who might be in the building. There are plenty of wooded areas just outside the village."

Tricia swallowed. Was the woman certifiably crazy or did she just possess a warped mind?

"And what makes you think I'd accompany you out of the library?"

Amelia's hand came up from under the table, clasping a semi-automatic pistol.

Tricia swallowed, a shiver of fear running through her. "I'm supposed to meet some people after this meeting. They'll report me missing almost immediately."

"Good. The sooner they start looking, the sooner they'll find our bodies. I presume you'd planned on leaving with David Price."

A rising terror threatened to choke Tricia. She didn't answer.

"Give me your phone."

"What for?"

"A text to Mr. Price should be all it takes to have him meet you outside the building by your car. You see, he needs to be punished, too, for bringing Lauren here to spread her filthy messages."

Holy crap. The woman *was* nuts!

"Unlock the phone and give it to me."

Tricia sat rock still.

"Give it to me or traumatize every child in this building."

Knowing what Angelica had gone through after finding a suicide victim, Tricia couldn't let that happen to a child.

She unlocked her phone and pushed it across the table.

Amelia picked up the phone, tapped out her text, reading it out loud so Tricia could hear. "Hey, honey. I'm almost done with my meeting. Meet me at my car out in the parking lot."

Tricia hadn't told him she had a meeting with Amelia. She'd never called David *honey*. Would that tip him off that something was wrong?

Honey! Unless moving the bees had already been accomplished, Larry Harvick might still be hanging around the parking lot.

The phone pinged.

Amelia looked at the screen and smiled. She read the answer aloud. "'Sure thing, bunnykins.'" She simpered.

David had probably thought Tricia had been messing with him and answered in kind.

The phone pinged again. Amelia read the text. "Just finishing up for the day. Meet you in five."

Amelia set the phone down and tapped in two letters: *OK*.

Tricia watched the analog clock on the wall tick, tick, tick the minutes away, feeling damp with perspiration as the two women sat in the deafening silence.

Finally, Amelia spoke. "We're going to walk straight out the front door. I'll be right behind you with the gun in my jacket pocket. Make a mistake, and I'll blow you away in front of anyone who gets in my way. Maybe them, too. Do you want that on your conscience?"

"No," Tricia said quietly, and rose.

Amelia pushed back her chair and stood. "Let's go." She waited for Tricia to open the door, then stepped in behind her, shoving the gun barrel into Tricia's back to remind her to do as she'd agreed.

Tricia walked slowly toward the reception desk, with Amelia practically breathing down her neck. No one paid them any attention.

Descending the library's front steps, Tricia walked slowly toward her car. The caution tape was still in place, but now someone in a beekeeper's suit had braced himself, holding on to a heavy-duty rope. Some kind of pulley system was now attached to the building.

Another suited someone hung over the edge of the roof, steadying several stacked hives slowly being lowered to the ground.

Closer, closer.

"Hey, Tricia," called the man on the ground. Larry Harvick.

Tricia raised her hand and gave him a one-handed wave.

Suddenly, the rope slipped through Harvick's fingers, and the hives dropped from at least ten feet, smashing into the ground. Instantly, a dark mass emerged from the broken case as hundreds of crazed bees escaped, buzzing around.

"Run!" Harvick hollered, but Tricia stood stock-still, too shocked to do anything.

"Run!" Harvick warned again as the bees swarmed, moving in Tricia's direction.

Suddenly, a gunshot rang out. Amelia was shooting, but not at Tricia—at the hives!

Harvick fell back as splintering wood, wax, and honey shot into the air as Amelia pumped ten shots into the hives.

As though identifying their enemy, the bees moved en masse straight toward Tricia and Amelia.

Tricia made a dive for her car, jumping into the driver's seat and yanking the door shut, but not before she'd been stung at least a dozen times. She clawed at the insects still clinging to the bare flesh of her face and neck, getting her hands stung as well. When finally she could no longer feel anything crawling on her, she dared to look out the window.

Amelia lay on the ground writhing in agony as the dark swarm covered every inch of her. Harvick was overhead, trying to swat the bees away but having little effect.

Tricia didn't have her phone; she couldn't call 911. All she could do was watch in horror.

It seemed to take eons before the bees began to dissipate. Harvick was shouting at someone. Tricia strained to see what was going on. David had arrived. He was on his phone frantically gesturing as he spoke—more likely shouted—to a 911 dispatcher.

Tricia dared to look at the disfigured body that lay on the ground. Amelia had been allergic to beestings. Already, her face was red and swollen. She clawed at her neck, as though gasping, writhing weakly—anaphylactic shock.

Oh my God, Tricia thought. *She's dying!*

Amelia Doyle was dead long before the paramedics arrived.

THIRTY

Tricia sat in the back of the ambulance, thankful that the paramedics had counted only twenty-two places where she'd been stung on her hands, face, and neck. It could have been a lot worse. Her face was already pink and puffy, and her hands would probably be useless in another hour or so. Still, she felt grateful to be alive.

David walked into view, holding his phone in his right hand. He leaned against the ambulance's open back door. "Angelica is going to meet us at your place. She's pretty upset."

"They want me to go to the hospital," Tricia lamented. "Just in case."

David nodded. "That's okay. I'll go with you. I'll let Angelica know in case she wants to come, too."

"Of course she'll show up. That's what sisters do."

David nodded. "I wish you would have let me know what was going on."

"I couldn't. Amelia had my phone, which is probably still on the library conference table. Would you have a look before you leave?"

"Sure thing."

"I should have been here waiting for you. It should have only taken five minutes to tie things up, but there was this little girl who—"

Tricia raised a swollen hand to stave off his explanation. "As it was, you saved my life."

David looked confused.

She raised her hand and gave him the same wave she'd given to Larry Harvick. It was something David taught many of his charges at the library. The hand signal conveyed two words: *help me.*

Harvick, a former sheriff's deputy, recognized the gesture. Had he been shocked to see it, or did he just lose his grip on the rope while lowering the bees? She'd have to ask him.

Harvick was busy trying to calm the still-hovering bees with smoke. His son had been dispatched to retrieve other boxes for the bees to be coaxed into. It was no doubt going to take hours to corral the usually affable insects.

Meanwhile, Amelia lay on the cold asphalt. She'd been covered with a sheet, and the medical examiner had been called. A small crowd stood outside another line of caution tape, and working his way through the throng was Ian McDonald. He halted before the ambulance.

"Well, what have you gotten yourself into this time?" he asked, sounding weary.

"It's not that long a story," Tricia said, "but can I tell it later? Apparently, I have a date with an ER cubicle."

One of the EMTs appeared in front of the door. "We're about to take her to St. Joseph's. You can follow if you want."

"I'll do that. It's a date," McDonald said. He took in Tricia's face and frowned. "That's not a good look."

"Thanks. I needed to hear that."

David insinuated himself between the two. "Tricia always looks beautiful to me."

Just then, Tricia saw Becca Dickson-Chandler standing on the periphery of the crowd. "Are you sure you can't talk to me tomorrow?" Tricia asked. "It seems like you might have other things to attend to."

McDonald looked back, waved to Becca, and turned back to Tricia. "My duty as an officer of the law comes first."

Uh-huh. Why did it bother her that Ian appeared to be infatuated with Becca?

It wasn't a question she wanted to ponder that evening.

The stings were beginning to burn and itch. Tricia hoped some doctor at the hospital could recommend some course of treatment to help it, but reconciled herself to a couple of days of discomfort.

Still, she was alive. Although Lauren Barker's killer hadn't faced earthly justice, Mother Nature had ruled and condemned her. Still, Tricia felt a weird kind of empathy toward her would-be killer. Amelia had lived with her torment for decades. Tricia had lived through a different kind of bullying from a mother who'd punished her for being the surviving twin of a SIDS death. Punished her every day by bullying her into starving herself to please a woman who could find no solace.

Tricia didn't want to think about it.

"Let's go. The sooner we get to the hospital, the sooner I can go home."

"It's a wrap," said the EMT, closing the ambulance doors, shutting Tricia inside, and cutting her off from her paramour and a man she still hoped was a friend.

She would have to parse that out later.

EPILOGUE

 Pixie took Saturday off from her part-time job at Booked for Beauty to cover for Tricia at Haven't Got a Clue. Angelica had insisted on staying the night to help Tricia dress, bathe, and even eat. Her hands were so swollen Tricia couldn't even hold a cup, but by Sunday, she was pretty sure she could be left on her own. Angelica was an excellent nurse, but after thirty-six straight hours with her sister, Tricia was aching to be on her own or at least spend a little time alone with David. Pixie took care of that, too, as she didn't hit the Sunday estate sales so that she could take care of the store along with Mr. Everett.

"People are dropping dead like flies," she said, then seemed to realize the phrase could be taboo to someone who'd just witnessed a death. "I mean, there'll be more estate sales next week."

So, Tricia and David watched a football game, and then they, along with Mr. Everett, set out for Antonio's and Ginny's home for their weekly family dinner.

Thankfully, the others were only concerned about her health and didn't press for details about Amelia's death. But, she noticed, they weren't afraid to ask David in whispered tones for details.

Tricia was glad to retreat to the kitchen to help Angelica.

"Your hands look much better than they did this morning, and so does your face. I predict by Tuesday, you'll be back to your lovely, smiling self," Angelica said cheerfully.

"I hope so," Tricia said.

"Would you ask Ginny to serve the pizza rolls?"

"Oh, I can do it. As you said, my hands are much better."

"Are you sure?"

"I can hold a tray," Tricia assured her sister.

"Okay," Angelica said doubtfully, but watched as Tricia carefully lifted it. She picked up the other one and followed her sister to the family room, where the others had gathered.

"Would you like a pizza roll?" Tricia asked.

"Tricia dear, sit down. Let me take that tray," Grace insisted.

"No, thanks. I need to feel useful."

"Are you sure?"

"Definitely."

Grace took one of the rolls, but before she tasted it, she spoke again. "Tricia, have you heard the good news?"

"News?"

"The library board will bring back Lois Kerr as director until they find someone else to take on the job."

"How does Lois feel about it?"

"Ecstatic. Apparently, she found retirement to be a dreadful bore."

Tricia laughed. "I'm not surprised. But I'm shocked David didn't mention it to me."

Grace looked embarrassed and lowered her voice. "Perhaps I ought to let him know before he finds out another way."

Tricia nodded. "Mum's the word," she said, and moved on to Ginny, who bounced baby Will on her lap. "Would you care for a pizza roll?"

Ginny made a face.

"They're good. I tried one," Tricia assured her.

"I don't doubt it, but someone needs a change," she said, and nodded toward her son. "Save a couple for me, will you?" she asked, and got up to change the baby's diaper.

Antonio was occupied with Sofia, who sat on his knee, whimpering after having tripped while chasing Sarge. The little dog sat nearby looking desolate, his brown eyes damp with what looked like unshed tears because his little human friend was in distress.

Sofia was soon placated with a pizza roll and Tricia moved on to the others.

David and Mr. Everett sat in a corner chatting. "Tricia's already abandoning plastic. Just think, if everyone jumped on that bandwagon, refusing to buy needless plastic junk, it would be a boon to the planet's health. Is this something the Everett Foundation might champion?"

"Tell me more," Mr. Everett said.

Tricia offered the tray of rolls to the men.

"No, thank you," Mr. Everett said.

David reached for one. "Thanks."

As Tricia and Angelica circled back to the kitchen, they heard a loud knock on the front door.

"I'll get it," Angelica said. "Who'd come visiting on a Sunday evening?"

"Maybe it's Ian. He said he'd probably track me down with more questions," Tricia said, following Angelica.

The knock came again, and then the doorbell was pressed repeatedly.

"All right, all right!" Angelica called, and flung open the door. Standing on the step, wearing a baggy beige raincoat that had seen better days, with a large, battered, brown string-handled shopping bag sitting beside her on the concrete, was Sheila Miles.

"Mother, what are you doing here?" Angelica cried. It was not a sentence said with joy—more like horror.

"Your father and I have come for a visit."

Tricia stepped closer, her mouth dropping open in shock and dismay. "Mother?"

"Oh. There you are, too. I figured you'd be wherever Angelica was. You two are as thick as thieves these days. It never happened when you were children," Sheila said derisively.

The woman was always ready with the insults—and usually aimed at Tricia. The sisters filled the doorway, almost as a blockade.

"Well, where is Daddy?" Angelica said, looking around the lone figure on the stoop.

Sheila bent down and reached into the wrinkled sack, withdrawing a black plastic rectangular box. She shoved it at Tricia, forcing her to take it. "Here."

"What is it?" Angelica asked with a look of distaste.

Sheila glared at Tricia, as malevolent a gaze as Tricia had ever seen. "Your father's cremains."

HAPPY HOUR
RECIPES

PUMPKIN HUMMUS

INGREDIENTS
1 cup canned pumpkin
1/3 cup tahini
1/4 cup olive oil
3 tablespoons orange juice
1 tablespoon toasted sesame oil
1 teaspoon ground cumin
1 teaspoon minced garlic
1/4 teaspoon salt
2 tablespoons olive oil, optional
1/4 cup salted pumpkin seeds
Baked pita chips, sliced apples and/or pears

In a food processor, combine the first 8 ingredients; cover and process until smooth. Transfer to a serving platter or bowl. If desired, garnish with the olive oil; top with pumpkin seeds. Serve with pita chips, apples, and pears.

Yield: 3 cups

PUMPKIN CHEESE PUFFS

INGREDIENTS
2 cups canned pumpkin
1 cup grated cheddar cheese
2 eggs, lightly beaten
1 cup self-rising flour (or 1 cup all-purpose flour, plus 1½
    teaspoons baking powder, plus ¼ teaspoon salt)
¼ cup chopped fresh chives, plus extra, to serve (optional)
Salt and pepper to taste

Preheat the oven to 350°F (180°C, Gas Mark 4). Lightly grease a twelve-cup muffin pan. Place all the ingredients in a large bowl and season. Fold the ingredients together until well combined. Divide the mixture among the prepared muffin pan. Bake for 25 minutes or until puffed and golden (they will sink a little upon cooling). Set aside in the pan for 5 minutes to cool slightly. Gently remove the muffins from the pan. Serve warm or at room temperature, sprinkled with extra chopped chives, if desired.

Yield: 12 puffs

TORTILLA PINWHEELS

INGREDIENTS
1 cup sour cream
1 package (8 ounces) cream cheese, softened
¾ cup sliced scallions
½ cup shredded cheddar cheese
1 tablespoon lime juice
1 tablespoon minced seeded jalapeño pepper*
8 to 10 8-inch flour tortillas, room temperature
Salsa or picante sauce

Combine the first 6 ingredients in a bowl; spread mixture on one side of each tortilla and roll up tightly. Cover and refrigerate for at least 1 hour. Slice into 1-inch pieces. Serve with salsa or picante sauce as dipping sauce.

*Wear disposable gloves when cutting hot peppers; the oils can burn your skin and eyes.

Yield: 5 dozen

Simple Sausage Rolls

INGREDIENTS
1 sheet puff pastry
All-purpose flour, for dusting
2 tablespoons applesauce or chutney
1 pound ground sausage
3 tablespoons cold water
1 egg, beaten (for egg wash)
2 teaspoons sesame seeds (optional)

Roll out the pastry to a 9- or 10-inch rectangle on a surface dusted with flour. Cut the pastry in half lengthways to form two long strips. Spread with a thin layer of the applesauce or chutney, leaving a border along the edges. Place the sausage in a large bowl, add the cold water, and mix together. Divide the mixture in half and form each into a cylinder. Put each portion of meat into the middle of a pastry strip, leaving a border at either side. Brush the pastry border and the top of the sausage mix with some of the beaten egg. Fold one edge of the pastry over the meat and roll to encase. Use a fork to press the pastry edges together. Cut the sausage rolls into 2-inch lengths and arrange on a lined baking tray. Chill for 20 minutes.

Preheat the oven to 400°F (200°C, Gas Mark 6). Brush the sausage rolls with the rest of the beaten egg and sprinkle with the sesame seeds (if using). Bake for 30 to 35 minutes until the pastry is golden brown. Transfer the sausage rolls to a wire rack and let cool for 10 minutes.

Make them a day ahead or freeze for up to a month; to bake from frozen, add an extra 10 minutes to the cooking time. This recipe can be easily doubled.

Yield: 12 rolls

PIZZA CRESCENT ROLLS

INGREDIENTS
1 10-inch-by-15-inch sheet puff pastry dough
½ cup tomato sauce
16 slices pepperoni or chopped salami
1 cup cheddar or mozzarella cheese, shredded
1 egg, beaten (for egg wash)
½ teaspoon ground black pepper (or to taste)
1 tablespoon Parmesan cheese, freshly grated
Marinara sauce (optional)

Preheat the oven to 375°F (190°C, Gas Mark 5). Line a baking pan with parchment paper and set aside. On a lightly floured surface, cut the puff pastry dough into 8 triangles. On each triangle, spread 1 tablespoon of tomato sauce evenly and top with 2 slices of pepperoni or salami and 2 tablespoons of cheese. Gently roll the crescent dough from the wide end over the toppings and pinch the sides to seal. Arrange the crescent rolls seam-side down on the lined baking sheet. Apply the egg wash evenly on each roll and sprinkle with black pepper and Parmesan cheese. Bake for 15 minutes or until golden brown. Serve immediately with marinara sauce, if desired.

Allow to cool to room temperature before storing in an airtight container and refrigerate for up to 4 days. To reheat cold pizza crescent rolls, place in a preheated oven for 10 to 15 minutes. Recipe doubles well.

Yield: 8 rolls